I0727448

Other works by Jack J. Wyatt:

Lions in the Water
Blood Stone Mountain

SCORN

JACK J. WYATT

First Edition, December 2022

Library of Congress Control Number: 2023900120

ISBN-13: 979-8370272035 (paperback)
ISBN-13: 979-8370274657 (hardcover)
ASIN: B0BQFSL4JK (Kindle)

Trade ISBN: 978-1-7341083-5-4 (paperback)
Trade ISBN: 978-1-7341083-6-1 (hardcover)

JackWyattBooks.com

Revenge is an act of passion, vengeance of justice.
Injuries are revenged, crimes are avenged.

— Samuel Johnson (1709-1784)

How it Began

Earlier events aboard the Amelia Island-based shrimping boat, *Gypsea Moon*, led Jed Salvador, Bill Myer, and Dennis and Bobby Tucker on the trail of a missing Golden-Age pirate ship. The men had unknowingly trawled over its remains which had sunk over 300 years ago.

However, it was the kindly Thomas 'Tommy' Kendrick who helped Jed realize that they'd uncovered far more than a few bits of gold and silver coins. Tommy's knowledge of the unsettled isle of eight flags and its stormy coastline supplied an incredible backstory of the doomed Spanish Fleet and helped his friend piece together clues in pursuit of the wreckage.

Meanwhile, David Brack, the owner of the *Gypsea Moon*, had drunkenly gambled the shrimp boat away to Eastern European mobsters. However, a transportation thug named Remo Gezzle, who was Brack's nefarious business partner, bought the ship and intended to use it for smuggling.

A reluctant Brack also became part of the deal, and Gezzle's plan was to use him as a frontman to take the blame if authorities ever seized the *Gypsea Moon*.

On the night Gezzle and his men intended to take possession of the shrimp vessel, an onboard battle with the boat's crew ensued, resulting in Gezzle's death and three others. David Brack had miraculously survived the ordeal, resold the ship to Jed Salvador for whatever cash he had on hand, and vanished from the area.

At roughly the same time, strange shipping activity in a nearby port on Alexandra Island caught the attention of the International Police

Agency, Interpol. Thomas Kendrick, who'd been passing himself off to locals as a 52-year-old retired history professor, was called into action.

Tommy the Welshman, a former British Intelligence officer, had been forcibly retired only two years prior by a new military regime that believed technology was the real future of intelligence. Distraught, Tommy considered his dismissal as 'forced obsolescence in this new soulless circus of automation.'

Nevertheless, Interpol needed his help. Tommy entered the shipping yard at Alexandra, opened one of its containers, and found remnants of illegal automatic arms. Someone was shipping these weapons from overseas to destinations unknown.

But before he could act on that information, another urgent call sent him on a rescue mission.

Four individuals in Columbia's South America had been kidnapped. With the help of a young UK-based Second Lieutenant Adler, Marine pilot Michael Bennett, troubled Navy Seal Ernie Nelson, and Sergeant Catalina Rosales, they affected a covert search of the jungle for the missing physicians.

Deep inside the unforgiving wilderness, what they uncovered shocked them all. Illegal mining of Coltan, Gold and other rare earth minerals were being pulled from the ground using forced labor.

The team found their assets, and even rescued one of the mine's workers named Lorenzo—a young man who incredibly made it all the way back to the states.

But the road home wasn't without tragedy.

Sergeant Catalina Rosales lost her life at the hands of one of the mine's henchmen. The would-be Green Beret perished in Kendrick's arms aboard the *Malusnavi* cargo freighter.

Kendrick promised to keep Rosales's daughter safe and ensure her share of the rescue reward went directly to the young girl.

But it's what Kendrick wouldn't understand for months that enraged him. Even more appalling freight was aboard the *Malusnavi* cargo vessel than he knew.

Kendrick's mission is now to find those behind the despicable shipments and bring them to justice.

Chapter

1

Gary Allan Oliver was murdered in a rundown strip mall north of Stillrock, Mississippi.

According to the written report, there were no suspects and no witnesses. The building's owners employed no electronic surveillance, and due to city cutbacks, the area's traffic cameras were little more than pricey bird nests.

Fortunately, Gary Oliver's partner, Rick Melton, was out of town at the time of the murder. Twice divorced, the 43-year-old took a monthlong trip to south Florida.

Police wasted no time and picked Melton up for questioning upon his return.

Thomas Kendrick had less than 20 minutes. He took a deep breath, timed the traffic, sprang from the curb, and scurried through the rain.

This would be tricky.

Once across the motorway, he came to a large two-story building and caught his reflection in its glass entry doors. He tweaked his collar, trued a crease in his trousers, and stroked a quick hand through his ash-black hair. After a long exhale, Kendrick tugged the door handle and entered the main lobby of the South Parish Police Department.

Inside, officers roamed the division's ivory passageways—as did a handful of detectives with badges fixed to their waistlines.

To Kendrick's right, arrowed signs instructed visitors toward the clerks' office and onsite courtroom. The lobby's mid-section saw rows of chairs for comers and goers, some waiting to pay a fine while others waited to visit an inmate. But on the lobby's left side rested a quarter-round information desk. The station was manned by a tall, uniformed officer scowling at his computer.

Kendrick straightened his posture and approached with a forced grin. "Damn technology, am I right?"

The officer glanced at him.

"I remember when we wrote things down." He delivered a tight nod, "Old school, you know?"

The policeman tapped his keyboard. "Simpler times. Sorry I missed them."

Kendrick removed a leather fold from his trouser pocket and flashed his counterfeit badge.

The tall man barely looked at it.

"You have a Rick Melton?"

The cop pointed to his left, "Came in an hour ago. Number six, through those doors, down the hall."

Kendrick closed the pouch and quickly returned the fake badge to his pocket. "Thanks, appreciate it."

The officer's attention returned to his fussy computer.

Kendrick strolled through the waiting area to a set of metal doors inscribed with the words 'No unaccompanied civilians past this point.'

He entered.

The long cinderblock corridor echoed with his footsteps. He wandered through the vacant area, rounded two corners, and came to a second junction. It held a large, barred prison cell.

Inside the lockup, a couple of sleeping drunks sprawled across its two benches while a sobbing young man in a tuxedo paced the cell's interior.

Kendrick hurried past the junction and, after another turn, entered a second door. It led him past the dispatch/records room to the witness and interrogation area.

A pair of chatting detectives in cheap suits glanced his way.

If either asked to see his credentials, he was done for. They'd toss him into a cell and laugh themselves into a coronary. Because who the hell impersonates a police officer and then strolls into a police station? A looney, that's who.

Still, Kendrick confidently bobbed his head and continued past the detectives without a word.

This looney was on a mission.

He found door number six a few steps later and rechecked his watch.

Down to 18 minutes.

Right now, this was his only lead. Even though time was limited, he couldn't rush things. He'd first ask basic questions to get a feel for temperament, and then, when his subject relaxed, he'd blindside the man and gauge his reaction.

Kendrick opened the door and stepped inside.

Tube lights hummed in the ceiling above. The interrogation room was paneled with chestnut pegboard and furnished with a metal table and three cushioned chairs. An unused handcuff bar sat welded to the table's upside, and a closed-circuit camera overlooked the small rectangular space.

The man waiting inside the room got to his feet.

Rick Melton was under six-foot with longish brown hair. He was dressed in a casual long-sleeved Polo with jeans. The holiday tan on his cheeks had already begun to fade. Melton didn't look like a typical attorney and reminded Kendrick of a scruffy weekend boater.

Kendrick closed the door, tweaked the camera upward, and held out a hand. "Mister Melton, I'm detective Thomas."

Following a quick handshake, Melton reseated himself, stroked his chin, and said in a smooth southern drawl, "Terrible, terrible thing that happened to Gary."

"Indeed." Kendrick took a chair, "And we need your help on this one."

"Your accent. It's British, right?" Melton smiled.

Kendrick supplied half a nod.

"Didn't sound Louisianan. You know I got an ear for that sort of thing." The lawyer appeared pleased with himself.

Kendrick ignored the remark. "I understand you were out of town when this occurred?"

"Right," Melton rubbed his upper lip. "Drove down to Key Largo," he grinned. "Beautiful little place on the water, did some fishing, and –"

Kendrick held up a palm—he wasn't interested in this man's holiday. He'd secured a copy of the police report through back channels. According to the information, Melton Oliver & Associates sat west of the rail tracks in a derelict shopping outlet called Warner Plaza. In more thriving times, the hundred-space parking lot and its dozen brick-and-board storefronts housed an oversized hobby store, shoe outlet, clothing retailer, two mom-and-pop eateries, and a microbrewery.

Today, the only tenants left in the open-air dwelling were Frank's Drive-By Liquors, a Payday Loan and Check Cash center, and the currently closed law offices of Melton Oliver & Associates.

Kendrick leaned forward, "How'd you and Gary Oliver meet?"

Melton rested his hands on the table. "Junior college," he began. "Neither of us had the grades or cash for university. We became roommates, shared notes, shared a few girlfriends—though Gary wasn't too keen on that," he chuckled. "Did our two years at Gulf Coast Community before transferring to Mississippi State. Gary majored in business management, and I went into economics. My old man was an accountant, and it seemed a natural fit."

Melton's body language was steady. As far as Kendrick could tell, he didn't sound nervous and had no random tics.

"Economics? But you both became lawyers?"

Melton straightened himself in the chair, and a slight smile crossed his lips. "There was this party. End of our junior year. Gary and I got drunk and started arguing, the way friends do."

Kendrick's voice piqued, "Arguing? About what?"

"About who'd earn more with their degree once we graduated." Melton swiped hair from his brow line, "Well, that turned into a debate on who was smarter. Then I bet Gary that I could outscore him on the LSATs."

"The Law School Admissions Test? Why?"

"Dunno," Melton shrugged. "The idea just popped into my head. We were competitive but in a friendly way. I was only half-serious, but Gary wouldn't back down. That led to us both studying like hell. I don't remember doing anything else during my senior year. We didn't want to be lawyers. We were just trying to one-up each other."

According to an entry in the police report, both men scored a 148 and wouldn't be attending Harvard.

"Still, we each had a mountain of debt from our undergrad degrees, and neither of us had any job prospects. What were three more years? He dared me to apply to some law schools, and I dared him back. By dumb luck, we were both accepted at Mississippi College. The courses were brutal, but we buckled down and earned our JDs by the hairs on our ass."

Kendrick tilted his head, "Then came the bar exam?"

Melton nodded, "Yeah. Louisiana's bar uses the essay format, which we both figured would be easier to complete because Gary and I had bullshitted our way into law school anyway. He passed it the first time. I had to retake the exam in July that year, but thankfully passed the second."

"What was your first job in practice?"

"Gary and I spent most of the next year fielding rejections from the big firms, then the small ones. We took odd jobs. I worked in a bank for a bit, and Gary did a bartending gig for cash. Finally, we pooled our money together at the end of summer and opened our office." Melton peered at his hands, "We specialized in injury law, thinking it would only be temporary until bigger opportunities arose. Though,

"One of your officers mentioned the key was inside the interior lock." Melton squinted. "We do that at 5pm, you know?"

Kendrick pressed. "Why? Explain."

"Well, when the last client arrives, we lock things up. That's when evening rolls around. Darkness brings out the riffraff. Addicts of all substances wander the area. If they see lights in the office, they'll give a tug at the door. Check if it opens. And, well…"

"Well, what?"

"Not sure I should go into too much detail." Melton ran curled knuckles against his face stubble. "When April Harris was still with us—she's our former secretary—anyway, she, Gary, and I worked late one night in the backroom. April went out to fetch some papers from a box when we heard a scream."

"Scream?"

"Yeah, she caught a homeless couple having sex on the lobby couch."

Kendrick raised a brow, "I see."

"Might've even been a third participant in the melee. She wasn't sure." Melton held up a finger, "Then a second time, April found a glassy-eyed junkie riding out his high in the restroom after hours." He shook his head, "She said the guy was 'naked as the day God made him'… course, April quit after that. Can't blame the unfortunate thing. Haven't been able to refill her position since."

Kendrick turned in his chair, "Understood."

Melton's eyes darted left, then right. "My guess is one of those junkies busted in and took Gary by surprise."

Eleven minutes remained.

While Melton had his own ideas, Kendrick knew Gary Oliver's killing was no random attack. It was a professional hit—almost personal. The perpetrator clocked the lawyer's routine and waited patiently until the end of the day when there were no witnesses.

According to the timeline, Gary Oliver was killed on a Friday, but his body wasn't discovered until Monday.

Police found him slumped over his desk, with three 9mm slugs through the front of his skull.

Someone wanted to make sure the man was dead—and stayed that way.

CHAPTER

2

"How about $2,500?" But David Brack wasn't after this man's money. He was on the run for his life.

He'd bounced between different motels in Alabama and Mississippi for more than a month. Anytime he drove, he stayed vigilant of the cars around him. Whenever he slept, he parked the Lincoln far from the motel.

Today, he was on the outskirts of Hillman, Mississippi.

The time had come to stop running and confront the attorneys who'd conned him out of $2 million.

Fumes of gasoline and WD40 swirled about. Racks of used wrenches, hammers, screwdrivers, and assorted pneumatic tools crowded the narrow aisle behind him. Below sat hundreds of ratchets and socket heads, mismatched and sold by the pound. Blenders, toasters, air fryers, and microwaves were farther rear: unboxed, and their cords dangled from the shelf.

Each item was mashed with a thumb-sized sticker, inking its starting price. Three chainsaws, as many lawnmowers, and a washer-dryer set flanked the south wall. Another section displayed used computers and handhelds—sold as-is, with a stern no-return policy.

Behind the pawnshop's counter, a glass case filled with swords, knives, nun chucks, throwing stars, and other weapons flickered beneath a row of finicky fluorescent lights.

And every item was eyeballed, tested, and valued by the old man he was haggling with behind the booth.

A patch of crumbs fell from the shopkeeper's chest. He turned in the chair, gazed out the store's grimy window, and raised his gaunt chin, "Steep ask. Best I can do is twelve-fifty."

Brack fingered the tip of his baseball cap and scowled, "I thought the price of used vehicles was going up?"

"Not for that damn dinosaur," grunted the old man.

Weeks ago, David Brack had fled west in the beat-up Lincoln, down the A1A, onto 17 south, then to I-10, while the car's wiper's thrashed at the rain.

That night, he'd thought briefly of returning to his place down in Jacksonville, but nerves—or maybe it was common sense—got the better of him. They'd most likely tossed the apartment. He could never return.

Even today, more than two months later, one of Gezzle's men was probably at his place, sitting on his couch, watching Sports Center, waiting for him to insert his key into the lock. A turn of the doorknob and the bullet would zip through Brack's head before he could release the handle.

He'd left behind a wardrobe of suits, shoes, and a beautiful ceramic-blue Rolex Submariner. But none of that bothered him—outside of the watch. Though he'd stopped paying rent, there'd soon be a notice of eviction tacked to his apartment door. Those possessions would shortly find their way curbside for picking, and the apartment's manager would undoubtedly keep the Rolex for himself.

But he didn't want any of those things following him.

Gezzle's people were cruel and cunning. They'd most likely bugged his place and hadn't stopped there. Were there geo-trackers on his stuff? Had they sewn AirTags into his clothes? Fixed trackers to his car?

Even though he was now over 600 miles away, Brack thought of this a lot. When he'd fled, he took a far out-of-the-way detour north onto I-75 into Georgia when he thought someone was tailing him. Once the Lincoln hit I-20, he sped west. At an all-night gas station in Douglasville, he grabbed three large coffees, filled his tank, and bought a new pair of windshield wipers. He also purchased blue jeans, a t-shirt, and a baseball cap with a Chevy 4x4 logo.

After he crossed into Alabama, he followed Highway 84 through the torrential rain until dawn and stopped a few times when the downpour let up to search the Lincoln for any hidden tracking devices. Thankfully, none were found. The long, out-of-the-way route would've also baffled any electronic pursuit.

When the Lincoln reached Alabama's River Falls, he stripped off his slacks, jacket, shirt, socks, shoes, and underwear and tossed them from a bridge into the water along with his mobile phone. He redressed in the gas station outfit and decided the Chevy cap looked cooler turned backward.

From there, he reversed direction, taking Route 137 south into Florida and onto I-10 west again.

During the entire drive, he'd thought about his life. How he'd once dined at tables with fanned arrays of silverware, white linens, chilled salad plates, and freshly caught specials. Where the slightest nod sent smoothly courteous waitstaff on missions to tighten up his scotch.

But that life was long gone.

He was almost forty and had nothing.

Looking back, there were so many mistakes.

This latest fiasco began because of that damn shrimp boat—the *Gypsea Moon*, that 79-foot pain in his ass. The one those fucking lawyers Rick Melton and Gary Oliver had conned him into buying.

That giant boat brought him pure trouble. A financial drain that kept him around those docks. But worst of all, owning the *Gypsea Moon* had put him into the path of Remo Gezzle.

Though, reminiscing about the chaos with Gezzle made him feel queasy. It was far too fresh.

It was time to move forward. To put that life and the mistakes he'd made behind him. There were other things in his past he needed to address. Bigger matters stemming from how it all started nearly ten years ago.

The old man rubbed his gray-stubbled neckline and turned again to the grimy window. "Damn ten years old. Tires near bald. And how am I to know if the oil's been changed on the regular?" The chair creaked. He tore off another piece of muffin, tossed it into his mouth, and chewed loudly.

Brack inhaled, deep. It was important he look disappointed. Make the man feel like he was making out well on the deal. Leave him a story he could brag about to his pawn store buddies. But most of all, Brack didn't want any questions.

"Would you do $1,800 in trade?" he shrugged.

"In-store credit?" The man in the chair leaned forward, "I can do you $1,700. Fair?"

Brack wouldn't need half that much. He dropped the Lincoln's keys on the counter, thrust out a hand, and the two men shook.

"Fair."

The old man grunted.

The return to Mississippi was only the first part of his plan.

The time had come to pay Melton Oliver & Associates a visit.

David Brack pointed to the flickering glass case.

"Let me see the Smith & Wesson."

Chapter

3

"Took three in the stomach, two in the chest, and another… Jesus! Another in the neck?" Doctor Tammy Rivers flipped through the chart and shook her head. "And he's still alive?"

Nurse Miguel Rios gave half a laugh, "I know, right?"

An unconscious man laid on the elevated bed attached to a whirring ventilator. The patient's chest rose and fell with the machine's cadence. An intravenous line supplied his nutrition, and various cables relayed his vitals.

"Unbelievable. Says a round passed between the jugular and the carotid. Are you kidding me?"

Miguel tilted his head, "Apparently the bullets were –"

"Full metal jacket, right." She flipped a page and scanned the notes. "No way a hollow point would've thread that needle."

Miguel rubbed his chin and nodded.

"Any family?"

"He's had a single visitor, who came only once. A stunning lady, brunette in her twenties or early thirties. She spoke with an Eastern-European accent, I think, and little broken English—but we couldn't find a translator before she vanished. I think she might've been a relative or a girlfriend."

"Hmm. And they believe it was some type of gang activity in the port?"

Miguel turned to the doctor, "Friend on the force told me they weren't sure who was involved. But this guy was dumped on the pier and pretty much left for dead. According to the blood trail, they think he might've been on a freighter from one of the foreign port zones. It looked like someone dragged him outside the area, then made an anonymous call. Otherwise, customs never would've been alerted. Authorities ID'd him as Russian from the tattoo on his knee."

"His knee?"

"Left side. Said it was a 'thieves' star.'" Miguel draped back a cover to expose the unconscious man's leg. "He must've spent some time behind bars. That tat is supposed to mean he bends before no one, or something like that."

Doctor Rivers chuckled. "Yeah. We're all tough guys until there's half a dozen holes in us." She checked his breathing tube and his intravenous line. "Anything else?"

"No name. Local PD ran the prints, but no hit. I think they sent them onto Interpol, but who knows how long that might take?"

"Interpol, eh? And no guard on this guy?"

"Cops left after the second day. Said hospital security was enough. I guess because they couldn't ID him, and he wasn't connected to any immediate crime, that they just sort of lost interest."

"You said he came off a ship?"

Miguel furrowed a brow, "Yeah, but that's the weirder part. By the time local authorities received authorization, they believed whatever vessel he was on vanished from the area."

"A disappearing freighter?" Doctor Rivers frowned. "That's a new one."

"Right?" Miguel chuckled.

The doctor rechecked a line, "Well, this is a bizarre case in of itself. By all accounts, Dimitri Doe here should be downstairs in the meat locker."

Miguel nodded.

Doctor Rivers turned to the x-ray film suspended on a lit wall panel. "Last lung image?"

"Pulse ox levels are normal, and radiology shows the wounds in the right lobe have healed." Nurse Miguel pointed to the x-ray, "I think he's ready for a wean, doctor."

"All this in only weeks," she muttered. "Incredible."

"Even consultation signed off. They're encouraged."

"Has attending weighed in?"

"Believe that's the next step, if you agree of course, doctor."

Doctor Rivers examined the patient's pupils then rechecked the chart. "You're one lucky Russian," she said. "Alright, lets run down Lawson for sign off. If this guy passes the wean, then we can de-trach. Move him out of intensive care maybe tomorrow or the next day. And once he wakes up, I'd be curious to hear what he has to say."

"Me too."

The doctor tongued her cheek and turned to the nurse, "You've been on this from the beginning?"

"Yes, doctor," Miguel straightened his back. "Since he came through the doors."

"Mm hmm." She paused. "Feel up for a challenge?"

"Yes ma'am, doctor. Always," Miguel nodded.

Doctor Rivers smiled, "Since Wilkens is off today, and the patient's history is, well, interesting, I'd like you to present this to Lawson yourself. Garner the approval." She handed the chart to the nurse. "I'll be by your side of course."

Miguel was taken back, "Really?"

"Really."

A big grin, "Thank you, doctor. Thank you for the opportunity."

Doctor Rivers smiled and the two left the room.

In the hall, they passed a young, attractive woman with long brown hair wearing a black hat. She sat on one of the benches and dabbed at her eyes with a large handkerchief.

Nurse Miguel whispered, "I think that might be her."

Doctor Rivers turned discreetly, "Who?"

"His visitor, the girlfriend or whatever."

"Ahh, the one who doesn't speak English?"

"Right."

"Text Marta, see if she can find a Russian translator. Maybe we'll get lucky?"

Miguel fussed with his mobile phone, "On it."

Once they rounded the corner, the sobbing woman in the black hat changed her expression, and she stood.

Alana Kerkovich entered the intensive care room and closed the door.

The breathing machine attached to the unconscious man ticked and fluttered.

Alana leaned over his bed, took his hand, and probed between his fingers. "Many innocents affected by what you have done." The man's hand twitched and she steadied it with a squeeze, "And for this I do not forgive."

Carefully, she reached into her clutch and quickly found the device she was after. She spread his middle and index fingers, and slipped off the needle's protective cap.

The barb pricked the skin, the plunger flattened, and the aconite slid into his bloodstream.

The machine's nasogastric tube filled with vomit in seconds. The ventilator chugged. Thick discharge inched from the patient's innards up the exhaust hose.

Alana grabbed the tube and crushed it closed.

The unconscious man's eyes sprang open.

His arms thrashed and he clawed for whatever he could grab.

Alana jumped on top of him, wrestled his flailing limbs to submission, and stared grimly into his eyes, "Now to next life."

The two struggled.

Soon, the vomiting man in the bed fell still.

A steady tone resonated from the heart monitor.

And Yuri Melnyk's terrified expression froze, forever.

CHAPTER

4

Inside the interrogation room, Thomas Kendrick rested an elbow on the metal table. What started with suspicious goods in a portside shipping container had exploded into a conspiracy of weapons, drugs, and kidnapping. He needed to understand how Gary Oliver's murder was connected.

According to the police report, a brush for fingerprints at the offices of Melton Oliver had yielded nothing. Fibers from the crime scene were also sent to a lab for processing. However, because the office was filled with threadbare carpet, and neither man was big on vacuuming or cleaning, hopes for a forensic breakthrough would likely go unfulfilled.

So far, Rick Melton had mostly kept eye contact. For a southern man, Melton wasn't overly expressive and, beyond regular adjustments, had remained steady in his chair.

Even so, Kendrick decided to fire off a few questions and watch for signs of deceit.

"Do you pay rent on time?"

Melton nodded, "Yes."

"Any issues with Warner Plaza's landlord?"

Melton reiterated that the place was a dump, but rent hadn't increased in ten years.

"Is the business in financial trouble?"

"No."

"Was Gary Oliver in financial trouble? Are you?"

No, and no.

"Do either of you have enemies?"

Melton laughed. "What defense lawyer doesn't?"

Then Melton discussed a prior client. A thirty-year-old named Ray Banks. A serial Workman's Comp litigant who'd tried to sue his last three employers in as many years.

"Ray was an interesting fellow," Melton said. "One afternoon, he stormed into the office and started chucking furniture around. He scared the shit out of the other clients. Ray threatened to 'torch the fucking place to the ground' if he didn't receive his 'cut' soon."

"Cut?" Kendrick asked.

Melton looked toward the ceiling, "Standard settlement rates for personal injury are 33 percent. But if we can't settle, the rate goes to 40 percent because we need to shift gears and file before the case goes to court. Ray's 'cut' would be the difference."

"Then what happened?"

"Well, Gary somehow kept Ray calm until Ray's wife showed up. She scolded Ray as only a southern wife can do, apologized, grabbed the hushed man by the elbow and drove him home."

Kendrick clasped his hands, "And that was the end of things?"

Melton shook his head, "A few months later, Ray's case was rejected for fraud. Some P.I. snapped photos of Ray working a second construction gig pouring cement while still claiming a back injury." Melton frowned. "Guess the guy couldn't face his wife's shame. He downed a fifth of Crown Royal, drove his pickup into a swamp, and drowned."

Kendrick nodded slowly, "When was this?"

Melton scratched his forehead, "This all happened seven, maybe eight months ago. Don't recall, really."

Kendrick nodded, "Did Gary Oliver have life or business insurance?"

"Yes, about half a million on the business, plus five million in professional liability." But life insurance? Melton wasn't sure, and Oliver never married.

"Five million for liability? Pretty sizable?"

"Gary was a cautious man," Melton said. "Also labeled everything, including his coffee cup. Didn't like sharing. Product of being an only child, I guess."

From the report, Kendrick recalled the dead man's address, "Can you confirm Gary Oliver's residence of 1661 Beach Blvd in Wavecrest, Mississippi?"

"Yes."

"On the beach?"

"Yes."

Wavecrest was a posh area with several multi-million-dollar homes overlooking the ocean. Despite this minor league practice and dodgy location, Melton Oliver & Associates was a thriving business.

"Do you have any partners? Anyone else with a stake in your business? Besides Gary Oliver and yourself?"

"Partners?" Melton brushed his nose, "No, no partners."

Kendrick leaned in, "But your business name includes '& Associates.'"

Melton exhaled, "That's just so nobody thinks we're a bakery or a massage parlor."

"Are you sure?"

Melton smiled, "We're definitely not a massage parlor."

Kendrick didn't laugh.

The lawyer cleared his throat, "It's always been just Gary and me."

"Any client that might've held a grudge against your partnership?"

Melton blinked, then shook his head, "No, I don't think so."

But Kendrick had seen the list of Melton Oliver clients—and one name struck him.

Sigma-Sea Imports ran a bustling freeport in New Orleans, which brought in goods from overseas, unrestrained by customs inspection or tax. The company claimed to import textiles and small electronic components.

Though Kendrick knew better.

Sigma-Sea was smuggling substantial amounts of contraband. Containers full of drugs, automatic weapons, other munitions, and illegally mined rare earth minerals.

And his close friend and colleague, young Catalina Rosales, had been murdered by someone connected to the organization.

Four minutes remained.

Somehow, Melton Oliver & Associates were linked, and the man in the chair across from him may be the only connection to any of it.

Kendrick stood, looked down at Rick Melton, and delivered his jab, "What kind of work was your firm doing for Sigma-Sea?"

Melton shifted his gaze, "Who?"

"Sigma-Sea Imports," Kendrick repeated.

Melton shook his head, "I don't know that company."

But Kendrick was unconvinced.

U.S. real estate holdings for Sigma-Sea included harbor and yard space in Port NOLA and a sizable warehouse outside the seaport. The company had two owners. A dummy corporation—which Kendrick had hit a significant dead-end trying to track its owner months ago. But its second proprietor was a recently missing man named Remo Gezzle.

"According to our records, we show them as your client. And you say you don't have a clue?"

Melton's hands fell into his lap. "You know, I don't... they might be one of Gary's old clients, maybe?"

This time Kendrick shook his head. "You're saying that you and Oliver, as partners, had a multi-million-dollar client you knew nothing about?"

Melton gazed down at the table, "He must have... I mean, back when we were in flux. Gary was working with other businesses. Just trying to make some extra cash. We both were."

"But Oliver had this client for 11 years, and you've never heard of them?" Kendrick tilted his head. "Did you two keep other secrets from one another?"

Melton's shoulders stiffened, "I don't—I mean, he may have mentioned them, but I don't… wait, are they the ones by the port?"

"Yes, the import company."

"Yeah, right, right." Melton put a hand on the table—as if trying to crawl out of a hole. "Don't know much about them, but yeah. I think Gary mentioned them a few times."

From 'never mentioned' to 'mentioned them a few times.' Most curious.

"What about the power cords in Gary Oliver's office?" Kendrick's eyes narrowed. "Do you know where his computer is?"

Whatever was on that laptop might be vital in uncovering his next clue. Kendrick recalled the police report's photos and description, which noted the incident as a robbery gone wrong. And that made sense. Beyond a missing laptop, detectives noted many cardboard boxes had been toppled and ransacked, and their files littered around the office. Somebody was looking for something.

"His laptop?" Melton went flush. "No. Probably the murderer took it." He paused and bobbed his head. "Might've been one of the junkies, I think."

Kendrick stared him in the eyes. "A junkie?"

"Hey, listen," Melton recoiled. "I had nothing to do with Gary's murder. And if I'm… if you think I'm a suspect, then I need my own attorney."

Kendrick sat back. Beyond Melton's suspicious reaction to Sigma-Sea, something else bothered him about the partnership. Why were two wealthy lawyers doing business in such a seedy office in a rundown area when better real estate was available just a few miles away? It didn't make sense.

Nevertheless, Kendrick had gotten the answer he needed. The inquiry about the import company had shaken the lawyer.

"I'm just trying to get to the bottom of things." Kendrick leaned back and checked his watch. "Let's take a break. Do you want a soda or a bottle of water?"

Melton's head lifted and he nodded, "Water, please."

Kendrick rose and left the interrogation room. He rushed past the two chatting officers in the hall and sped by the records room.

But before he could exit the maze of halls and reach the main lobby, three stone-faced detectives entered the south passageway.

Kendrick made a quick left and hustled from the hall to its only enclave.

The drunk tank.

Behind its bars, the two men sleeping on its benches hadn't stirred, and the weeping lad in the tuxedo still paced its floor.

Behind him, the detectives neared.

In his best southern accent, Kendrick pointed at the crying man in the tux and said sternly, "Quiet down now, son."

Thankfully, the detectives marched by the enclave without stopping. Though, through their chatter, Kendrick heard one mention Rick Melton's name.

He had to leave the premises before they caught him.

But unexpectedly, a low, sobbing voice muttered, "Can you please help me?"

Kendrick turned.

Fair-skinned, blonde, and barely out of his teens. The kid's tousled hair had lost its part. Decked out in dark gray formalwear, his unfastened rosy, pink bowtie matched his cummerbund. Though, most peculiar, down the young man's left side—from elbow to ankle—were odd blobs of crusty, white matter.

"I... I didn't mean to drink so much, officer. I swear it." He wiped a cheek with his jacket sleeve and choked back a sob.

In Kendrick's periphery, the three detectives vanished through the doorway toward the interrogation area.

He had only seconds—but for some reason, he felt sorry for the tuxedoed kid.

Kendrick eyed him, "Wedding?"

"Best man," came the weak response.

"Got any blood on you?"

The kid's eyes widened, but he shook his head.

"Good. Then nobody was killed." Kendrick turned to leave. "So, relax. You'll be out of here in a couple of hours."

The tuxedoed kid lit up.

Kendrick hurried down the hall toward its exit.

"You really think so, officer?" the well-dressed kid shouted. "But what about the cake? Do you think they'll make me pay for it?"

Despite impersonating a police officer, his trespass into this police facility, and executing an unlawful interrogation that—if caught— would land him in prison for a long, long time… Kendrick chuckled.

CHAPTER

5

Along with the Smith & Wesson, David Brack negotiated a ratty oxford briefcase, a red duffel bag, and the pawn shop's most expensive burner phone.

Brack then pointed to a stack of used garments on the south wall, "Mind if I take some of those clothes?"

The happy shop owner clutched the Lincoln's keys, "Shit, you take as much as you can carry."

Brack stepped to the pile. Six pairs of pants and two armfuls of shirts made their way into the red duffel bag.

"Course this makes us even," the old man shouted.

Normally, there'd have remained a sizable in-store credit in Brack's favor. But such was the cost to skirt a firearm background check.

Brack tucked the handgun under his shirt, thanked the old man, and hailed transportation through his new mobile phone

Outside, an older model SUV Sportwagon pulled up within minutes. The passenger side window was down, and a woman in her mid-twenties with sassy blonde hair in a tousled bun sat inside, "Where y'all headed?"

Brack approached the vehicle and bent at the waist, "Not sure how far you're willing to take me, but I'm going to Biloxi."

A bent smile crossed her lips. She rubbed at her nose and said in her strong southern accent, "Mister, you're in luck. I'm from Gulfport."

Weird, because the coast of Gulfport was a solid hour south, in light traffic. "What're you doing all the way up here?" Brack asked.

She pointed to the dash, "Gotta little mouth to feed. I go where the fares take me."

Taped on the console was a photo of a boy, maybe three years old. He sported a wide smile and wore a Superman cape.

"Got some luggage, if –"

"Need help?"

"No, it's just a case and my packs here."

"I'll pop the hatch."

Brack put the gray case, large duffel, and his backpack inside.

The young woman called, "Give it a slam for me? Latch is a little wonky."

On the second try, the hatchback held.

Brack jumped into the vehicle's backseat, and, thankfully, didn't detect the usual scents of marijuana or alcohol that saturated so many taxis in big cities.

"Buckle up for me, please, sir?"

The belt clicked into place, and the Sportwagon meandered over the gravel and dirt onto the asphalt, heading south.

She shot a glance into the rearview, "Music or conversation?"

"Neither, if that's okay." Mindless chitchat with a twenty-something would, like, literally, make him want to jump out of the vehicle. Moreover, there were more pressing matters on his mind.

"Alright," she replied.

"But I have a question. I'm not familiar with this area." This was more lie than truth. He knew Biloxi-proper very well. "I'm hoping you might know a place I can stay?"

"Sure, lots of fine places in the city. From bed and breakfast to chain hotels, it's…"

"No," he said, a tad louder than needed. He wanted someplace lowkey, someplace he could stay invisible, someplace cheap—but near the city.

"Okay," she said. "What are you looking for?"

"Hotel, inexpensive. I don't want to be downtown. I just need to be close."

"Uh-huh," she uttered. "Quiet place or just trying to stay off the radar?"

She'd hit both nails with one swing, "Yes."

The young woman glanced his way again through the mirror, regripped the wheel, and focused on the road. The Sportwagon's hum was the only sound for more than a minute.

"Anything come to mind?" he asked.

"Well, I'm just trying to figure out your tolerance."

"Tolerance?"

She snickered. "Where you fall between comfort and absolute shithole."

He chuckled, too. "Alright. Walking distance to a restaurant or two? I'm not finicky, but if we could also steer clear of absolute shithole, they'll be a bonus in it for you."

She nodded, "Then I may know just the place. Ranks two-stars, but there's a new owner. Outside Beauvoir but right on the water, about 15 miles from Biloxi itself. Quiet, cheap. Might fill your needs?"

"Sounds promising."

"'Promising' might be a strong word," she snickered again.

They drove in silence for several miles before he took her up on the music, readjusted the Smith & Wesson from mid-pelvis to his hip side, slunk in the seat, and watched the highway's low grasslands and trees pass by outside.

The shrimp boat *Gypsea Moon* was gone. He'd sold it to its first mate, Jed, for $13,811 in assorted bills—which he'd jammed into a Whataburger takeout bag because most of the money smelled of dead fish.

The vessel, though, was worth far more than he'd sold it for, but he'd decided things in a hurry. He wanted to get away from it, purge himself of that enormous burden and the life it brought. Though, that fateful night, the biggest purge in his life had drowned in the storm. And for that, he was grateful.

Bondage to a notorious thug like Remo Gezzle would've meant his eventual imprisonment or death. The man, his organization, had no scruples. And he'd been sucked into it because of one stupid fucking night that plunged him into horrendous debt. A debt he knew he'd never get out from under.

He'd kept the Lincoln as bait, knowing that if Gezzle's men had hidden a tracker on it, he'd know they were after him.

Selling the Lincoln put further distance between himself and those worries. He couldn't stay on the run forever and needed to start fresh.

Brack would hunt down the men who'd stolen from him. If he could recover the money, he could restart his life, get a new place, and return to the financial sector again. It was where he belonged—not living in some low-rent apartment and tending to a damn boat.

An hour passed when the Sportwagon exited I-10 and headed up a two-lane road toward the hotel.

It was as she'd said. The tourist area stopped about a mile east. Lots of vacant land separated the facility on the west from a large shopping center far, far in the distance. But the hotel's road and its immediate area here looked forgotten, like it'd been skipped over. There were a couple of mom-and-pop stores, and an eatery but little else.

Eventually tourist facilities or the sprawl of shopping centers would overtake the area, but possibly not for decades. Meanwhile, this quiet hotel sat in the middle of nowhere as commercial growth inched at it from both sides.

The Sportwagon stopped at the hotel's two-level structure. A pale-yellow stucco exterior with charred brown accents. Paint chips flaked in several areas, but repairs were underway. Random patches of a ruddy red primer dotted the walls, making it appear the entire hotel had the measles.

The lot's parking held only a few cars, and not a soul was in the area. The Sportwagon's rear hatch sprung open, and the young woman jumped out. Brack unbuckled and they met at the vehicle's rear.

She fussed with a tie in her hair, "The 'Big B' should fit the bill, unless you want me to take you someplace else?"

The hotel's giant changeable-letter sign touted clean rooms, Wi-Fi, and free HBO.

Brack nodded, "This should work." He reached into the open hatch to retrieve his belongings.

But the Smith & Wesson slipped loose from his waist.

The gun hit the Sportwagon's bumper and plummeted to the asphalt.

He gasped. The weapon was in plain sight between he and the young woman.

Though he didn't expect her reaction.

"Nicala," she stuck out a hand. "Nikki for short."

Her grip was firm.

"Here's my cell number." She handed him a business card. "I'm around the area all the time, and I'll charge you less if you contact me directly."

She shot a down glance at the handgun.

"And I keep my mouth shut."

He bent, snatched up the weapon, and returned it to his waistline under his shirt.

Her eyebrows raised, "By the way, there's a shooting range up the road. And you may want to get a holster for that."

Brack chuckled nervously, "Good idea."

He paid the fare in cash and slipped her an extra $200—half for the ride and hotel recommendation and half for not freaking out when she'd seen the gun.

Nikki gratefully accepted the cash.

"This means a lot. Thanks again. Anytime you need a ride, I'm available to you 24 hours."

They said their goodbyes, and Nikki and the Sportwagon sped off.

Brack scanned the area for any suspicious vehicles, then lugged the case, duffel, the backpack, and himself through the hotel's doors.

CHAPTER

6

Strong mildew drifted in the air. Goldish carpet tarnished by a decade or more of foot traffic covered the hotel's mid-sized lobby. On the nearest wall, stacked ten- or twelve-foot-high rested chairs, tables, soiled linens, and at least three bedframes with discolored mattresses.

Brack frowned. Was the 'Big B' moving this pile of crap in or out?

At the foyer's far end, a man with short, dusky-brown hair wrestled a commercial-sized carpet cleaning machine. He switched off the mechanism as soon as they made eye contact.

"Afternoon, traveler!" he chimed. "Welcome to The Big B. Might I give you a hand?" His nametag read 'Charlie,' and he seemed perhaps forty-five.

The slender man enthusiastically jogged Brack's way before he could stop him. Charlie grabbed the duffel and hustled toward the check-in counter.

"Plenty of space available. And you're in luck. We have suites with scenic ocean views at a nominal upcharge. How many nights can we keep you comfortable?"

Charlie the sprightly salesman.

And a 'suite' at a rundown hotel, why not?

Brack nodded, "Sure, let's do the scenic."

"And how many nights?"

"Five weeks to start, and can I extend without too much trouble?" After the words left Brack's mouth, he almost laughed. If this place were even ten percent occupied, he'd be shocked.

"Not a problem. I'll put the room in reservation lockout indefinitely. If you do extend, there will be no need to change rooms."

Brack gave half an eyeroll and muttered, "Excellent."

Charlie clacked the keyboard, humming to himself.

"Name?"

"David B—Brannon." He hoped the man wouldn't ask for ID. Though, Brack would fish out a hundred from the Whataburger bag inside his backpack if Charlie pressed him.

"Welcome, Mr. Brannon. The room is on the second floor and has a queen-sized bed, if that's okay?"

"Fine." Please, God, let it be clean.

"I'm afraid we have no bell or meal service. Our goal is to remain a budget-conscious facility for the like-minded traveler."

Brack eyed the pile of furniture and assorted crap in the lobby. Budget-consciousness stacked floor to ceiling.

"We have a pool in the center quad, but there's no lifeguard."

Did he drown, or die in one of the rooms?

"Near your suite is a water and ice machine down the west corridor, which uses new high-quality filters for the freshest cubes." Charlie seemed incredibly pleased by this.

The lobby's mildew-chemical smell was making Brack's eyes sting.

"In the office here, we offer coffee, a range of soda pop, and vending machines with assorted offerings should you require a quick snack." Charlie waived an outstretched hand to show their direction.

A bank of three machines filled with carbonated beverages, Yoohoo, rows of upright candy bars, and plastic-wrapped pastries stared back at Brack like diabetic soldiers.

"Great," he said flatly.

"And across the street, we have a magnificent diner open 24 hours. Serves delicious tuna melts. Plus, each Tuesday is bottomless pancake day. All-day, topped with whipped cream." Charlie smiled.

Wonderful. Carbohydrates smothered in sugar.

"There are also several take-out eateries a few blocks north, and a laundry mat should you be in need," he said still clicking the keyboard. "I'm assuming just the one key?"

Brack nodded.

"And which credit card will…"

"Pay you cash if that's alright."

Charlie smiled, "That'll be fine. Alright, the room, with applicable federal and state taxes, comes to $171.27 a night."

Nikki was right, this place was inexpensive. Brack expected to pay at least twice that amount for a beachfront room. But given its two-star status and current disarray, perhaps this was the best price the innkeeper could get.

"We do have a mandatory maid service charge for longer-term stays. Wednesdays and Saturdays. Fresh towels, sheets, vacuum, and wipe down. Though, there is a ten-dollar charge per visit. This brings up your per night charge to $174.07."

Brack squinted. "I think you mean $174.13."

Charlie looked at him quizzically.

"The seven-day surcharge for a weekly $20 comes out to a rounded $2.86 a night, not $2.80," Brack said. "The math is wrong."

Charlie plucked a few keys and tilted his head.

"I believe you're correct and right on the nose. Yes, $2.86 rounded up. Thank you for being so honest, Mr. Brannon." Charlie clicked his tongue. "I confess I have no talent with numbers, and my sister's husband, my brother in-law, did all the program settings in this damn accounting software."

"Happens," Brack shrugged.

"Yes. But an honest man is hard to come by."

If poor Charlie only knew.

"Again, I'd help with your bags to your room, but I'm afraid it's only me right now. As I said, we're not staffed to offer bell service."

"That's fine."

Brack prayed there weren't an army of cockroaches under his bed preparing for a fight, since the Big B apparently weren't staffed for that battle either.

Charlie handed him the room's key. An actual metal key and not one of the more modern card slides. Budget-conscious, Brack figured.

"Anything you need, don't hesitate to ring from your room. Local outbound calls are also free."

He wouldn't be making any of those but nodded his acknowledgment.

"Have a pleasant stay, Mr. Brannon."

Brack lugged his bags up a flight of stairs to room 231.

As Nikki, the driver, described, The Big B wasn't quite a shithole, but they were cousins.

A single room with a queen-sized bed, cheap flatscreen, small desk with chair, a maroon pushbutton phone, and a manufactured shower with fake tile inlays.

An earlier occupant had tried to redecorate, adding a fist-sized hole in the shower's fiberglass shell, currently covered in a mesh of duct tape. He wondered if Charlie slapped on the adhesive, or some offending 'budget-conscious traveler' attempted the repair.

Nonetheless, room amenities did include tiny soaps and shampoos, two plastic cups, plastic tongs, and a bucket for the ice machine of which Charlie was so proud.

To his surprise, the bed and its sheets were clean.

There was also an incredible view of the ocean, just outside his window. An unspoiled scene which Charlie had really undersold. It included a small balcony accessible through a slider. He could watch both sunrises and sunsets with its southern view.

Inside, the room also came with a wall-attached dresser large and sturdy enough to hold his belongings. He'd launder the clothing items from the pawn store before wearing, because who knew where they'd been?

Next, he focused his attention on the backpack.

Inside, along with shaving cream, razors, and a few items of clothes, was the last of the money the shrimper had given him for the boat—precisely $6,993.

In the bathroom, he found a safe spot. The ducted exhaust fan above the toilet had a removable cover and plenty of room to stash the money.

First, he removed $300, then, using the toilet as a stair, opened the vent and jammed the Whataburger bag full of cash into the hole.

He snapped the vent cover closed and hopped off the toilet.

He rechecked the room's door lock, placed the handgun on an end table, fell onto the bed, and shut his eyes.

CHAPTER
7

David Brack was sure they were hunting him.

Before Remo Gezzle's well-deserved death, he owned and operated Gezzle Lift & Haul—a North Florida-based trucking company that ran over 60 semitrucks to and from seaports throughout the southwest.

But the organization was anything but legitimate. Illegal imports, stealing from customers, intimidating rivals, arson, and rumors of outright murder plagued the business.

Remo Gezzle had drowned weeks ago trying to commandeer the *Gypsea Moon* shrimp boat which Brack had lost gambling. Although the man was dead, he had many partners and underlings—some, Brack feared, eager to collect on his debt and bury him in the ground.

He knew this because he'd worked with them. Gezzle's company was only one part of the criminal network, which spanned cargo freight as well as trucking. Large organizations that trafficked unlawful goods nationwide, whose captains and crew were on the take, and transported their illicit goods from their ships onto Gezzle's trucks.

But many of Gezzle's other affiliates were simple business owners. A dry-cleaning establishment, a bicycle store, a hair salon. Most of them had been unwilling to participate in Gezzle's shenanigans until they were strong-armed into compliance. Each otherwise legitimate business was a vehicle for Remo Gezzle and his colleagues to run their ill-gotten gains through.

And this is where Brack's financial expertise had once been valuable to Gezzle. He'd met with dozens of them, spread phantom inventory across their books, and moved revenue in and out for profit, breakage, and loss. Brack even went so far as to personally hand-enter extra transactions into their point-of-sale systems to hide inflated funds.

He was mindful to avoid red flags—like a pattern of unexplained lump-sum payments, or blindly registering sales without thought to compare their dates to the store's working schedule.

In one instance, Gezzle was laundering through an Indian restaurant owned by Kiran Patel. Patel would never work during Diwali—as Indian holidays are especially sacred. Brack noted several 'transactions' on that week and changed the books, because any smart government auditor would make that connection and flag it.

He paid extra special attention to details like that. He was excellent at what he did for the gangster Gezzle and his buddies.

Too bad they wanted him dead now.

When he'd first gone into hiding, he'd considered dying his hair but then decided on a high crop cut, which got rid of his brownish bangs. A manicured bit of stubble added to the look, and the casual clothing he'd picked up from a thrift store meant nobody would give him a second glance.

Over and over, he replayed his getaway. He knew he hadn't left anything to chance.

He'd sold the Lincoln and said nothing of his comings or goings to the pawn dealer who'd bought it. He paid cash for the room and, fortunately, the Big B didn't ask for his ID when he'd checked in. He made no phone calls. His former clothing, credit cards, and mobile phone were in a river someplace or swirling in the greater Gulf of Mexico.

Since being on the run, he'd eaten all his meals from vending machines. He couldn't stomach another Honeybun or Powerbar. He was starved for real, delicious food. Charlie's recommendation of the 24-hour diner across the street made his stomach rumble.

He rose from the bed, sorted himself, grabbed the room key, and left through the hotel's lobby. The carpet shampoo machine rumbled down one of the halls, and a 'text or call for service' sign sat atop the check-in desk. Charlie was a busy man.

Brack made his way across the street. The diner had a lengthy counter, fitted with swiveling stools. Four-person booths aligned the walls, and larger tables could seat perhaps eight in each corner. The grill area ran the entire back wall behind the counter, where a lively chef flipped meals on its surface.

A curvy, mature woman in an apron shouted, "Got another to-go!" She ripped a ticket from her check pad, slid it onto a rail over the grill, and then came his way.

"Just you, hun?"

The stitching on her blouse read 'Deena.' Her long, red hair was bound in the back with what looked like two chopsticks.

Brack grinned, "Yes."

"Counter or booth?" She pointed her Bic to one section, then another. "Any where's fine, really, but I can serve you faster at the counter."

Her false lashes fluttered to a nearby stool.

Brack nodded, "Counter it is." He wasn't in a hurry, but he'd picked up on her preference.

The only other customer in the place sat a few stools away. An older man, perhaps in his 50s, brown curly uncombed hair, slightly overweight, with a silver scruffy beard. His tweed jacket rested sloppily over a second stool. He sipped a large coffee and fussed with a stack of papers, plucking at a cheap calculator, and grunting.

If Brack didn't know any better he'd think the man slept in his clothes. Probably many nights in a row.

"Something to drink?" Deena asked.

Brack peered over at the soda station behind the waitress but felt a sour rumble in his tummy. In the last few months, he'd drank enough carbonated drinks to last him a lifetime.

"Coffee's fine."

The man beside him looked up from his calculator and chuckled. "No, it ain't."

"Now you hush up, Dax," Deena giggled. "That's your third cup. If it's so bad why you still here?"

Dax gave a belly laugh, "Nothing else open in this damn area."

Deena turned and bent to retrieve a fresh cup from below the coffee station.

Dax rotated his head, leered at Deena's hind quarters, and smirked. Before she turned back around, the older man's stare broke, and he resumed rifling through his papers.

It was either sweet or creepy.

"Wisenheimer over there comes in on the regular." Deena placed a paper coaster and cup on the counter before him and nodded toward Dax, "Always working. Does taxes and such around town."

"Best CPA in five counties," Dax grunted.

"Right. But he's forever working."

"Can't find any good help," he grumbled.

Deena shook her head, "You know it ain't good for you. All hunched over those papers all the time."

"Yeah, but who'd take care of you if not me?" Dax said. "Can't trust those other shitheads. Shortcut calculations, missing deductions."

"He's right," she said excitedly. "Dax helped us all last year, and it only cost me a needle and thread." She smiled and pointed to the name embroidered on her work shirt.

Dax peered Brack's way, "Damn IRS stopped letting service staff deduct the cost of their uniforms. Said most of the time the garments could be used outside the workplace." He shook his head. "And that, therefore, made them ineligible for write-off."

"Yeah, can you believe that?" Deena said.

"Crooks," Dax added before his stare returned to the paper stack.

"But then sweet Dax gave us all the wonderful idea of adding our names to our uniforms. Called it branding." Deena smiled big, "Now we can deduct them."

The chef, a large man sporting a netted frohawk, turned and pointed to a stitched pocket on his dark trousers. It read, 'Alvin.' He grinned and nodded, then resumed his duties at the grill.

Deena glanced the man's way kindly, "Dax's been good to all of us."

Brack sensed a peculiar gleam in her eyes.

She and Dax were about the same age, and given they seemed to know one another, he figured Dax's earlier ogle at Deena's rear end was mainly harmless. Then again, Deena was a curvy woman that looked like she could take care of herself.

As coffee poured into his cup, Brack wondered who might dominate in the relationship if these two ever did get together. Given the ample size of Deena's chest, his wager was on the waitress.

Though beyond all that, Dax had stirred an idea.

Life on the run wasn't cheap. Food, motels, and hotels. He spent only on the essentials. But, after living expenses, he was down to less than seven grand.

Those funds wouldn't last but a couple more months.

The use of credit cards was also out of the question. And any withdrawal from his bank in Jacksonville was too risky. Besides, at last count, he had less than $1,400 parked there, and it wouldn't help much. But any type of electronic transaction would alert someone watching his financial footprint—and lead them directly to his location.

What he needed now was a good, old-fashioned job. A position not too demanding but one that could sustain him while he worked on his other plans.

Although, if he were going to personally interact with people in this town, he couldn't use his real identity. The false name he'd made up to check in at the hotel should work.

He removed his cap, brushed a quick palm through his hair, and extended a hand toward Dax, "Dave Brannon."

The two men shook.

"Dax Langford."

"Good to meet you, Dax." He looked down at the man's papers. "I think we might be able to help each other out."

Chapter

8

In the morning, Thomas Kendrick traveled back to his place in northeast Florida. He put the Audi's top down once Alabama's cloudy skies cleared, and a warm wind struck his skin when he hit Interstate 10 in the panhandle.

Despite his unlawful escapade into Louisiana's PD, he didn't have any actionable evidence. But he was waiting on another, critical lead.

During his last assignment in South America, he'd made friends with Second Lieutenant Adler, a U.K. Intelligence officer. Adler was a techno-geek and could feed him information about anything from any place. Though they'd never met in person, the young man's exceptional skills had saved Kendrick's life and the lives of his team months ago. And even though Adler was behind a keyboard, on another continent, thousands of kilometers away, he was Kendrick's intelligence ear-man.

Kendrick voice dialed through his mobile, and his trusted pal answered on the second ring

"Sir, Second Lieutenant Adler."

"Hey mate," Kendrick laughed. Adler always addressed him with unnecessary formality, and they'd even talked about it. But Adler insisted out of respect for the uniform. They just didn't make soldiers like this dedicated young man anymore. "Good to hear your voice. How are things across the Atlantic?"

"Good, sir. But I'm still waiting on assignment. They've got me reporting to a Brigadier after my superior officer and his C.O. went AWOL."

The pandemic had caused a ruckus early on, and apparently, a few of Adler's brass had abandoned their posts and left the poor second lieutenant with no boss.

"A Brigadier? Really?"

"Yes, sir. But nobody's reached out. I know it's only temporary, but I don't have much to do now."

"You want to change that?"

"Absolutely, sir."

Months ago, on that mission in South America, Kendrick bore witness to several disturbing crimes. Crimes that culminated with the kidnap of hostages aboard the supercargo freighter, the *Malusnavi*.

The massive merchant ship had left a Columbian port full of illegally mined minerals, along with two doctors, one British and one American, who'd been kidnapped from the region. Kendrick's team had tracked and hunted down the vessel to Port New Orleans in the southern United States.

After hasty planning and an incredible amount of good fortune, they were able to board the freighter and rescue the two women. Though, it hadn't come without the terrible price of Sergeant Catalina Rosales' death during the ordeal.

But the incident went well beyond illegal rare earth minerals. At the *Malusnavi*'s intended port, they'd also found opium in one of the freeport's containers. Thousands of pounds of hand-scored deep brown resin tucked inside a foreign trade zone—where U.S. Customs didn't have jurisdiction.

Now, Kendrick's purpose was to find out who was behind it all. Who imported the drugs? Who was buying the illegal minerals? Did the purchasers realize the ore was cultivated using forced labor? Who ran the vile smuggling operation? And, ultimately, who'd cost Sergeant

Catalina Rosales her life?

They had one suspect he was counting on to provide him with answers.

Kendrick spoke over the vehicle's light hum, "Can you give me an update on our friend?"

Adler could talk and type simultaneously, and Kendrick had gotten used to the constant clicks on his end of the conversation.

"Already on it, sir. Wait…"

More clicking.

"Oh, bloody hell," Adler cried. "Err, sorry, sir."

"Informal, Adler. You know me."

"Sir, there's been a change."

Kendrick eased off the gas pedal, "Change?"

"His status was listed as stable. I even looked at his chart over the wire. All was normal. I don't understand?"

"Don't understand what?"

"Sir, according to this… he's dead."

"Dead? But –"

"I know, sir. I don't get it. The cause of death isn't listed yet, but I'm confused. I thought he'd come around in another few weeks, and you could… I don't know what happened."

Oh, shit—their only real suspect—the Russian. The man aboard the *Malusnavi* who'd orchestrated the shipments and ran most of the illegal mines down there. Kendrick had counted on gaining insight once Yuri Melnyk could speak.

It was imperative to understand the intricacies of the operation. Unfortunately, after the *Malusnavi* incident, the giant ship took off from the port and returned to the Gulf. Kendrick and his crew couldn't help authorities track the vessel. All communications were jammed. The 200,000-ton cargo freighter had maneuvered through the channel and vanished into the open sea.

He knew the only answers he'd get would come hard-earned. Local law enforcement had no authority over potential crimes inside foreign trade zones unless they looked to run through a gauntlet of bureaucratic approvals. Find Judges who'd risk their judicatures on the bench to issue an international warrant.

Beyond that, Kendrick was a Welsh National and didn't have citizenship in the states. He was former British Intelligence, but that didn't hold any credibility with dismissive agencies like the state FBI. He'd been there before, and they treated him like some toy they found in a cereal box—even mimicking his unusual accent but never truly took him seriously.

Thankfully, Interpol, a collective of devoted agents worldwide, did take him seriously. But the organization didn't have much financial muscle. It relied on people like Kendrick to flush out the bad guys for a takedown.

Kendrick pierced his lips.

"Autopsy isn't expected for some time, sir," Adler said. "I'm very sorry about this."

"Yes, me too."

Kendrick had worked the small crumbs and chance leads these long weeks, waiting to interview that Russian once the hospital stabilized his gunshot injuries and he was awake. But now they'd get nothing.

Yuri Melnyk was gone.

It was a major loss, one Kendrick wasn't prepared to absorb.

But if his last mission had taught him anything, it was to have confidence in others. And right now, to keep his investigation moving forward, he needed someone to rely on, with skills to complement his own.

He needed serious help.

Help from a field-seasoned warrior as formidable as himself, someone who could show up at a moment's notice and wouldn't back down from an impossible challenge.

He stared out at the palm tree-lined road and nodded to himself.

"Adler, I need you to locate someone for me."

"Who, sir?"

Kendrick would return to Louisiana quicker than he thought.

"Find me that flying Marine."

CHAPTER
9

The next day, David Brack dressed in black slacks and a casual collared white shirt, which he'd ironed using the hotel room's amenities. He grabbed the gray briefcase he'd bought at the pawnshop, made his way downstairs, and supplied a quick wave to Charlie who returned a grin and a pleasant, "Have a fantastic day, Mr. Brannon!"

About a half mile's walk from the hotel, Brack found the office Dax Langford had directed him to last night at the diner. It was a small, simple storefront with a yellow and black lettered sign above its entrance that read 'Dax's Taxes'—which turned out to be as gruff and straightforward as the man who ran it.

"Taxes are the penalty we pay for being alive," Dax announced after they greeted.

He wore a cream-colored collared dress shirt with the sleeves rolled to the elbows. He sported a Timex with a black leather band. His disheveled hair sat in a midway part, while his cheeks held the day's stubble.

Inside his small office lobby, half a dozen chairs sat around two sets of low tables, waiting for customers when tax season arrived, or last-minute filers showed up. Though it didn't appear Dax had too many visitors. The furniture itself was 60s kitsch. The armed chairs were a soft pea green, and the tables held a faux teak pattern. Each seat was accompanied by a mustard yellow pillow to complete the effect.

Magazines, probably dating back to the 1990s, were littered about their surfaces.

Dax led them toward the rear and its three desks—though, Dax seemed to be the only employee. Every workstation was built of no-nonsense dark oakwood and sported an oversized large blotter calendar covering the writing area.

Dax's camel jacket sat draped over the backside of one of the chairs while the two other vacant desks held computer monitors plugged into docking stations and laptops.

Buzzing overhead, fluorescent lights filled the drop ceiling. The restroom was in the back down a short hallway. The small hall space also included a drinking fountain hung on the wall. There was a coffee machine somewhere. Brack could smell the burnt aroma floating about.

As the two men walked deeper into the tax facility, Brack noticed that despite the dull interior of golds and pale greens, the place was clean. All physical files were placed into a bank of tall tan-colored cabinets arranged along each of the main walls. On top of the cabinets, a few ferns soaked up whatever sun managed to beam through the five floor-to-ceiling windows at the entrance. A couple of plants toward the rear showed their displeasure with crispy brown leaves and sagging branches.

A large white fan whirred in a corner, blowing the edges of Dax's papers in regular cycles.

Dax continued, "Our mission is to get our clients to pay as little as possible."

Brack nodded, "Gray areas?"

Dax pointed, "Charcoal as that case you're holding."

"Risk of an audit?"

Dax grunted, "Don't give a double shit about those IRS assholes. But liability insurance is expensive, so they better not find us in the wrong."

"Got it."

Dax eyed Brack for a moment, "Also, I need to verify your creds before I hand you these files. You understand?"

Brack straightened his back, "Education background check will show I graduated, South Carolina."

"Clemson?"

"Yes."

Dax began typing, "Go Tigers."

"But there's a thing," Brack leaned on Dax's desk.

"Thing?"

"It's about my last name."

Dax stopped and looked him in the eyes.

"It's a long story," Brack said. "But this is where we become good friends, or you kick me out of your office."

Dax flexed his cheek muscles, "You wanted?"

"Not by the authorities, no," Brack said.

"Uh-huh. You in good standing?"

"Yes."

Dax squinted, "You lying to me?"

Brack dropped his shoulders. "No. But I have to trust you. People in my past will come after me if they find out I'm here. There's a situation…"

Dax put up a hand, "Which is why the last name. Sure, I get it."

"Right," Brack said.

Dax bobbed his head, "We all have secrets."

Brack's nerves eased. He supplied his proper last name and made Dax promise not to repeat it to anyone.

"We'll take precautions and pop into the VPN to check you out. Don't want a trail," Dax muttered.

"Thank you." He held as Dax loaded up the IP masking service, logged in, and verified his records. He'd surrendered an unusual amount of trust to a man he'd only met yesterday. But Dax seemed to more than understand—and without much question. It was a strange feeling for Brack, though.

Dax nodded to the screen once he was satisfied.

"Alright, enough of that shit." Dax logged out, closed the VPN service, and then looked over Brack again. "You an honest man, David?"

Where Dax and his business were concerned, Brack was and would do things by the book, "Yes."

"Then prove it to me."

Dax pushed a stack of files toward him, then pointed to the only other desk with a computer, "During your employment, that laptop is yours to use and take with you should you need to. Fuck it up, and you buy me another."

"I won't fuck it up, then."

Dax grumbled, "Alright, Mister Brannon, get to work."

Brack found the coffee station and poured himself a cup before starting. The beverage was scorching, probably because it'd been brewing since the turn of the millennium.

Back at his desk, he found most of the files Dax supplied him held small business clients. And their disciplines varied wildly, from actual individuals to businesses in farming, auto parts, hotel management, and restaurants.

Dax did everything for his customers. Tax advice, planning, payroll, audits, forensic accounting to look for fraud, and good old fashion bookkeeping. Dax tried to be a one-stop shop for everything and seemed to be working himself to death.

What was interesting, though, was the man's dedication to all of it. Dax worked non-stop, as Deena said. Whether here in the office or enjoying the coffee and staring at the waitress's behind at the diner. It was as if he'd sentenced himself to the work for some reason.

Once Brack acquainted himself with the clientele in the files, Dax spoke to him about each client, many of whom, it seemed, he knew personally. If Brack didn't know any better, he'd say Dax had a peculiar affection for each—like a momma bear looking after its young.

Brack tried to focus as Dax laid out all the exceptional circumstances affecting his cubs—from late filers to those he had to nudge for proper invoices. He spoke passionately about each person and company, and none seemed less important than the next.

Brack took in a deep breath. He'd dedicate himself to the work at hand. However, during Dax's discussion, Brack's thoughts drifted back to the events of the last ten years.

Finding the lawyer and uncovering what happened to his $2 million would take time.

But he'd find those son-of-a-bitch lawyers, and soon.

C H A P T E R

10

David Brack, rather Dave Brannon, grew up in a lower middle-class section outside Villa Rica, Georgia. His mother was a K-6 substitute at the elementary school, but he never recalled her being on the job more than a day or two in a row.

She told friends working parttime was so she could spend the rest with her son. But young David could only recall wafts of nail polish, hairspray, and the ruffle of clothing bags when she'd reappear in the afternoons to pick him up from the sitter.

His father Mick was a hardworking airplane mechanic who commuted to Hartsfield before sunrise. At sunset, he sauntered back home at the end of his shift, stripped off, showered, and nursed a tallboy while flipping through the late-night shows—until he'd eventually drift off in his recliner.

There were some memorable times, like when the three would venture to Los Cowboys on weekends for a meal. Or enjoy a movie in the small town's theater when the family budget allowed. One summer, the tiny movie house ran a revival and featured a different Peter Sellers film on each of its screens. It was the only time his father skipped work—bringing his son along to enjoy the hearty laughs.

But young David had much larger ambitions. He didn't want to stay in a pint-sized town of less than 4,000 souls. There was a great big world out there, which he'd discovered in books and on the internet. Exciting places full of opportunity where he become anybody he wanted.

All he needed were means to escape.

College was the first step. He spent more time online and researched a career path where he thought he could make the most money possible in the shortest amount of time: finance.

Then choosing the right college. Too close to home meant his parents would never go for the expense of him living on campus, and demand he fight the traffic and live at home. No, out of state was his only choice.

Clemson in South Carolina offered an excellent education in the field and was far enough away that he wouldn't be expected to return, but from school breaks. Also, since 99 percent of his college-bound classmates were going to UGA or Tech, nobody would know him at the out of state university. David Brack could reinvent himself.

He fudged a few references and figures and secured his student loan.

While his mother was anxious about him moving away, his father was surprisingly supportive. The day of his departure, Mick handed David $1,000 in small bills—which he knew the man couldn't afford—and gave him a pat on the back.

"Didn't get to go to college," his dad confessed. "Suck it all up, son. Let them wild horses loose but buckle down when you need to."

Then Mick looked his son in the eyes and said something David Brack wouldn't fully understand for almost two decades.

"Advice I never took but should've. Moderation and dedication. Those two words will keep you healthy and wealthy." After that, the large man hugged his boy, which he hadn't done in years, and quietly retired to his recliner.

College life was at first confusing, but Brack kept focus. As an undergrad, he fitted himself with collared shirts and slacks. He knew to be the part, he had to dress the part. Be noticed. He introduced himself to his professors, lugged his heavy laptop to each class, and turned in every assignment on time. He read everything and studied not only the main topics but any nuance that intrigued him. Especially ins and outs of making money in gray areas like penny stocks, IPOs, and commission scales. Any practice, system, or tool that could help fast track him to fortune.

After graduation, he spent a year in the real world at a no-name firm to study the industry. At the same time, he did what he needed to earn his Series Seven License. Soon, with money saved, he moved south, rented cheap space in a seedy Miami office complex, and settled into a second-floor office with a finicky fax machine and two phone lines.

Though he wouldn't be there for long.

David Brack was a financial advisor. He'd researched the essential tricks of the sales trade, and lured customers in with offers like 'Free, no obligation, portfolio review.'

Interested customers were hooked by 'Premium services at huge discounts,' and he reeled in the doubters with 'Imagine the huge change this could make to your life.'

The fiscal fantasy is yours, just sign here.

In a few short years, Brack Financial Services, LLC, had made him a very wealthy man. Executing trades and supplying investment advice to over 200 affluent, older clients who were a generation removed from the online day trading trend. And they absolutely loved him.

The best part was that no matter what stocks or funds he put his clients into, his business received a commission.

Steady cash rolled in. The day his personal liquid holdings broke $4 million he stopped keeping track. It was money enough to be comfortable with for the rest of his life. He'd set a goal to be a multi-millionaire by 30 years-old and had done it by 28.

Next came Vella. A parttime model, they'd met at Lucky's Porsche dealership. Brunette, tall, tan, and exotic. She was modeling on site to push the dealership's yearly sale. He chatted her up. She flirted back. Then he bought right off the lot, in cash, to impress her.

It worked.

Though voluptuous Vella turned out to be more than a car dealer's window dressing. She spoke two languages, had earned a Bachelor's in Marine Science, and was working toward her Master's.

They got hitched after a six-month courtship.

He spoiled her, and she adored him for it.

He bought a 3,000 square foot house in West Palm Beach. A nice four-bedroom place with views of the water.

Vella quit her job at his insistence to focus on schooling. But school soon took a backseat to Vella's new full-time job: draining the inventory of every store and mall in the area. Bags and bags of clothes. Countless receipts for shoes, jewelry, and treatments.

Shit, he'd married his mother.

Still, he made a lot of money and could overlook that. But after only a year, he came to the realization that life in the coastal suburbs didn't suit him. It was boring. He'd landed a hell of a trophy wife, sure, but was this all there was? Growing old, fat, and watching her spend all his money? Sex became less frequent. He loved her—at least he thought he did—but gradually found himself longing for the big city after each visit 'home.'

Work was 80 miles south in Miami—and so was his $2 million condo. Right off Collins Avenue, overlooking the boardwalk. The views there were also stunning—especially the female variety.

Maybe he'd married too young? Hadn't tamed those wild horses yet? Or possibly he was one of those people who shouldn't be married. His lust for success was strong, and maybe that's the way it was for all over achievers?

On the weekends he'd return to West Palm and play husband. But on Sunday nights he'd zoom back to Miami in his Porsche on the intercoastal.

Miami was dream living, filled with the best of everything, and he over indulged. The clubs, parties, fishing trips with clients. Amenities flowed freely, from the music and drugs to the parade of women looking for hookups with wealthy men. He gorged on all of it. Ingesting, partying, and blowing through his cash.

But in 2008 the unexpected happened. By late November, the DOW lost over 49 percent of its May high and was still dropping. Brack was on the phone with clients non-stop, trying to keep panic to a minimum.

Nothing worked. His largest clients didn't want to risk the exposure in a rollercoaster market. Most of his other customers held in cash and commodities. Fees were drying up.

Brack put off filing chapter 11, believing several well-placed investments with his personal funds could save his core business. But things happened too fast. No rebound came. By December, fiscal restructuring was no longer a possibility. He was forced into chapter seven. Brack Financial had fallen to the carnage.

Yet, it wasn't losing his business that ripped apart his life.

The biggest hit to his personal finances was the divorce. When the markets were crumbling, and he struggled night and day to keep his last clients, the papers arrived at his condo. There'd been no warning, or maybe there had, and he'd been too stupid to realize it.

The home in West Palm, and the savings, all went to Vella.

During the whirlwind ordeal, his fucking lawyers had told him to liquidate his other assets and hide them in a business. Something Vella couldn't touch. He sold his beloved Porsche, his artwork, and most of his expensive jewelry. Then, he overpaid for a huge diesel-powered shrimping boat once the doors to Brack Financial closed. The idea was, he was told, that this asset would act as his sole source of income and no judge would make him liquidate it.

On paper, David Brack was now in the shrimping business.

Vella hated the open ocean. It scared her. He knew she'd have no interest in the venture. And, because she received the bulk of the marital assets, he doubted she'd fight him for any stake.

His lawyer's grand plan was that when the divorce was final, they'd fund a sale of the *Gypsea Moon* through an intermediary to repurchase the boat at the same inflated price. Voilà, the old cash-for-trash game.

The ruling further allowed him to keep his primary residence. The Miami condo. A nice piece of property with a doorman and all the finest comforts and services. If money grew tight, he could sell it for a tidy sum.

But the market collapse sent everything into disarray.

Panic struck. The major drain was the condo. Three bedrooms, three and a half baths, oversized kitchen, tenth floor—the same level as the workout facility and indoor swimming pool he never used.

After five months of screaming at his realtor, the place sold at a considerable price drop. He'd lost all equity and then some. At least he was no longer on the hook for the insane mortgage or the $50k a year in association fees.

Worse yet, the *Gypsea Moon*'s resale to the intermediary never happened. The lawyers stopped returning his calls. When he tried to get rid of the vessel on the open market, there were no takers—and he'd dropped the price to half its actual value. He was stuck with a 79-foot 'asset' costing him a pretty penny in maintenance and dock fees.

Finally, after the downturn and the divorce, he moved far away from Miami, from Vella, and from every scrap of his former life. An area outside Jacksonville kept him close to the ocean. Owning the boat limited his options and he needed to stay near the water until he got rid of it.

A summer passed with no sale. He had to change his strategy. It might be another year or longer before he could rid himself of the giant craft.

A captain charged him an arm and leg to shuttle the *Gypsea Moon*, a double-diesel behemoth, up the coastline to its new harbor in Fernandina Beach. The dock fees there were far more reasonable, but they weren't free.

That huge ship was just sitting there bouncing against its berth. He needed income, a crew to work the waters. After a rough search, and two no-shows, he found an honest man named Bill Myer to run the helm.

Myer was a no-nonsense skipper. He insisted on hiring his own deckhands. But shit, that was a blessing. Brack had no knowledge of this industry, much less experience sizing up the skills of good fisherman-types.

Ironically, for most of the past decade, that damn shrimp boat had been his only source of steady income. It wasn't much, a few thousand a month, but consistent money that covered food and rent.

Then he met Remo Gezzle at the docks. Gezzle owned a fleet of trucks, and the two started chatting. Looking back, it was this conversation that got him into this latest mess. His stupid fucking mouth, bragging, coupled with his desire to return to the extravagance of his former life.

It started out small, but Brack began working Gezzle's books and laundering cash. A few thousand at first, ramping up to well over a million each month.

Brack wasn't earning much for his efforts yet, but he knew there was a good chance if he kept Gezzle happy that the man would eventually make him a larger part of his operation and his compensation would follow suit.

Then came the night Brack lost everything. It was all still a blur, the drinks, the woman, the cocaine fueling his confidence with the Eastern European men at the poker table. Brack's drunken arrogance was on full display, again. But when he'd lost all his cash and then double-down thinking he could make a comeback, that's when Alexei Kozlov took the *Gypsea Moon*.

Alexei's business partner, of course, was the notorious Remo Gezzle. They'd worked out a deal where Gezzle would take control of the boat and move anything Alexei demanded.

But, as all things with Gezzle, there was always more to the deal. He considered Brack himself as part of the transaction. Gezzle had 'rescued' Brack from Russian gamblers by taking possession of the vessel. And now Brack was in Gezzle's debt, forever.

The plan was to run illegal goods on the shrimping boat up and down the coast, keeping Brack as its owner on paper. If anything happened to the *Gypsea Moon*, well, David Brack would take the fall for it and Gezzle could walk away from the mess unscathed.

But when they went to collect their floating prize at the docks that evening, a sea chase began. A heavy storm, gunfire, and Brack had come within seconds of losing his life.

Gezzle and his two men had drowned in the chaos.

That was months ago.

Brack had miraculously escaped it all.

Though he now lived in a nowhere hotel, on the coast of Mississippi, with everything he owned crammed inside two bags, and was about to get a refresher course on individual tax law from Dax Langford—a man he'd met only the night before at a random diner.

But in the back of his mind, there were things to correct. A life to get back to, one before Remo Gezzle and Alexei Kozlov came along and wrecked everything.

What he was most angry about, though, was the damn boat. He trusted those shitbag attorneys and paid $2 million for a floating turd that he was forced to turn into a money-maker just to feed himself.

The more Brack thought about it, the more it infuriated him. The intermediary story, had it all been bullshit? Some ruse to unload an overpriced boat on an unsuspecting sucker?

Was the idea to screw him over all along?

Chapter

11

Alana gazed through the bar's open pergola at the rolling ocean and smiled. "An entity without beginning or end. Vibrant but arranged all at once. Like a magnificent painting that steals a breath."

Her rocks glass clinked his high ball.

Oh my God, this woman was beautiful.

Possibly twenty-five or thirty, but from her open-toed sandals to the spaghetti-straps falling off her bronzed shoulders—gorgeous didn't do her justice. Her long, silky brown hair tussled in the light breeze. If he didn't know any better, he'd say she was a model or a movie actress.

"To the ocean, from whence we all came," she whispered.

Hank nodded and grinned to himself. What the fuck was she talking about? It didn't matter. Her accent was like an angel's. Sultry and smooth. Though, despite traveling to almost every seaport in the world, he couldn't place the pronunciation. Czechoslovakian maybe? Shit, he didn't know, or really care right now.

Despite all the open seating, they sat one stool apart at the bar.

The Sand Orchid wasn't crowded, unlike those cheaper dives inland, polluted with their loud, bass-pounding music that rattled Louisiana's drunkards around—like the cheap Electric-Football game he'd played with as a kid.

No, here, in this quiet open-air tavern, the only sounds were the rolling ocean and the heavenly woman next to him, currently gazing out at the sunset.

Her stunning, buttery-brown eyes stared into his, "You are a captain?"

Had he told her this already? He'd downed two Vieux Carrés. Strong cocktails often brought out his salty side. Yet he knew tossing 'shits' and 'fucks' into this conversation would likely eject this enchanting woman from her stool like a combat pilot taking on hostile enemy fire. He'd have to manner up and do his best to keep his mouth and brain in check.

"Yes." Hank sat up straight and flexed a bicep, "I command a large freighter and crew." The arm was more fat than muscle, but he hoped she wouldn't know the difference in the evening's dim light.

She leaned his way, "Tell me of it."

A scent of vanilla warmed his cheeks. Her perfume was intoxicating.

He lifted his high ball glass and glanced at her breasts again, "Right now, we're in port for onload. Headed through the canal, crossing the Pacific to a place called Xiamen. That's in China, you know?"

She licked her plump lips, "Yes, I know. And that must be a large ship you command? Able to go all that way?"

He suppressed a belch and flexed his arm fat, "Uh, yes. Mine's a biggin for sure, the *Okeana*. She can transport around five to seven thousand tractor trailer loads. Around 15,000 containers. But it all depends on how they hitch things, you know?"

He'd needlessly added the last part and it was doubtful she'd understand what he meant. But he was nervous and wanted to keep the conversation moving.

"Are these twenty and forty-foot containers?"

The question surprised him, "Uh, right, though it's mostly the forty- and sixty-foot-long intermodals, and we get bigger custom loads, too. But usually the regular twenty-foot equivalent TEUs are carried by smaller boats. They're too expensive to stack on a cargo ship like mine. Twice the crane work for the same rate."

She nodded with a smile, "Imagine it would be."

This was the longest conversation he'd had about his job with a woman in almost twenty years. She also seemed to have some knowledge on the subject. It was near as impressive as her perfectly enhanced chest.

She gave out a hand and announced, "Alana."

"Raskin, Hank," he said. Last name first? It'd been so long since he'd introduced himself to a beautiful woman that everything felt out of balance.

Her soft palm took his, "Pleased to meet you, Hank."

"Gratefully pleased to meet you, Alana."

Gratefully? He'd meant to say 'very,' but cocktails...

Nevertheless, he hoped for a smile. That would let him know there might be a slim connection, an interest to at least keep the banter going. And he'd buy another round shortly if awkward pauses became too many.

Then something unexpected happened.

The breathtaking Alana slid into the stool beside him.

Oh shit.

Normally, no creature like this would ever give him the time of day. She was either half-blind, extremely tipsy, or horny.

Maybe he'd hit the trifecta?

He was forty-three, not unfortunate looking, and could still suck in the middle parts when the occasion called for it. Generously sized shirts also hid his growing love handles. But insofar as any of it working, honestly, it'd been so long since he'd been with a woman, he'd stopped torturing himself with the hope.

She touched his forearm, and a forgotten warmness filled his limbs. Was this really happening?

"How long does the ship take to make it to China?"

He stared at her soft hand caressing his arm.

"Uh, like, er, like three or four weeks depending on the load, weather, which affects speed and such."

Alana looked at him with concern, "That is a long time, Hank."

She squeezed his skin.

He almost dropped his drink.

"Yeah, uh, it can be for sure."

"Imagine it is tough out there, alone?"

Hank tried to control his smile, but his cheeks betrayed him. He must've looked like a cross between a chipmunk and a puppy begging for a snack.

All he could manage was a blushed nod.

Under the bar, she kicked off her sandals revealing her beautifully manicured toenails, "What do you transport?"

Hank's face was cemented in a lunatic grin, "Oh, oh, all sorts of stuff. Finished goods from refrigerators to motorcycles, raw materials, food, ore, a bunch of items."

Alana's long eyelashes fluttered, "Any contraband?"

Strange question, but not the first time he'd been asked.

Hank laughed. "Sure, there's some of that. Plenty of blind shipments, from buyer to seller."

Alana tilted her head, "Blind shipments? Drugs, or?"

Hank was determined to impress her and play this up. He leaned her way and spoke in a low, deep voice, "There's been occasion, yes. Back and forth from one country to another. Kilos, weapons, other things."

"And you have seen this?"

Hank smirked even wider, "Honey, nothing gets on my freighter without my say-so."

Alana tapped a nail on her glass, "Nothing?"

"Nothing."

"And the pay for this is good?"

Hank nodded, "Oh yes, very good."

If she was a pro, this is where the negotiation would take place. She may speak in code, or just come right out and tell him what the charge would be for her company. He had plenty of cash but would be a tad disappointed if things came to that.

He glanced at her soft neck and supple chest again.

Okay, maybe he wouldn't be disappointed at all.

She finished her drink, and he asked if she'd like another.

"No, no. I am fine but thank you."

Moments passed where neither spoke, and he knew from experience that a working girl wouldn't have wasted this much time.

She rose from her stool, gathered her sandals, her purse, and stretched her backside. Her curvaceous body caused his jaw to drop.

Shit. It would have been nice to see a real-live woman naked this year, but this was too much to hope with the lovely Alana. She had a magnetic beauty that reached at the pit of his stomach. Any man would kill for her.

They'd probably just shake hands and he'd supply a respectful goodnight. Meeting her would relegate itself to a recall fantasy—something to conjure up to help him fall asleep in the nights ahead.

But then Alana hit him with another surprise, "Would you like to show me your ship?"

Boy would he! Hank slapped $20 on the bar. Or maybe it was $50. He didn't care and didn't check. The Sand Orchid could have his wallet, wristwatch, and anything else they wanted—except Alana. She was his.

Alana draped his arm, holding it tight.

Several customers stared in envy as he and the barefoot goddess passed. Even the women ogled, and it wasn't at Hank's tummy tucking.

Who's the luckiest idiot in the world? Hank beamed. This Guy!

They made their way into the parking lot and to his rental car. An eco-friendly Toyota hybrid something or other. He pressed the keyless entry and walked her to the passenger side, opened the door, and quickly ushered a collection of wrappers from her seat.

Alana's curvy body brushed his as she got in.

Hank nearly tripped over his own feet when he'd shut her door. But he managed to round the driver's side without looking too much like the clumsy imbecile he was feeling.

Once he was also inside the car, Alana leaned his way with excitement, "This is like an adventure."

It's a fucking miracle is what it is, he nearly blurted.

She eagerly asked him questions along the short drive. Most of them about landmarks and such. He answered what he could, summoning whatever interesting bullshit came to mind, while sneaking glances at her bare legs. They made his mouth water.

Evening blanketed the sky when they arrived at port 31W. The Toyota's headlights found the entrance, passed the sorting buildings, and entered the container yard.

Ever the recent gentleman, Hank found a parking space, sprang from the car, and hustled over to Alana's side. He offered a hand to guide her up from her seat, which she took without hesitation... and didn't let go once she'd exited the Toyota.

Hank's heart pounded.

The seaport was dark and quiet, except for the sound of lapping swells against the pier. The current supply-chain slowdown had the cranes running only during the daytime now.

But because his freighter had crucial perishables, which they'd smartly stacked on the bottom rows, his cargo ship was pushed to the front of the line while other ships waited their turn in the harbor. As well, the freeport he'd berthed in wasn't hampered by the usual delays and inspections from U.S. Customs.

His reload was also more than halfway finished and, if things stayed on schedule, he could summon his crew back tomorrow morning for an afternoon cast off.

Though, right now, none of that shit mattered.

Alana's vanilla perfume hit his nostrils again and he floated in extasy beside her.

"So many beautiful ships," she exclaimed looking out at the berthed vessels. Then she pointed, "Wow, what is that huge one?"

Hank smirked and squeezed her hand gently.

"Alana, I'd like you to meet my freighter, the *Okeana*."

She spoke with such excitement, "Oh my gosh. It is so gigantic. I cannot believe. Amazing!"

Not as amazing as you.

"Like to go for a tour?"

"Absolutely, I would love that!"

It was too bad none of his crew were around to see his triumphant walk up the gangplank with this mesmerizing beauty. If they were, he was sure they'd cheer like he was royalty. He'd wave to their applause and take a bow once he and Alana reached the top. Yeah, yeah, gentlemen, your captain's still got it.

As they strolled the deck, he described several items aboard before Alana made an odd request.

She pointed to a container, "Can we go inside one?"

"Inside there?"

"Yes, I have always wanted to see. Is it roomy?"

Roomy? His quarters in the accommodation tower had a nice mattress with pillows and blankets. But if she couldn't wait, then neither could he.

All cargo aboard was locked and tagged, save for one intermodal that the crew used for storage. Padlocked, forty-foot, maybe half-full, and only a short deck-walk away. Hank felt for the ship's keys in his pocket and his fingers were greeted with the familiar metal clump.

Though not a 'real' commercial container, crew storage was filled with boxes, trinkets, a motorbike or two, sometimes a rug, a piece of furniture, or whatever his men bought in a port market—things like that. But Alana wouldn't know the difference between industrial packed goods and the crew's junk box.

Hank held her hand tightly, "Right over here."

It was pitch-dark now, especially between the high rows of containers. He felt for the cylinder's hole. Thankfully he'd used a bit of med tape on the crew storage key to remind him which one it was—and now that decision was blindly paying off.

A click, a twist, the lock popped off, and he raised the container's handle.

He let go of her hand and fished out his mobile phone, "One second." He pushed a few buttons and turned on the phone's flashlight, shining it into the space.

Alana's scent whisked past him, and she entered the container. "Wow, this is really something."

Hank almost giggled.

He turned to close the intermodal's door.

But a flash, a crack, erupted behind him.

A pinch hit his shoulder blade.

He'd felt something similar one other time. As a kid, when he and a friend were exploring a neighbor's unfinished swimming pool, he'd fallen backward onto a piece of untrimmed rebar. That wound tore into his back and needed eight stitches. He recalled the tears he'd shed peddling his Mongoose back home.

But this pain grew increasingly worse.

Hank dropped to a knee.

The ache radiated to his chest.

Blood soaked the front of his shirt.

Alana stood over him, outlined in the mobile phone's beam.

What was happening?

A suppressed gun in one hand, and her open handbag in the other.

"Nothing gets on freighter without your say-so?"

He cried, "What? Wait…"

The weapon targeted his forehead.

"No, no, please!"

Alana stood, stone-faced. A steady finger hovered on the trigger. The deadness in her eyes sent a chill through him he'd never known before.

He pleaded, "No, God, why are you doing this?" His palm pressed the oozing wound on his chest while his other reached outward toward her in defense.

Alana shook her head and squeezed.

Another flash.

Hank's body fell.

Alana searched his pockets, retrieved the keys, and then grabbed the glowing mobile phone. Using her purse as a kind of glove, she stepped outside, closed the container's panel, swung the lever back into place, and snapped on the padlock.

She found the correct key and inserted half its body into the lock's cylinder before bending and twisting the cast metal, snapping it in two. She jammed the key's broken lower half deep into the lock's cavity.

Carefully, she stepped to the freighter's railing. The ship keys and Hank's phone disappeared with a splash.

Alana looked out at the moon, then back at the container with Hank's dead body locked inside.

"Greedy fuck," she muttered.

Charlie was his usual chipper self when Brack returned to the Big B hotel from Dax's office with a stack of files.

Brack hadn't worked a full day in forever. His ass hurt from sitting, and his breath stunk from charred coffee, but mentally he felt good.

Though this wasn't stock trading, he was in the numbers again. And it used a part of his brain he hadn't tapped in a long while. Not the most exciting work, but aspects of tax law challenged him enough to supply a forgotten sense of satisfaction when he got everything to fit into place.

"Good evening, Mr. Brannon," Charlie said. He was dressed in shorts and a large sunhat, and it appeared he'd done some gardening. Behind the hotel's check-in desk stood a young man with long hair who Brack had never seen before. He and Charlie had been speaking to one another. Maybe Charlie had managed to hire another employee?

Brack nodded their direction.

Slender Charlie took several steps Brack's way, "Lots of paperwork. Do you need a hand?"

Brack did, in fact, need another arm. But he shook Charlie off with a "Thanks, I got it" and headed for the stairway. The lobby work was done, and Charlie had moved out, or in, the stacked furniture that was there just yesterday. The place smelled fresh and clean, and most carpet stains had vanished. This guy knew his business.

Charlie called out before Brack hit the stairs, "I'm having a beer by the pool in a few minutes if you want to join me?"

Brack was hunting down a devious lawyer who stole $2 million from him, hiding out from notorious knee-capping thugs who might kill him on sight, and finally, had just started a new job and currently had an armful of tax returns to get through.

He turned to Charlie and smirked, "You bet." Because why the hell not?

Upstairs, the suite was how he'd left it, which was a relief. He'd imagined images of an old movie series he saw as a kid where a crafty ninja attacked the main character each time he returned home. Thankfully, Kato was not inside the hotel room to lunge from the shadows at the Pink Panther.

He left the stack of tax papers on the second bed, splashed a handful of water on his face, unbuttoned the placket of his shirt, stretched his neck, glanced around once more for Kato, then headed back to the lobby area to join Charlie.

A bit of conversation and a beer might be nice.

Some of the rusty red primer patches in the hallway had been covered with fresh paint. That Charlie was busy today.

At the front desk, that skinny, long-haired kid stood with a smile.

He greeted Brack with an awkward, "Top of the evening."

Brack nodded and headed to the hotel's courtyard.

Charlie, as usual, was hard at work trimming hedges along the pool. The large hat shielded the sun and a white sweat cloth dangled from the back pocket of his swim trunks.

Charlie smiled, "Well, hello, Mr. Brannon."

"Yes, sir. I was promised a beer."

Charlie laughed. "Well, saddle up to the table, and I'll join you in a minute." Charlie finished the section he was working on, put the hedge clippers away, ducked back inside the hotel, and returned with a bottled six-pack.

"I sure appreciate you pointing out the mistake in the software the other day." Charlie handed Brack a beer.

For a moment, albeit brief, Brack realized he'd not touched a drop of alcohol since that stormy night on the shrimp boat when Gezzle had died. And its absence had come with unexpected benefit—the loss of more than thirty pounds in just a couple of months. As he twisted the bottle's lid off, he promised himself to keep it to two or three and no more.

"Yes, sir, don't get many honest ones here," Charlie continued.

Brack took a swig.

Cool, crisp spirits hit his tastebuds, and he swallowed. It felt like heroin, or what he thought heroin felt like. He took a second, longer swig of beer. The magical alcohol found the throbbing pain in his hindquarters and battled the ache. After another swig, his neck loosened.

"I'll look at the software settings for you if you want?"

"Oh, Mr. Brannon..."

"David, please." After all, Brannon wasn't his real last name, and it made him uncomfortable Charlie kept using it.

"Mister David, okay. You don't need to go through any trouble."

"It's no trouble. I'll just check the figures, ensure they're where you want them, and that things add up properly. Good maintenance, really."

"I could comp you, of course, if that works?"

Brack laughed. "No, no. The beer is quite enough."

"Someone not looking to take advantage of ignorance. That's also rare."

Yes Charlie, but if you stumble across my $2 million, please give me a shout, would you?

Brack sipped, "No problem, happy to do it."

Charlie raised his beer, and Brack did the same.

"I see you doing all this work on the place. It's really coming along. How many properties do you own?"

"This is my first place," Charlie chuckled. "I've worked in the industry, of course. Beverage and entertainment for various establishments in

Biloxi. But I've always wanted to find someplace to run, fix it up. Put some good old sweat equity into it."

"Speaking of rare, it doesn't seem like many people want to work that hard nowadays."

Charlie wiped a bead of sweat from his forehead, "Don't I know it? It was all I could do to bribe my nephew to come and help run the front desk. You know that little shit—excuse me—wants $25 an hour just standing there, checking people in? And it's not like we've got a rush of customers or anything."

Brack nodded. The place had good bones and was off the beaten path. But without sparkling, working amenities, a place like this would likely never climb out of its two-star status.

"Dang it, that sun is hot. You know I'm starting a gazebo project out here next week. It can get scorching outside."

All Brack could do was nod and drink. The fact was that no rush of customers would come pouring in without a restaurant, beach chairs, or drink service. But he held those comments to himself.

Brack reached for another beer and torqued the top.

Charlie grinned, "Quick drinker."

Brack exhaled, "Long day." Really, it was a rollercoaster life. But he was feeling good now.

Charlie tongued a cheek, "Try to keep myself from indulging too much. Moderation, and all. I treat beer like cupcakes. Too many will make you fat and lazy."

Both men laughed.

But Charlie's statement was more factual than he knew. Brack hadn't realized how overweight he'd become until he started losing the pounds, and his trouser belt didn't have enough holes. Had he really been that big? Apparently, yes.

Brack set the fresh beer on the table, trying to put some distance between himself and his next sip of alcohol, "Hey Charlie, have you always wanted to be in the services industry?"

The man looked down and set his beer on the table across from Brack's, "Not always. But life leads us in some strange directions."

I'll fucking say. I used to live in a beachfront condo, had a mansion in West Palm, scores of girlfriends, a sportscar, a beautiful shopaholic wife, more drugs than I could do, and not a care in the world.

Brack snatched his beer and downed a healthy swig, "It does."

"Would you believe I was once in the seminary?"

Brack gulped, "Like religious seminary?"

"Yes, with God, the Bible, our heavenly apostles, and everything."

"What happened?" Then Brack felt strange for asking. He was prying into a man's life he hardly even knew.

Charlie outstretched his arms and glanced around the courtyard, "Always enjoyed helping people. But we never stop growing as individuals. What we believe we want, who we think we are, changes. We become different with each experience. You know?"

Brack snickered. "Couldn't handle the chastity, could you?"

Charlie gave a half-smile.

Brack chided, "C'mon, we're guys here."

The beer and a half, coupled with his weight loss, was already affecting his inhibitions. But hey, a little friendly rousing was in order.

Charlie gave half a nod, "Right, something like that."

"But you found your place here. And you're obviously enjoying what you do. I've seen the work you're putting in, fresh paint even in the halls. It's like you were made for it."

"I do. I do enjoy it."

"Aww, don't tell me you're second-guessing the life?"

"No, no. Nothing like that, I…"

The hotel's courtyard door swung open. Charlie's nephew waved him over. Brack couldn't hear what was said, but when Charlie returned, he excused himself and gifted Brack the rest of the six-pack.

David Brack finished his second beer and made his way through the lobby to return to his room

Yet a haunting scent, that of vanilla, hung in the air.

A woman he'd half-recognized scurried across the lobby silently speaking on her mobile phone. There was a familiarity about her, almost ghostly. But after no more than two seconds, she rounded a corner and disappeared.

He followed.

The next hall turned quickly to a corner section, then another. He could hear her footsteps and some of what she was saying but couldn't quite manage to catch up.

At a confluence of halls and a staircase, he turned.

A heavy door someplace echoed to a close but knowing its direction in this maze of corridors was impossible.

Brack found an unnumbered door a few steps later and opened it.

Inside were metal prepping tables, two mixing machines, non-running refrigerators and freezers, and an entire mess of hanging cookware near a bevy of large sinks.

But no beautiful woman.

The large kitchen area looked as if it'd been sitting unused for at least a couple of years.

Brack left the area and shook his head.

Maybe it was the alcohol?

He didn't know that woman.

He couldn't have.

He returned to the lobby.

Charlie's long-haired nephew supplied a wave as he passed and wished him a pleasant evening.

Maybe because of his frustration at losing the mystery woman, Brack wanted to march over and tell Charlie's young nephew that back in the day that he had to work like hell for $25 an hour. But he resisted. He did promise himself, though, if he caught the kid sleeping at the desk, he would give the money-hungry slacker a nice, short trim with Charlie's garden sheers.

Brack ascended the stairs, strode down the hall, and decided to tuck the remaining three beers into the ice machine. Whoever came along might enjoy one. He'd had enough for the night. Moderation, mysterious women, and all.

Plus, a stack of tax returns was waiting for him to dig into.

CHAPTER
13

Alana steered the Black Cadillac Escalade onto Interstate 59 and spoke into her mobile phone, "What is wrong?"

The caller, though, was silent.

"Tell me. You know we keep no secrets." She peered down at the SUVs gas gauge and took the next exit.

Alexei Kozlov uttered sadly, "Cousin."

Alana found a filling station and pulled in. She'd returned to the hotel—a small seaside place outside Biloxi—before heading out again. She tried to move every couple of nights, but never too close to her targets. Out of the way areas where she wouldn't be hassled by the town's drunken woman chasers or courted by the faux white night types that felt she needed protection from the world, while they tried to charm their way past her undergarments.

"What of cousin?" Alana parked next to a pump and opened the Escalade's door.

Gas fumes wafted about. Next to her vehicle, an elderly woman pumped unleaded into her cinnamon brown Acura.

On the mobile, Alexi cleared his throat, then said gloomily, "My cousin is dead."

Alana tried to summon a tear, but when that didn't work, she spoke slow and tender, "I thought he was on the mend. How could this be? I am so sorry Alexei. What may I do?"

Alexei sniffled, "Report from hospital was positive, right until… they say he aspirated."

"Oh, my Alexei. I am sorry."

He cleared his throat before continuing, "Do you know what it means? This aspirating?"

Fuel pumped into the Escalade, "Is this something with lungs?" But she knew well what aspiration was—she'd seen it. The vomit filling the tube, trailing back into Yuri's blowpipe when she'd cut off his airway, and compressed his chest. Though really it had been the undetectable aconite poison she'd injected that sent the man to his maker. Squeezing his tube and making him choke was simply added torture she'd inflicted—and it was totally unnecessary, but the motherfucker deserved it.

Alexei asked again, "I have never heard of such a thing. Have you?"

"Alexei what may I do? Do you want me to return?"

Even under the circumstance she knew what his answer would be. She was his eliminator, paid to silence those connected with the bad shipment. Each had to be found and shitcanned. And there was at least one more target.

"No, we cannot. You must stay on task there. Find the man on watch at seaport and do what is needed. His men should have protected boat when it arrived but failed."

"The security man at port?"

"Yes, in zone. He is on payroll. I want him removed."

That location was near enough. She could stay at the Big B hotel until that job was done, then move again or return north to Alexei once she completed her duties, "Watchman at port, okay."

Alexei went quiet. She thought she heard him shout something with his hand over the phone at one point but did not understand what was said. When he returned to the call, Alexei was breathing heavier, "When you are finished, then I want you to find doctor."

"Doctor?"

"At hospital."

"Find the doctor, why?"

"Find her and kill her."

He'd never used such direct language on the phone before, she could tell he was thinking with emotion, "Alexei don't –"

Alexei shouted, "You understand, do you not?"

"Yes, but Alexei –"

"She failed me. She failed Yuri!"

"But Alexei –"

"You will kill them and anyone who gets in your way!" he yelled.

Alana sighed, "Okay, okay."

Alexei took a moment before speaking again, "I am sorry. It is very painful for me right now. I am beside myself, dear Alana."

In Alana's periphery, a suspicious looking man in baggy clothes was approaching the fill up station. She discreetly clocked his movements before she returned her attention to Alexei, "Okay, I will take care of it, I promise."

Alexei collected himself, "And get the lawyer."

"I have retired him, some days ago, as requested."

"No, no. The other one."

"The other one?"

"Yes. He has found nothing and now talks with police."

Alana topped off the Escalade's tank, "Alright, okay Alexei."

The baggy clothed man came from the filling station's west, nearing the old woman in the Acura opposite her Cadillac.

"You mean world to me, my precious, you know this."

"Yes, Alexei. Still, I do not think doctor is smart move."

Alexei held quiet.

Alana replaced the pump into its receptacle, "But I will do as you ask."

"Good, thank you."

Soon after, they said their goodbyes.

She still had Alexei's trust, his confidence, believing she would do anything for him that needed to be done. And now the death of his cousin had thrown him off-kilter. He was making emotive demands now and was no longer the strictly methodic man she'd known these past years.

Yuri's death had really fucked him up, even more than she'd calculated. She rethought her decision but knew in the greater scheme it had ultimately been the right choice. She still had Alexei's devotion and love and, right now, those meant everything.

The strange man in the baggy clothes walked under the gas station's awning to the Acura.

He pulled on the vehicle's passenger side door handle.

When it didn't open, baggy clothed man confronted the aged woman.

She was startled, "What do you want? What are you doing?"

He shouted at her, "Gimme your purse, bitch!"

He tried to wrestle away her keys and pushed the elderly woman to the ground.

Alana grabbed her 9mm from the Cadillac's center console and approached the two.

The man swiftly turned her way and drew his own firearm.

Alana sent two quick rounds into his knee cap.

The would-be robber screamed in pain.

He and the pistol fell to the station's concrete fueling pad.

Alana retrieved his weapon.

The terrified woman gazed at Alana with confusion.

"Sorry for trouble miss," Alana helped her from the ground. "But try to have good evening."

The trembling lady returned a shaky smile, "You... you too."

CHAPTER

14

Colonel Michael James Bennett appeared the next day on Kendrick's front stoop on Amelia Island.

The brown-haired Bennett wore casual slacks and a t-shirt touting Pink Floyd's Dark Side of the Moon. T-shirt casual was his style and, while not a snappy dresser, at least the man had solid taste in music.

For the most part, he looked the same as he had when they'd met months ago, but with two cups of coffee and a broad smile plastered across his face.

Kendrick stuck out a hand, but Bennett came in for a hug.

"I know this is gonna be fun," the Marine smiled.

Kendrick led them into his modest two-bedroom lodge. Built in the 1950s, a few blocks from the ocean in a not well traveled downtown section, the place was far enough away from the bars where he didn't hear the loud music but close enough to migrate toward the sounds when he needed a pint.

It was a furnished rental with fixtures at least two decades behind trends. On the main room's wall hung an early model flatscreen that pulsed strangely when Kendrick turned the television on to check the weather.

Bennett was a 48-year-old pilot who came up through the Marine corps. He'd earned his stripes through mud and blood, as he was often fond of saying. He hadn't gone to college and resented almost anyone who did. He'd spent much of his profession in-theater, as Kendrick had, and knew how to handle a weapon. Though, now he was in the latter half of his career. He mainly shuttled military bosses around the country on his aircraft. This left Bennett with a lot of free time, which was good.

The quirky six-foot-one Marine could pilot anything with wings. He was also loyal and didn't take any shit.

However, the two hadn't begun their relationship under the best of circumstances. Still, things had changed a lot during the previous mission on the *Malusnavi* freighter. Nothing bonds like a crisis. After their last harrowing adventure, Bennett spent more than a month in the hospital recovering from a gunshot wound from a hijacker which punctured his lung. But now the Marine was healed, and on both feet again.

Through that ordeal, Bennett had proven to Kendrick he was a true soldier. Courage, focus, follow through, and the mental wherewithal to manage objectives no matter their differences early on. None of the team would've made it back alive to the states without his abilities. In fact, the two men had saved each other's lives at least once.

Kendrick had been the one who drug Bennett from the crashed jet's pilot's seat when it slid off the runway into the ocean.

Through it all, Kendrick also learned to put trust in others. In their ability and their thinking. As an operative, in his younger years, he often went on missions alone because he believed it was always best not to involve others. But the truth was now, at 52 years-old, he couldn't do everything himself. Not at this level and not at this age.

Kendrick's covert investigation into the origin of the freighter and its cargo had gotten exceedingly complex. As well, the deeper he dug, the more he was sure his life would soon be in danger. He needed someone he could rely on, someone who always had his six, someone who could get them anywhere his investigation demanded. And there was only one man for the job.

He and Bennett sipped their hot beverages on the rental's living room couches.

Bennett snickered, "Love what you've done with the place," He stroked the bright, red, and green fabric on the floral sofa. "Very festive. Is Santa showing up later?"

Kendrick shook his head, "It came with the unit, and —"

"Sure, it did," Bennett laughed.

"It's too early in the morning. Don't make me shoot you."

Bennett grinned, "Just having some fun. Man, it's good to see you."

Kendrick set his drink on the tarnished walnut table between them, "You too."

Bennett drew a long pull from the coffee and swallowed, "Alright, amigo. What's got me flying down here? Lay it on me."

Kendrick leaned forward and shook his head, "I tried to get the manifest but couldn't find anything in the database. Adler had nothing of substance on the PELG containers, but he's still searching sources. We did find more details on Gezzle. His organization was working with a law firm out of Louisiana. A Melton Oliver & Associates. Oliver was killed weeks ago, and the man had three bullets in his head."

Bennett whistled, "Three?"

"Three," Kendrick confirmed.

"Sloppy or professional?"

"Tight grouping."

"Guess you're on the right trail," Bennett sipped.

"Yeah, but nothing makes connective sense. As far as Adler and I could uncover, the man Oliver just handled the paperwork for Gezzle's outfit."

"What about his partner?"

"Yes, Melton. He was out of town at the time, alibied and all. But I'm not sure he's completely clean. He seemed a little relaxed during the interrogation."

"Wait," Bennett shook his head. "Interrogation?"

"In Louisiana," Kendrick said matter of fact, "I snuck into the station and —"

"Woah, woah!" Bennett gasped, "You actually walked into the police station and questioned him?"

Kendrick shrugged.

"Ballsy, ballsy move, amigo." Bennett shook his head. "You're in deep, that's for sure."

Kendrick nodded.

"Alright, then," Bennett stretched his neck to one side. "What else did you find out?"

"Gary Oliver was Melton's chum," Kendrick resumed. "His best friend since university. And the guy was murdered in their office. Yet, and I can't put my finger on it, but Melton appeared matter of fact about the whole situation. He even posed a theory for the murder, which was oddly convenient. Said vagrants in the area often busted in."

"Sign of guilt?"

"Maybe. Or there was some knowledge he wasn't forthcoming with. Can't put my finger on it."

"You said that. And?"

Kendrick shook his head.

Bennett sipped again, "I know that look. You don't trust the fucker. Do we follow up?"

"Not yet."

"Okay, so what else?"

"Been searching for the captain of the *Malusnavi*. Figure if we can't find the ship, at least we find who was running it during the South American route. Maybe glean a few answers?"

"Got a name?"

"A Hank Raskin. Career guy, supposed to be in the area right now. Adler's trying to find his vessel to track him down."

"Hoping for a manifest on the last freighter?"

"Precisely. But what we really need are solid connections. The more I delve into this, the more muddled it gets."

"Muddled?"

"Sigma-Sea Imports, we know Gezzle worked with them, and the ship was registered to a company called Pellgrin International. But after that, things go pear-shaped. A maze, a mess. No names, just corporations that link to other corporations, and the trail fades into the back-and-forth mire of paperwork and legalese. There's no overall 'owner' that we could find."

Bennett nodded, "No big guy."

"No big guy, right."

"Well, seems the next move is to locate the captain and find out what he knows, right?"

"Agreed. Like I said, the man is somewhere in the port area, likely loading or unloading, so we need to find him fast."

"And you want to fly over there?"

"Yes, that's what I was hoping."

The two sat back and nursed their coffees for a long moment. Kendrick stared silently looking out a window.

"Hey, partner. You in over your head?" Bennett asked.

Kendrick turned to his friend, "May very well be. But there are many that…"

"No, no, I get it."

Kendrick looked his pal over, and suddenly realized he was thrusting him into a situation that could get them both killed. He turned to Bennett, "I never asked. This all could get bloody dangerous. You okay with –?"

"Hell, amigo," Bennett grinned. "You know me. Without scars, life's boring as shit."

The two men chuckled anxiously and finished their drinks.

CHAPTER

15

After a shower, Brack dressed in a plain pair of black pants and a light cotton blue flannel. It was the last of his clean clothes before he'd need to launder everything, including the pre-worn garments he'd gotten at the pawnshop.

As he readied himself in the bathroom, he noticed the looseness of the clothing. His belly had flattened, and his once puffy eyes and cheeks shrank considerably. The strong jawline he'd last seen in his twenties was coming back.

Had he changed himself that much? The absence of drink and a lighter diet?

Last night, he took a break from the tax returns and did an online search. Rick Melton's partner, Gary Oliver was dead. A murder—which didn't shock him. He knew the part of town they were in had become rundown over the years, and that the clientele could be precarious.

Gary Oliver had been one of the lawyers responsible for handling his divorce, and he and Rick Melton had convinced Brack to buy the *Gypsea Moon* to hide his assets. The fast-talking attorneys had assured the younger Brack that they knew how to hide properties from judges.

Now that he was wiser, Brack knew they'd likely scammed him. His education had focused on handling market monies, not the underworld, laundering, and concealing. But he'd learned a whole lot since then.

Rick Melton was still alive, and Brack knew that if he could get a look at his finances, he'd know just where to extract the cash owed to him. The trick would be getting into the damn office and finding where he kept his holdings.

Next, Brack couldn't help himself and searched for Vella's profile on social media. Within a few clicks, he found her.

His ex-wife was as beautiful as ever. Jade eyes. Long, deep brown hair. That glistening movie star complexion.

Though her smile was somehow different than he recalled. It was more extensive and more vibrant.

Vella still lived in West Palm and worked part-time at an aquarium. That was good. She loved marine life. Though, after scrolling down her page, Brack's heart skipped a beat.

Vella was engaged. Gavin Highland—a psychiatrist with his own practice. The guy looked like something out of a GQ magazine. Perfect physique, piercing blue eyes, and a grin that matched Vella's. The wedding was in four months. An evening ceremony at the five-star Breakers Hotel. The town's mayor was a family friend, and she and her husband would be there. Guests were encouraged to attend the event in white tie and evening dress.

Fuck.

He pondered things before finally falling asleep. Even if he could recoup the $2 million from the lawyer, that wouldn't be near enough to win her back, and he knew it. Vella was out of his league for good.

Still, he'd push forward. Forge his new life. Vella or not, he'd get what was owed to him, find a new place, somewhere like the condo in Miami, and buy a new Porsche the moment he could afford it.

Brack finished getting ready, grabbed the tax files, and headed downstairs.

Charlie greeted him in the lobby.

"Hey, good morning," Brack said. "I'll have a look at your software when I get back this evening if you're around?"

Charlie smiled, "Oh, Mister David. That would be great. And I'll get the beers."

Brack put up a hand, "Let's keep it to sweet tea if that's okay? I don't wanna meddle with something I shouldn't. Give your rooms away for free by mistake."

"Ha-ha. Sure, I'll whip up a cold pitcher then."

"Perfect."

"Have a pleasant day, Mister David."

He didn't know what it was, but chipper Charlie always put a smile on his face.

Dax's Taxes was a half mile up the road. Instead of walking the roadway, Brack strolled along the shoreline, listening to the sounds of the rolling waves. The fresh sea air made him feel good, and he'd forgotten how invigorating it was.

He left the sand, crossed the road, entered the office, and found Dax hunched over his desk, mumbling to himself.

"Where do you want these?"

Dax waved him forward and took the stack of files from Brack, "How many did you get through?"

Brack nodded toward the pile, "All of them."

"Twenty? You finished twenty individual tax returns?"

"Yes."

"In one damn night?"

Brack nodded.

"That's at least fifteen hours of work, maybe twenty. How late did you stay up?"

"I don't know. Midnight. I guess."

Dax scanned the paperwork, "You completed Hank's Berries? How?" He paused. "Wait, wait. This isn't right. How can Hank's deduct a… what is this? An XL-18? What the hell is an XL-18?"

"It's a flamethrower."

"A what?"

"Flamethrower."

"Is one of those even legal to own?"

"He's a farmer. After harvest, he uses it to burn away residue and enrich the soil before replanting. I deducted the device and the fuel he bought."

"What account did you locate it?"

"It was misclassified on his inventory 'for sale' list. I checked with the client and found it was, in fact, a fixed asset he uses."

Dax flipped through the file, "That damn inventory list was forty pages long. Did you depreciate all of it?"

"Yes, every item."

"Shit, and I thought I was good." Dax shook his head and looked up at Brack, "Still… twenty full returns?"

"Already entered in your system. I did that from the hotel. Ready for your approval and e-file."

Dax checked his computer, "You some kind of superhuman?"

Brack shrugged, "Well, I can do most of the math in my head. Numbers just make sense."

"Extraordinary."

Brack smiled. He hadn't worked with anyone this closely in many years. Dax's accolades felt surprisingly good.

"Hell. I've got another dozen here." Dax waved a hand to a second stack on his desk and snorted, "Should take you only a couple of minutes, apparently."

Brack chuckled. "Sure, no problem."

Then Dax drew his brows together, and he rubbed his chin, "Listen, there's something else you might be able to help with."

"Anything."

"Doesn't have much to do with numbers, but a smart guy like you might be able to figure it out."

"What is it?"

"Asset management.

"Yeah?"

"I have a client who passed."

"I'm very sorry to hear that."

Dax nodded, "Good woman." He leaned back in his chair. "Margaret ran a small business trading exotic pottery. Her son says that she has several unclaimed packages at the water port. But I haven't been able to verify it. Honestly, I just don't have the time."

"Do you have bills of lading, or?"

"Well, that's the thing. Margaret was an honest woman. I've no reason to think her son isn't the same. But there's no documentation beyond some receipts which do not show the shipping location."

"Ahh."

"However, the packages are apparently inside a warehouse outside port NOLA. Though I can't get anyone on the phone." Dax gnashed his bottom lip. "I even tried visiting once, but the place was like a fortress, and they didn't allow me past the gate."

"What can I do?"

"Chase down what you can. See what you can find out. There are potentially thousands of dollars' worth of products in there. Margaret's son needs it before he can sell the business. Otherwise, he's –"

"Upside-down in inventory."

"Exactly."

"Where is this place?"

Dax took on a serious expression, "That's the other thing. Because the packages came from overseas, they're in a warehouse. It's a facility inland, but it's technically part of the foreign trade zone at the port. Restricted. So, it isn't as if we can get a permit and search for the merchandise."

"That is a challenge."

"Yeah, but I figure with that Clemson brain of yours, you might figure out something I haven't."

Brack relished the challenge, "Sure, I'll see what I can uncover."

"Thank you, and thanks for this." Dax nodded to Brack. "Excellent work, really."

Brack's smile widened.

That was a statement no one had said to him for a long, long time.

CHAPTER

16

Dusk found Bennett and Kendrick at the Starfish Bar downtown. The unique place was nestled cattycorner from Centre Street and was among many small businesses in the town's zone contained within their original homey residential structures.

The pub's insides were once a three-bedroom, two-bath abode but had long since been transformed into a favorite funky hangout for coastal locals. The business altered the household's configuration and erected a giant 14-stool oak bar for patrons where the home's living and kitchen areas once existed.

The tavern's walls were covered in a hodgepodge of groovy artwork, including an old bicycle that hung from the ceiling alongside wave riders and massive bohemian cloth coverings.

Outside, the establishment also kept its original, generous wrap-around porch. Colorful lights dangled from the rafters, and a walk-up ramp helped to seat guests in rocking chairs and by tableside where they could enjoy open-air live music from the local talent.

The bar home's adjacent lot was also in on the party. Green picnic tables, a secondary performing stage, and a brick patio with wobbly metal tables seated even more merrymakers under an immense canopy of oak trees draped with thick Spanish moss. And, within those trees hung all manner of seaside knickknacks, from fishing nets to surfboards.

Bennett and Kendrick rocked on the tavern's deck halfway through their third pint of Red Stripe. They were listening to a delightful brunette and her tall, bearded bandmate cover 'When the Levee Breaks' on an acoustic guitar when the two men began trading war stories.

"Shit, man," Bennett began. "I can't tell you the number of times I barely escaped with my ass."

Kendrick gulped and nodded.

"Had this one thing over Afghanistan. Night mission in an F16. We're coming in low and I'm cruising just above stall speed. They wanted recon photos for enemy troop numbers. I wasn't taking the pictures. My mission was escort only. Clear a path and all that."

Bennett finished his Solo cup and Kendrick handed him his refill.

"Comes these dudes out of huts and holes absolutely lighting up the sky. Bullets, surface-to-air missiles, fucking kitchen sink. Looked like the fourth of July down there. I mean, shit."

Kendrick leaned Bennett's way, "That is hairy."

"Plane's getting dotted with piercers, and I start to notice some sluggishness in my turns but no big deal. There's booms, bangs, and bullets everywhere."

"Blimey."

"Anyway, I get back to the forward operating base, and this guy at the FOB is inspecting the F16 and finds this hole the size of my fucking head in one of the wings. Said a surface to air went right through my left flank but didn't explode.

Kendrick gulped, "Bloody hell."

Bennett nodded, "Would've been. Got shit lucky, that's for sure. An instant explosion would've done me in before I could eject. Not that I'd have been in any better shape trying to hump my way out of Dodge on the ground."

They sat listening to the music for a moment.

"What about you, amigo?"

Kendrick swallowed.

"I can't fly a plane."

Bennett crooned, "Well, nobody's perfect. But you've been in nail biters, right?"

Kendrick cocked his head to a side, "I have, indeed." Though, he'd never actually shared such a story before. Life in the intelligence business wasn't about boasting. In fact, it demanded the opposite. But since they'd sacked him into retirement, and if he didn't give away national secrets— not that he knew any—he was free to talk about whatever he wanted.

"Iraq." Kendrick took a long pull, swallowed, belched low, then settled back in his rocker. "After the bombings. Turns out there's this General Qadir third or fourth in command. Anyhow, this guy was a high-value target that was supposed to be killed in the primary bombing raid but wasn't, you see."

"And they sent your unlucky ass in to get him?"

"Affirmative." Kendrick sipped, "Somehow, they'd tracked him to the northern highlands by radio and satellite. I was airlifted by midnight chopper into those mountains and told to take him out."

"Just you?"

Kendrick nodded, "For three days, I'm going back and forth with command on where this guy is, tracking him through the hills, staying out of sight. During the day, there are farmers and others about, and I'm wearing customary garb to fit in."

"Customary garb? What does that mean?"

"Not to arouse suspicion, you see."

"As a customary what, exactly?"

Kendrick mumbled, "Herdsman."

"A what?"

"They dressed me like a damn goat-herder!"

Bennett busted out a gut laugh, "Kendrick the goat-herder! Full turban and a kurta? Did you have a cane too?"

Kendrick nodded reluctantly.

Bennett choked out another laugh, "Oh my God, I love it!"

"Finally," Kendrick raised his voice, "I came up over a ridge, and I can see their camp. Now why they didn't just bomb the place when I called it in, I don't know. Something about the 'degrade not eliminate' bullocks of scope."

"But they wanted Qadir dead?"

Kendrick nodded, "Head of the snake. As if that ever works with these types."

"Yeah. Relief command in those regions sprout like mushrooms around an outhouse shitter."

Kendrick considered the curious simile then continued, "I waited until night and crept into the area. There are guys everywhere, but I manage to hide behind equipment and the light vegetation."

"Wouldn't imagine there'd be much of that?"

Kendrick shook his head, "Mountain desert and all, no. But I get into the occupied space and wait until most of the enemy are asleep. There're only two tents erected out there, and I figure Qadir must be in one of them."

"Did you find him?"

Kendrick nodded, "In the first."

"Lucky."

"Crawled under his cot. Covered his mouth. Used my knife. It took only a couple of minutes until Qadir bled out."

"Jesus."

On the Starfish Bar's deck, the bearded man switched to an electric guitar. He fervently broke into 'Heartbreaker' as the energetic brunette beside him belted out the lyrics.

This caused Kendrick and Bennett to further increase the volume of their own chatter.

"I hike out, but I'm exhausted. Ran out of water almost two days before. I did manage to steal some of theirs, but my legs are weak from heat depletion and activity."

Bennett nodded and raised his beer.

"So, I find a flat place to camp for the night until I can get to a safe spot for extraction the next day."

"That's pretty hairy."

Kendrick finished his pint and grabbed his secondary, "We haven't gotten to that part yet."

"Oh shit."

"Morning comes, and there's smoke in the air."

Bennett shouted over the music, "Smoke?"

"Yeah. And it smells good."

"Smells good? What does that –?" Bennett's eyes grew huge, "Oh, holy hell!"

Kendrick lowered his head and shook it, "I'd fallen asleep inside the bloody perimeter of the enemy's camp, on its other side."

Bennett howled.

"When I wake up there's pots and pans and chatter all around me. Men rolling up their cots, trapsing everywhere, gearing up for the day."

Bennett exploded in laughter and beer splattered his shirt.

"These guys are fixing breakfast!" Kendrick cried.

Bennett caught his breath, "What the fuck did you do?"

"Got to my feet, brushed off, grabbed my cane, and hobbled my goat-herding arse out of there!"

Bennett roared.

"That's the funniest shit I've ever heard!"

Kendrick couldn't hold his laughter either.

CHAPTER
17

At the hospital, Doctor Tammy Rivers replayed the scenario repeatedly in her mind, and it still bothered her. Their patient was ready to be taken off the ventilator. His vitals were solid. Pull the tube, get him breathing on his own, then it was back to gen-care. He'd have sailed through joint review, and they could've transferred him from Level III into non-intensive.

What the hell did they miss?

She took off her lab coat, hung it inside the locker, and redressed. Her shift ended at midnight, and it was already three-quarters past because she'd spent the extra 45 minutes reviewing the dead man's charts.

Due to a staff shortage, she was also expected to return to the hospital in 24 hours. She'd been promised a 48-hour break but whatever. So much for work-life balance. Still, she couldn't wait to unwind with a warm bath and a good book.

She found her gray BMW in the parking deck and tapped the keyless entry. The lights flashed, and the haptic chirp sounded.

Behind the wheel, she drew in a long breath. It wasn't good to focus on a patient's death. It was distracting, and she needed to get beyond it. The autopsy may find something, some abnormality in the lungs, or poor history on the patient that might've caused a drug reaction they weren't expecting. She couldn't think of anything else that could've gone wrong. Everything had been handled textbook. Everything on her end was clean.

She backed out and headed down the ramp to the garage's first level.

A cold sensation hit the back of her neck.

Tammy froze.

"Drive," the voice said.

A glance in the rearview revealed a shadowy woman with long dark hair.

The gun she held had a long muzzle, like the ones she'd read about in DeMille's suspense thrillers.

"Who are you?"

"Take left out of garage. Do as I say."

Tammy turned, but her hands started to shake.

"Drive north."

"Where are we going?"

The woman in the backseat did not answer.

"If you want the car, please just take it. It's not worth –"

"I am not after vehicle. Get on highway at next turn."

The woman's accent was strange, Eastern European maybe.

"What do you want? I have some money, but not much. Despite what you hear, health care pay is shit nowadays."

"I do not want your cash."

"Then what?"

"Focus, doctor. Drive."

"That's really fucking hard to do with a gun pointed at my head, you understand?"

Curiously, the woman at once removed the pistol from her neck, sat back, and buckled herself into the BMW's rear seat.

The car's headlights found the onramp for Interstate 110. She used the turn signal and, for some reason, was overly mindful of the speed limit.

Doctor Tamara Rivers had never been married and had no children. She had a cat named Oscar once, but an apartment neighbor's eight-year-old daughter, whom she'd paid to look in on the feline, had fallen in love with him. Eventually, after a string of double shifts, she figured it was only proper to surrender the attention-starved kitten to the little girl.

There was no appeal of motherhood, or ailing family, or even a lonely cat to make the woman in the backseat feel bad and let her go. There was nothing at her place but a stack of unread mail and a refrigerator full of single-serve salads and stale condiments.

If the woman hadn't clicked in, she might've sped up and ended this hijacking by driving into a wall or causing some type of accident with another vehicle. But the thought hadn't occurred earlier, and now it was too late. If she did so now, the airbags might deploy, causing confusion, but a crash may only make things worse—unless the gun miraculously flew into her hands during the melee.

She'd need to talk to the woman. Work in her name, humanize herself before it became too late.

"I'm scared and confused. If you could –"

"Drive, doctor."

"My name is Tammy, and –"

"I know Doctor Rivers. Please keep driving."

She muttered, "Okay," and kept focus on the road.

They drove through the darkness north for ten miles, but it seemed like a hundred. There were few cars at this late hour, and she didn't pass one police officer. Not that it would have done any good. For all she knew, the woman behind her might shoot her and take the wheel herself if she tried to signal for aid.

The strange woman pointed over her shoulder to a green, glowing exit sign, "Turn off here."

Instinctively, Tammy activated the turn signal and took the offramp.

Oh great. A deserted industrial area. A strange sulfur smell hung in the air. The car's headlights flashed on rows of large, abandoned buildings. A stray dog crossed the street and she slowed. The creature's eyes reflected on the BMW's beams. The pooch held a moment and then scurried off to scavenge whatever he was hunting.

Tammy cringed.

Murky night, huge, deserted buildings, and a homeless dog to pick at her bones—shit, she'd driven right into a Karin Slaughter novel.

"Do you see place on left?"

Tammy nodded.

Yup, a defunct convenience store with a busted sign peddling Camel Lights for $1.39 a pack. Not only would she be murdered, but the morning's photos would juxtapose the low price of smokes from twenty years ago as background to her pixilated corpse.

"Good, pull in there."

The turn signal clicked. Why did she even bother?

"Slow to stop, now."

She did.

Fuck, this was it. There was nothing she could do now but beg for her life. Years of medical school and knowledge would be snuffed out by a weapon accidentally invented by a Chinese hunter who was only trying to figure out a way to hurl a faster spear at his prey.

The woman in the backseat leaned forward, "You do not know me, but I have been sent to kill you."

Tammy's hands remained gripped to the steering wheel. If she removed them, they're shaking might become uncontrollable.

"Several days ago, you had a patient die in your care."

Oh no, this was about the Russian. She glanced into the rearview, and a vague recollection of this woman surfaced. This was the girlfriend on the bench.

"I'm so, so sorry. We did everything we could. Honestly, I still have no idea what happened. I think it might have been a negative drug reaction, and I've looked at the files, but –"

"Stop!"

The woman's insistence scared her.

"You said you have money?"

"Yes, some. I can drive you to the bank in a few hours, and you can have it all. But please don't hurt me."

The woman unbuckled and leaned between the BMW's two front seats, "You, you were not meant to be part of this. The man's demise was not accidental. I am the one who killed him."

"What?" This made no sense at all. Why would his grieving girlfriend kill him? Tammy squinted. She must have misheard the woman.

"He was horrible man. He, he…" she trailed off.

Tammy wasn't sure whether to speak or not. But none of this was making any sense. What could the man have done to set his lover off like this?

The woman in the backseat composed herself, "I want you to take most out you can from bank."

"Yes, yes, it's yours."

The woman shook her head, "You need to go someplace."

"Huh?"

"Go someplace for at least one month. Do not use credit card. Do not call anybody. Do not go back home for anything. Do not let work know where you are. Do not contact family."

"I don't understand?"

"This is opportunity for your life which you must take. Do not socialize or go to restaurants. Get as far away from here as you can and stay hidden. When you return to work at end of month tell them you had some brief mental or physical episode. Make it public to achieve compassion. They will have to take you back."

Tammy's hands calmed.

The strange woman then asked, "Do you understand?"

"Yes, yes. I think so. But –"

"There is bounty on your head. Many bad people. If they find you, they will kill you for what happened to Yuri."

Tammy nodded carefully.

"I am taking care of that, but you must vanish. Okay?"

"Yes, okay."

The woman tucked her weapon in her purse.

"You are tangled in dangerous situation. One beyond your understanding. I am sorry for trouble. But one month, not single day sooner. You understand?"

Tammy focused on her breathing, "Yes, I understand."

The woman opened the BMW's rear door and left without another word.

Tammy quickly locked the doors and exhaled. A single tear fell down her cheek. She popped opened the glove compartment, and her passport was still there. She eyed the fuel gauge. Half a tank. Hurriedly, she tapped a few buttons on the vehicle's glowing console and selected a route.

The time was 1:21am.

The Canadian border was 1,500 miles north.

Tammy's heart raced and she stomped on the gas.

CHAPTER

18

At last call, Bennett and Kendrick took their drinks on the go and strolled back to Kendrick's place through Amelia's residential streets.

Neither man was feeling any pain.

The quirky walk led them through the island's historic Victorian homes. Fish scale shingles, steeply pitched gable roofs—many rising to a third level with balconies. Turned porch columns with milled railings, coal chutes, milk doors, and iron boot scrapers at the home's entry step. Many residences also included high turrets with giant bay windows trimmed in decorative stained glass. Fantastic places that were indeed the craftwork of another time.

Many of these post-Civil War Victorian dwellings also sported a large rectangular stone block about two feet high and three feet wide at street level. Most were also etched with the year of the home's construction. A long, thick t-shaped pole about six foot high accompanied the block.

Under the streetlights, Bennett pointed to one of the knee-high stone blocks as they passed, "What the hell is this stone for? Is it an old seat? Like a bench?"

"I'll give you a hint," Kendrick said. "See that pole?"

Bennett eyed the rod curiously, "What is it, a lamppost?"

"Close. It's a hitching post."

"Hitching?"

"And that block is a step-down."

"What the hell's a step-down?"

Kendrick chuckled. "These swankier older homes were built in the 1800s—and there weren't any automobiles back then."

"Okay?"

Kendrick motioned to another large four-sided steppingstone protruding at the sidewalk's edge as the two strode past, "Horse and carriage riders used that stone to step onto when they disembarked from their animals and carts. And they hitched their horses to that post."

Bennett stopped to examine both apparatuses, "No shit?"

Kendrick pointed to himself, "I am shitless."

"And we tease kids today about not understanding how to use a rotary telephone," Bennett gulped his beer. "I had no idea."

The two restarted their walk.

"Galloping obsolescence," Kendrick crooned. "The hallmark of progress."

"What?"

"Nothing important," Kendrick sipped.

"You know something, amigo?" Bennett turned his way. "The more you drink, the weirder you get."

Kendrick chuckled. "That's a fine phrase for one of your t-shirts."

His rental home was a simple modern ranch with a brick façade. The pub's music faded into the night once they reached his flat's front door and entered.

"Man, that was a cool bar." Bennett raised his empty cup, "Got any more?"

Kendrick motioned to his ice box in the kitchen.

"Grab me one, too?"

Bennett snickered, "And another for your goat?"

"Ha-ha. Funny, chap," Kendrick replied before his mobile phone rattled inside his pocket. He swiped open the call.

"Sir, Second Lieutenant Adler here."

"Major Thomas Ryan Kendrick here. Former Intelligence Officer, loyal British subject, and sparkling conversationalist at your service, Adler."

Kendrick laughed, and so did Bennett.

"Sorry to bust in on your evening, sir."

Kendrick plopped down on one of the floral couches, "You know, Adler, we wish you were here, mate."

"Me as well, sir. But I have some news."

Kendrick took the fresh bottle from Bennett, downed a swig, and his expression changed, "News? What's happened?"

"Development, sir."

"Well, don't keep a drunk major in suspense."

"Sir, it's not good."

"Not good?"

Bennett and his beer manned the other sofa, but he turned Kendrick's way.

"Hank Raskin is missing."

Kendrick straightened his back, "The captain is missing?"

"Raskin?" Bennett whispered.

Kendrick nodded.

"Sir, yes. Crew said he didn't report this morning."

"Trail?"

"They found his rental car in the port's parking lot. I pulled up his cell number and tried to call. Straight to voicemail. Then I bounced a direct trace through a satellite, tracked it through… well, that doesn't matter. Sir, Raskin's phone isn't pinging. It stopped last night at 22:37."

"Local time?"

"To you, yes, sir. The last location was the docks, and I think something might've happened to him."

Hank Raskin was the captain of the disappeared freighter *Malusnavi*—the boat from which they'd rescued the hostages. It'd taken a while to track down the crew list, but by sheer luck, Raskin had been placed on another ship, the *Okeana*. It had come to port in New Orleans a few days ago.

Although Kendrick doubted the captain knew much about Yuri or the others aboard his giant vessel, he was hoping the skipper might supply them with a reckoning list of cargo aboard that missing freighter. That list would allow Kendrick to investigate where the shipments were headed.

But now he was missing.

Kendrick repeated aloud Adler's statement for Bennett, "Last known was around 10:30pm yesterday."

Bennett leaned forward.

Kendrick set his beer on the walnut table, "But Raskin lives in the states?"

"No, sir."

"Can we track his residence?"

"He has a condo in the Northern Territory. Jabiru, in Australia."

Kendrick turned to Bennett, "Australia?"

Bennett mumbled, "I ain't going there. Giant snakes, fucking crocodiles. Angry Kangaroos wanting to kick my ass." The Marine moved his head side to side, took a swig of beer, and swallowed. "Forget it."

"Right, sir. Raskin's usual route took him through the Panama Canal into southern Asia."

"Home at the halfway point."

"That'd be my guess, sir."

"Alright. Keep me posted on any updates."

"Will do, sir."

With that, the call ended.

Kendrick rose from the couch, grabbed his drink from the coffee table, and glanced out a window. From what he knew of cargo captains, they could be a rough bunch, but when it came to their obligations, they were professional. Like commercial airline pilots, they needed to arrive on time for their shipping duties. Millions in freight were at stake, much of it perishable.

Bennett called from the couch, "So, what the hell do we do now?"

Kendrick thought for a moment, "We should still fly to the port first thing tomorrow. I'll confirm where the ship is docked with Adler and see if we can somehow get aboard for a quick look."

"We also looking for the man?"

"It'd be nice to find him, but his mobile died at about half past ten last night."

"You sure he wasn't picked up? Might be in the slammer?"

"No. Adler said the last ping was at the port."

"That's not a good sign."

"No, not at all."

"Possibly, he had enemies. Pissed someone off?"

"Maybe."

"Well, I say we get some rest, and start fresh in the morning."

"Agreed."

Kendrick took a long sip. Two questions were brewing. Who in the hell would want a ship captain dead? And why?

CHAPTER
19

Alana drove down the Pontchartrain Causeway, heading south across the lake's 24-mile span over water. At the end of the bridge, she made a right onto Route 61, parallel to the winding Mississippi River—whose waterways every cargo freighter headed to or from the various ports in New Orleans passed through.

Would her family approve of her actions?

Time neared 9pm, and the night was clear. Although this was a simple exercise in reconnaissance—she would not act. Points of entry, zones of activity, pathways for escape—whatever information she could gather would help her plan.

The Escalade turned down a sideroad, edged by chain-linked fences on both sides, which led to a gravel path barely wide enough for the large SUV to pass through.

Alana slowly steered through the narrow lane and switched off the vehicle's headlights.

Far west were high yellow gantry cranes used to lift the cargo to and from freighters at the water's edge. The immense structures were lit from top to bottom against the night sky, ostensibly as markers for the passing ships and low-flying planes that might cross over the area.

The gravel path ended about half a mile, reaching an asphalt road running east and west. She might have stayed on Route 61 and hit the same side street, but this allowed her to spot other possible routes for her coming venture.

Alana sat inside the idling Escalade and scanned the entrance to port 49L. Semitrucks entered and departed the yard along with the occasional operations vehicle to the west. Those were usually vans or pick-up trucks piloted by dockworkers in hard hats. Goods were shuttled in and out of the area about every ten minutes, but there was one thing she noticed right off.

No guard protected the port's gate entry.

Slowly, Alana put the Escalade into drive and followed the paved road to the entrance. Once inside, she drove past a sorting building adorned with the Sigma-Sea logo. This building had an elevated loading dock for smaller loads and offloads. Two hard-working men transported pallets of goods from a semitrailer using a push dolly.

East of that, Alana noted several surveillance cameras in the zone overlooking the yard's shipping containers. The maze of high intermodals stretched to the pier beneath the giant gantry cranes, and their stacks ran wide in both directions as far as she could see.

The shipping yard was like being in the middle of a sprawling mini-city. But the buildings were of corrugated steel and jammed together to use every piece of available real estate.

Floodlights brightened most of the area but for a section to her right side. There sat a small dark parking lot that accommodated three vehicles in its four available spaces. Yards beyond those was a small shack with a sign over its entrance that she could not read due to the distance.

Up an embankment to the west end was a three-story office building about half the size of a home improvement store. Its exterior was dark. Its workers had gone for the evening.

As far as she could tell, the only significant activities occurring at this late hour were in the yard. The cranes were not running because no ship was birthed at the port. But the regular movement of containers to and from the area on tractor-trailers continued and probably did so 24 hours a day.

To the far east, a stocky uniformed man spoke with one of the van drivers and provided directions with broad arm movements and nods. He wore a grayish shirt and pants with a hefty belt that held a sidearm. He checked something off from his clipboard, motioned north, and the van driver switched on his headlights, waved, and left the area.

Next, the guard turned Alana's way.

As far as she'd assessed, there was only one entrance and one way out. Overhead lights and cameras blanketed the area. Three buildings—one a sorting dock, another a small shack, and the distant office building—housed her possible target. There wasn't much to learn unless she left the vehicle on foot. But if she did that, she'd be exposed.

The port guard approached the Escalade and put up a palm.

Alana slid the Lebedev between her legs and covered its barrel with her short skirt.

The guard approached, "Good evening, ma'am. Are you here to see someone?"

Alana leaned forward, shook her head, and used her best American accent, "I am so sorry. I was driving to the bridge, trying to get to my sister's home, but somehow got all turned around, and..." She lifted both hands from the steering wheel in frustration.

"Easy to do. These roads run wonky through this area because of the river and all. I completely understand." He held the clipboard and motioned with his free hand as he spoke. "What you wanna do is whip a U-turn out of here and go due east. That means a right turn on the first major road here."

Yes, she knew which way east was.

"Follow that for the better part of half a mile, and you'll see the signs for the Pontchartrain crossover. Follow those, and it'll take you to your sister."

"Oh, sir. Thank you so very much. I was so lost until you showed up."

The guard came closer and grinned. On his shirt was a chrome badge and a nametag that read 'Mike.'

"Tell you what, ma'am," he said. "Carl just showed up to relieve me from dayshift. Hang tight here, I'm going to grab my truck, and I'll lead you out there. Perhaps we can get a drink at the bar on the other side of the lake? I know this nice little place, one minute."

Before she could object to bulky Mike's invitation, he rushed to the shack area with his clipboard.

She could simply leave, but it might cause difficulties. A man like Mike might also get suspicious enough and check the cameras to find her license plate. And if he dug too far, he'd know the plates themselves were fake, which would throw her planned activities into turmoil.

Alana scanned the three vehicles at the shack where Mike had entered. One was a small white two-door Acura, another a green Toyota sedan, but the third was a large black Ford 4x4 truck.

Mike's truck.

She quickly eased the Escalade a few feet into position, cautious to avoid her driver's console from being seen by any cameras. She pulled up the Lebedev and took careful aim.

The muzzle flashed.

A perfect strike.

She shoved the smoking Lebedev under the front seat.

Since the gun had discharged inside the vehicle, the Escalade's tinted windows absorbed most of its flare. She also turned the Cadillac's AC on full blast to clear any smoke and smell.

In only a few moments, Mike bounded down the shack's three steps with a set of keys and a wide smile.

He waved.

Alana waved back.

He shouted, "Let's go get that drink."

Alana nodded with a grin.

Mike started up his truck, but when he clicked into reverse, he knew something was wrong.

Alana held as he got out and saw the problem.

His rear tire was flat.

The big man barked, "Ah, shit."

Bullet holes will do that.

Guess they wouldn't be getting that drink after all.

Mike approached.

Alana turned down the AC.

Mike rested a palm on her door, "Let me see if I can borrow a vehicle from one of the boys."

Alana put up a hand, "I must go. I am incredibly late. But another time, okay?"

Mike slunk his shoulders.

Alana smiled, "Can I get your phone number, perhaps?"

Mike flashed a smile. He supplied the number as she punched it into her burner phone.

He leaned toward her, "I hope to hear from you."

She smirked, "Oh, you will."

Alana sent a quick text to his phone. It read, "Hi Mike."

The stout man looked up from his glowing screen and beamed.

"Hi back," he coyly said.

Alana glanced at the time on her dash, "You've been so very nice. Thank you. But I am extremely late."

Mike turned, examined his truck's flat tire, and scratched the back of his head.

His disappointment was clear, "All right, then. Stay to those directions and have yourself a good evening."

Alana swiftly put the Escalade into drive, supplied a courtesy wave, and exited the lot.

In her rearview, Mike looked down at his mobile phone and kissed its screen in victory.

That should buy her 24 hours before the anxious man began rooting through the surveillance footage to track her down for that drink.

CHAPTER

20

"Good morning." Bennett was up and brewing the coffee. Today's t-shirt celebrated a 1994 tour by The Eagles.

"Morning," Kendrick rubbed his eyes.

"Plane's fueled, and we can leave whenever you're ready."

Kendrick grunted, "We'll try to keep this one in the air, yes?"

"Good one." Bennett raised his eyebrows, "And how much spit would you like in your coffee?"

Kendrick snickered, "How long a flight is it?"

He handed Kendrick a freshly brewed cup, "We're in a Riley-Rocket, twin turboprop. Now, this is no Gulfstream, but once we're in the air, the flight to Louisiana shouldn't take but a couple hours. Figure we can hit a place for a nice seaside lunch by mid-afternoon and complete the plan?"

"Do we need to go through security?"

"With the Riley? We take off and land at municipal airports. They're open 24/7, and most of the time these places are unattended. Pilots and a few passengers come and go, but that's about it."

Kendrick tilted his head.

Bennett smirked, "No pat downs or detectors, amigo."

"Good." Kendrick unzipped a large case on the kitchen bar and pulled its flap open. "First choice to the pilot."

Bennett examined the half-dozen handguns and grinned, "I brought my own. I knew we weren't going mini golfing." He fished out a weapon from beneath his undershirt and held it by the barrel, "Trusty .44 caliber Desert Eagle."

Kendrick nodded, "Solid weapon." He reached into the case, grabbed his SIG Sauer 9mm, and tucked the pistol into a holster around his backside. Like Bennett, he wore an untucked, overshirt. His was navy blue and its long fabric hid the weapon.

Twenty minutes later, the men were on their way to Fernandina Beach Municipal Airport in Kendrick's two-door convertible Audi roadster.

Bennett spoke over the soft wind, "Didn't figure you for a ragtop man."

Kendrick grinned, "It's the coast. Fresh ocean air. Leaning into the life, as it were."

"Good for you, pal."

They turned off Amelia Island parkway onto Airport Road. Kendrick parked the Audi in the tiny airport lot and gathered their duffle bags.

"Ever been here before?"

Kendrick shook his head.

Bennett pointed to the municipal airport's reception building, "Modeled after a Corsair. The WWII fighter plane."

The building's entire roof mimicked a large, winged aircraft. The jutting tail section also served as a drive-under for pickups and drop-offs, and the craft's rudder was marked 'FB' after the airfield's name.

Bennett nodded slowly, "The artist was on his juice that day."

The inspired outbuilding also put a smile on Kendrick's face. To borrow a stateside idiom, it was very cool looking.

Bennett pointed to the field's airstrip, "I filled her up on the fly-in."

"Good. Got your sidearm?"

Bennett turned, "Yeah, and I also brought my putter, you know, in case there was minigolf?"

Kendrick laughed. "Next time, mate, I promise."

The two made their way inside the building, which was more like a tiny museum commemorating the airstrip's storied past since opening during WWII. There was a full-sized army jeep and other historical paraphernalia on display in the lobby.

Bennett motioned toward a small reception desk, "Let me check in with these good folks. There's a pilot commissary back there," he pointed to his right. "Grab us some snacks?"

Bennett headed to the two-person desk and greeted a lady who seemed to know him.

This place wasn't like a commercial airport at all—or for that matter—any military airstrip Kendrick had ever been on. There were no metal detectors, no dogs sniffing bags, and nobody waiting on anything. No security lines, shoe removal, baggage carousel, or ticketing counters. People simply came and went from the runway like they owned the place. They might throw a courtesy wave at the desk upon entering or deliver a little chitchat when they paid their landing fee, but there were no hassles. It had none of the push-and-shove cattle roundup elements of military or commercial boardings.

Around the side, Kendrick found the unmanned commissary. It, too, was very cool. A large pinball game sat next to a pair of tall vending machines. One machine dispensed drinks and the other treats. On a second wall, an honor bar held wine and beer. These air jockeys knew how to live.

Kendrick fished out some cash and bought two bottled waters and two bags of crisps. He sat at a small table and admired the wall's framed black-and-white and color photos. Some were taken during the war, but others more recently. Each displayed happy pilots and their flying machines.

A shout came from outside the room.

"Hey, amigo. We need to take off now. Got weather moving in the panhandle."

Kendrick quickly gathered his things and Bennett met him in the lobby, "Weather?"

"Thunderclouds and rain."

Kendrick's face went pale.

Bennett nodded to the airstrip's glass doors, "Faster we leave, the less chance we have of hitting it."

Kendrick hustled toward the door.

Bennett snickered. "Thought that might get you moving."

Outside, the airfield's giant orange windsock blew northeasterly.

Bennett marched them across the taxiway toward a red, twin-prop aircraft with white stripes. The plane's fuselage looked freshly painted.

"This old girl is mine. I rebuilt her from the ground up." He turned to Kendrick, "So, no puking."

Kendrick quipped, "If you can keep the aircraft's door from flying off, that shouldn't be a problem."

"Careful. I can send you into a swan dive from 10,000 feet."

Both men laughed.

There was seating for two pilots and four passengers.

Bennett climbed inside, "Reupholstered her myself."

The aircraft's matching maroon interior was gorgeous. The inner carpet was also a complementary shade of burgundy, and its clean smell meant it was freshly installed. Every knob, wood surface, and chrome accent inside the craft shined like brand-new.

Kendrick admired the craft, "Labor of true love."

Bennett made his way forward, "Well, she'll never leave me and take half my shit."

Both men squeezed into the cockpit, and Bennett handed Kendrick a pair of headphones, "Your cans, amigo."

Kendrick buckled into the copilot's seat and adjusted the headset over his ears.

The airfield's windsock fluttered in the light breeze.

Bennett tuned the craft's radio to 122.7 and spoke on something called UNICOM. After a minute of confusing back-and-forth chatter, Bennett turned to him, "We're clear."

The twin-prop taxied to the runway as Bennett throttled the propellers. The speeding aircraft left the ground in less than a minute and banked toward the west.

When they reached the shoreline in the panhandle, Kendrick caught his first glimpse of those thunderclouds Bennett was talking about.

CHAPTER

21

Working for Dax was great. Brack could come and go as he pleased, and the man was delighted with his work.

Last night he visited the laundry mat Charlie recommended. It was a short walk from the hotel. He washed all the clothing from the pawn store and the four outfits he'd worn repeatedly while on the run these past two months. He also finished the dozen individual tax returns for Dax between loads.

In the morning, he packed the tax files and headed downstairs. Charlie's text or call sign was on the desk again. The man was always working on the place.

The beach walk to Dax's office turned into a jog since the loose clothing from the pawn shop allowed his legs room to move.

Oddly, he was getting used to the scorched coffee in the office. It had a weird bite but did the trick.

Dax was at his desk, "Done with all of them?"

Brack plopped the files on the counter and nodded.

Dax shook his head, "You're like that savant from that movie, the one who took the casino for a run."

"Definitely, definitely deducted everything. Of course, Wapner in ten minutes."

Dax roared, "You're a funny guy, Brannon!"

Brack smiled.

The office's main entry door opened. A slim, elderly man walked inside.

Dax made a beeline for him.

Brack didn't overhear the conversation, but Dax took some money from his pocket and handed it to the gentleman. The old man put a hand on Dax's shoulder and thanked him before leaving.

During their conversation, Brack glanced at Dax's screen. Accounts payable. He was charging many of his clients way below market value for his services. In fact, the lower the return, the lower the fee. Was it a sliding scale? A few of the returns he'd done last night were large but not making much money, and sure enough, Dax wasn't charging them a fixed rate.

The man could run his business any way he wanted of course, still Brack found it very unusual.

Dax returned to him at the desks, "Oh, yeah, reminds me." He dug into his pocket again. "A Benjamin for every completed return. That's thirty-two, and I don't know how you did them so damn fast."

He handed Brack a stack of bills.

"Thank you, and thanks for keeping it off the books."

"No problem. I keep some cash in a safe in the back. Give out small loans sometimes or try to help people out when they need it." He motioned to the door that the elderly man had just exited. "Wife just had surgery, and bills are piling up." Dax cleared his throat, "Good folks just trying to make ends meet, you know?"

The gesture struck Brack in his chest. Despite his gruff exterior, Dax was an incredibly kind man and sincerely cared for the people in this small area.

Before Brack's eyes got misty, he changed the subject. "I'm thinking I might run by that warehouse. Check it out for Margaret's son today."

Dax cleared his throat and grabbed the coffee cup off his desk for a refill, "Yeah that place, it's a couple of miles north of the port. Need to warn you, though, lots of security. Fences, cameras. Not an area you can just walk into. It's like a prison compound." He filled his cup from the sizzling coffee pot, tossed in a single sugar, and stirred, "And we absolutely don't want them to ID you."

Brack exhaled, "Yeah, that'd be bad."

"Right. So, don't do anything you can't walk away from. Could cause a shitstorm for a man in your situation."

"Got it."

They returned to the work area, and Brack sat at one of the desks with his laptop and worked up a few more returns.

Between files, he found a satellite map website online, typed in a location, and located the warehouse area. The pictures were quite good, but he could only zoom in so far. Still, things were as Dax said.

A fenced perimeter surrounded the parking lot. Then, a set of gates led from the lot to another interior wall. That wall was of some height and topped with razor wire, encircling the warehouse on all sides.

The warehouse was a large building, thousands of feet in square footage, and was two or three levels high. It was difficult to tell from the online satellite photos. There was a loading dock and a double entrance on the building's adjacent edge.

But how could he get inside?

Brack exited the satellite view and switched to street level. These photos were better and showed the building was four levels in height, not two or three. The parking lot also didn't have many cars, maybe four or five. Security guards, most likely.

What he did notice was a second lot entry on the interior wall. The first entry he'd seen on the satellite view had a walk-up guard station from the parking lot.

But if he could somehow park, make his way to the west on foot, to that second entrance, he'd be able to enter the building. If he could avoid contact with the guards inside, he could snoop around and see if Margaret's goods were in their inventory. That could take a while, though. He didn't know their tracking system or stacking methods.

Shit, things could be a mess in there, and he'd never find anything if he was expected to climb over pallets of packed goods and stay hidden.

He closed the browser and opened another tax file.

He needed to find a way to be invisible. He'd further need to wander about for a while, undetected, inside of a compound with armed security guards. It was also an area considered mostly foreign soil, being a free trade zone. If he was stopped, who knew what they might do to him?

Be invisible.

Then, an idea. It wasn't perfect, but it might get him inside.

He finished the file, hit enter, closed the laptop, and turned to Dax, "I'm heading out."

Dax looked up from his screen, "Warehouse?"

"Yes."

"You remember the name of Margaret's company?"

"I do."

"Find anything, you come back here so we can discuss the next steps. It'd be easier to claim if we had lading numbers or shipping tickets."

"If I find something, I'll make sure to get those."

Dax sipped his coffee, "David, you be careful, man. If you're caught trespassing, old Frank at the station won't be able to get you out of it easily. You got me?"

"I got it."

The men said their 'see ya laters,' and Brack left the office.

He jogged along the shoreline back to the hotel.

Dark clouds hovered about the sea's afternoon horizon.

And the winds were blowing in his direction.

CHAPTER

22

Drops fell from the night sky. Alana found a parking space for the Escalade outside the fenced port area behind a row of long containers.

As she'd seen the night before, the freeport's yard spanned several acres of asphalt, and its perimeter was fortified with high steel barbed fencing, elevated floodlights, and security cameras. Thousands of shipping containers, some stacked eight or ten high, filled the vast yard's interior. Wide paths between the intermodals allowed the yard's semitrucks to pass.

Nearest to the water port's side were towering yellow cranes which loaded and unloaded the cargo freighters. Because the ships were thousands of feet long, these enormous, heavy cranes moved back and forth on rail tracks to fix their talons to the gigantic boxes, like a colossal version of an arcade Claw Game.

Alana brought an umbrella that served two purposes. The first was obvious, but the second concealed her from the yard's security cameras.

Her espadrille sandals splashed in the wetness during the long walk as rain collected in puddles at her feet. When she reached the fenced perimeter, she held for any guards wandering about in the downpour. She saw none.

She quickly dashed across the wet gravel lot.

The four spaces saw only the Acura and Toyota parked near the shack. Mike's dayshift had ended, and he and his repaired truck were

121

most likely awaiting her text.

The small wooden shack in the distance kept an outside spotlight over the yard's containerized merchandise. As she got closer, over the shack's single-door entry was a sign that read 'Bond Security.' She splashed forward quickly through the pouring rain.

There was no guard around.

Alana ascended the three wooden steps and entered.

The security office was small. A file cabinet sat opposite a single-person desk with stacks of papers, three surveillance monitors, and a tiny television with an antenna. In the corner was a mini fridge with an open energy drink on its topside. There wasn't much space for more than two people.

"Jimmy, that you?"

A separate doorway led to another attached room at the shack's rear. The voice had come from behind that door.

Alana said nothing.

"Jimmy?"

Pattering rain struck the shack's rooftop.

"C'mon now, if that ain't –"

The guard appeared from the attached area and stood face-to-face with Alana. He was young, in his mid to late twenties. His blue-gray company uniform included an arm patch, a small chrome badge, and a nametag that read 'Carl.'

He looked over Alana's wet clothing, "Woah. Gosh, umm…"

"Where is he?"

"Who, Jimmy? I thought you might be, but –"

Alana shook her head, "No, your boss. Man who is in charge of the yard."

Carl held up a hand, "He's on-site elsewhere. But miss, can I please see your yard badge?"

"I am not part of this place. Where is your boss?"

Carl, the guard, shook his head and pointed to the door, "Listen, miss, this is a restricted area, and I will have to escort you from the premises unless you got proper ID."

Alana swiftly raised the Lebedev 9mm.

Carl gasped, "But that works, too!"

She held the pistol on Carl while at the same time ejecting the security recorder's solid state hard drive.

"Is this only recorder?"

Carl kept his hands in the air and nodded.

Alana examined the device and found the removable solid-state drive slot in its rear. She ejected the credit-card-sized module and tucked it into her skirt band. Then, she wiped her fingerprints from the recorder using the bottom of her blouse,

"I ask again, where is boss?"

"Everett?"

"Yes, Everett. Where is he?"

Carl motioned to the outside, "He's at the administration building up the way."

Alana looked Carl over, "Okay. Strip down."

"Strip? For you?"

Alana nodded.

Carl removed his belt, which held a radio, sidearm, and a convenient pair of handcuffs. Next came the shirt, the pants, and the shoes. He even removed his socks.

Then Alana learned how literal Carl took her orders when he began lowering his boxer shorts.

"Stop!" she exclaimed.

Carl did, and thankfully the trunks remained on his waistline.

In the facility's attached room was an electrical and storage area. There were no phones or computers inside. Instead, pipes ran the wall length to junction boxes from floor to ceiling and held high-voltage wires.

She motioned to Carl, "Go inside there."

Carl and his boxer shorts entered.

Alana threw him the handcuffs, "Attach one wrist to pole."

He did.

She waved the Lebedev, "Click tightly."

Carl complied.

She moved his security belt to the main room on top of the mini fridge, where he couldn't reach it. She bent down, picked up his pants, and pulled out his ID, "Your name is Carl Tullberry?"

"Yes, ma'am. I'm sorry for whatever this is."

"Carl, I am not here to hurt you. But now I know where you live, and if you utter a word of my description, I will find you. Our next meeting will not be so pleasant. You understand?"

Carl nodded anxiously.

"Good. Lean forward for me."

Carl was confused, "Lean?"

"Bend at waist and put your head down."

He did as she instructed.

"For this, I am sorry, Carl."

"Huh?"

Alana swung the pistol's handle across the back of his neck, and Carl fell unconscious to the floor.

A landline phone sat on the desk, and Alana cut its line.

The shack's door squeaked open behind her.

It was Jimmy.

CHAPTER

23

Bennett shouted over the heavy rain, "Hold on to anything but the stick. This could get nasty."

Outside the aircraft's front window, thick raindrops pummeled the plane like stones.

"Taking her down to 8,000."

Immediately, Bennett put the aircraft into a dive. Kendrick felt a lump grow in his throat. His stomach, too, started to turn. Suddenly, he felt unfortunate things brewing at both ends.

When the Riley leveled out, Kendrick took a deep breath and exhaled, "Why did we descend?"

"Because we can't pressurize." Bennett's stare remained forward. "Cabin windows are original. Haven't had a chance to test them and probably need to replace a few seals. Which means we gotta fly under 10,000 feet with no pressure."

"Can't we just get above this? Do we have to go that high?"

A sheet of rain battered the plane as they flew through the downpour.

Bennett made some adjustments and eyed the dash gauges, "These rain clouds could extend upward 25,000 feet or more. If we could pressurize, which we can't, we could normalize force inside the cabin to the equivalent of 8,000 feet above sea level. That would allow us to fly higher where the air is thinner and the drag is far less. Of course, pressurizing pops the ears and fractionally lowers oxygen, but we're fine. If a leak happens in the fuselage somewhere, we should have plenty of time to put on our masks and descend to a safe level before going hypoxic."

Kendrick swallowed, "Hypoxic?"

"Altitude sickness. Develop pulmonary edema and such. Chest tightens, skin turns blue. This is because the blood isn't getting adequate oxygen, and our brains could swell. We lose bodily coordination, become confused, and develop blurred vision." Bennett turned to Kendrick and grinned wide, "We become lethargic vegetables—like drinking at that bar last night."

Kendrick didn't return a smile.

"We'd factually lose our minds, and this plane can't land itself."

Kendrick checked his seatbelt, "Can't land itself, right."

"But my worry with these windows is explosive depressurization. If one of these panels blows, in less than half a second, all the air in our lungs will evaporate." Bennett clapped a palm on his thigh. "There's no time for hypoxia. We become victims of our altitude. And—this is just my theory—we smoosh like an empty beer can."

Kendrick swallowed hard, "Smoosh like a can."

Christ, they should've taken the train to New Orleans.

Bennett's attention returned to piloting, which was good because he stopped scaring the shit out of Kendrick. After a few minutes of jostled flying, the Marine spoke again.

"Runway in range," he pointed to a panel on the dash.

Kendrick's shoulders relaxed.

But the twin prop Cessna dipped wildly.

Bennett jerked the cockpit's yolk.

"Turbulence!" he cried.

Kendrick clawed the seat's armrests. The spinning in his stomach started again, and he almost gagged.

The aircraft felt off-kilter as Bennett fought the yolk.

He shouted, "C'mon, baby! C'mon, little more."

After several seconds, the plane leveled out.

But Kendrick's heart continued to pound.

The rain lessened, and Bennett called in their intent to approach. Then he turned to Kendrick and shook his head. "Storms, amigo."

Kendrick took several deep breaths but didn't share how close he'd come to redecorating the man's cherished Riley Rocket with accents of brown.

Bennett managed to line up the runway and land them safely.

It was still pouring rain when the plane taxied toward the hangers, parked, and the two men grabbed their gear.

They headed across the tarmac to the airport's outbuilding.

"Guess that seaside lunch is off the table?" Bennett shouted.

"Let's grab a car and head to the seaport." Kendrick's insides hadn't settled yet, and he doubted he could keep anything down anyway.

Inside the municipal's foyer, Bennett paid their parking and landing fees while Kendrick presented his ID, paid cash, and retrieved the keys to a blue Chrysler Sebring.

The two men drove through the rain to the harbor and circled outside the freeport's lot. Despite the weather, they saw the container cranes but no freighter where Adler had told them the ship was docked.

Bennett scanned the zone, "Might've left already?"

Kendrick fished out his mobile and dialed. Despite the early time, his confidant answered on the first ring.

"Sir, Second Lieutenant Adler here."

"Hey, Adler. How's your morning over there?"

"Good, sir. Playing Call of Duty. It's a combat video game.

"Excellent. Keep those field skills sharp. Never know when I might need you over here."

Adler chuckled strangely but then said, "Sir, you've landed. Good flight?"

Kendrick shot a glance at Bennett and frowned.

"Yeah, we're here," he said. "But no ship. Do you –"

"Sir, I knew you'd call. I watched the *Okeana* freighter via satellite before the storm turned over Louisiana. When the clouds got in the way, I switched to thermal, and… sorry, but the ship left port about two hours ago."

"Headed to the Gulf?"

"That's right, sir."

"Ship left a couple of hours ago," Kendrick said to Bennett.

"Dammit," Bennett said, steering through the drops.

Kendrick switched the call to speaker so both men could hear.

"Sir, they also towed Raskin's vehicle from the area."

"What the hell do we do now?" Bennett said. "Pick through the garbage?"

The Marine had a point. Checking out that freighter was the primary goal of flying out here in the first place. Now the rental car they were hoping to search had been carted off by lorry, and the ship they needed to explore was cruising toward the open sea.

Kendrick gathered his thoughts as Bennett circled the port area. If Hank Raskin was involved, there may be other clues they could track down, which may produce leads.

"Hey, Adler, can you check Raskin's finances?"

"It'll take some time, but yes, sir."

Bennett turned, "Thinking if he was in on things, someone might've been paying the man on the side?"

Kendrick managed a grunt. They were running out of leads again, and a wave of disappointment washed over him.

"Sirs, speaking of finances, I finished looking into Rick Melton's latest transactions. Bills, credit card usage, and such."

Kendrick gnawed at his lower lip, "Find anything?"

"No real large purchases, sir. Beyond his recent vacation to Key Largo. A charter boat fee, a meal at a place called Only Clams." Adler snickered for some reason. "And another at a pricey restaurant called the One-Hundred Double L. Then I see various hotel charges, but –"

"What?" Bennett stopped him.

"Sir?"

"You said a place called the One-Hundred Double L?" Bennett said. "Spell that for me?"

"Yes, sir. Numerals one, zero, zero, and alphas lima-lima," Adler replied.

"How much?"

Adler clicked, "Looks like almost $300, sir."

Bennett glanced at Kendrick. "You said Rick Melton drove down to Key Largo, didn't you?"

"That's what he told me, yes."

"Interesting," Bennett muttered. "Because 100LL isn't a restaurant. It's an abbreviation for one hundred low-lead, avgas."

"Avgas?" Kendrick frowned.

"Thinner, Kerosene-based gasoline. Doesn't freeze at high altitudes." Bennett steered them down a side road. "Unless his car ran on aviation fuel, I believe our lawyer flew down to Key Largo in a small plane because that's a refueling charge."

"He flew?" Kendrick was stunned. Why would Melton lie about flying and not driving? Did he fudge his alibi? It was time to pay the lawyer a visit. "Hey, Adler, do you have Rick Melton's address? To his residence?"

Clicking erupted, "Pinged from your location, his flat is east, on the south shoreline—about seventy miles, sir. An hour's drive."

"Thanks, Adler. Can you send directions to my mobile?"

"Sir, already tracking your vehicle. I sent a travel map to the car's GPS. You should see it on your navigation system now."

Sure enough, a map appeared on the Chrysler's touchscreen, and a female voice sounded from the vehicle's sound system, "Drive one mile, then make a right turn."

"You're too good, Adler," Kendrick said.

Then Adler chuckled. "Sir, it's good you're on the way to see Melton now. Don't want the guy drowning or eaten by an alligator before you can question him."

A sharp tingle hit the back of Kendrick's neck.

Adler was right.

He couldn't believe he'd not considered this before.

First, Gary Oliver is murdered via three rounds to the head.

Next, Yuri Melnyk dies when all signs point to a full recovery.

And now Hank Raskin goes missing with no trace.

Were they connected?

Each one seemed to be linked with the cargo freighter, *Malusnavi*.

Was someone hunting them down?

Kendrick turned to Bennett. "Let's get there as soon as possible, yes?"

Bennett nodded as the vehicle sped through the raindrops.

Chapter
24

Jimmy was less agreeable than Carl.

But when Alana discharged her weapon and the bullet grazed his leg, the brave but stupid Jimmy became very compliant.

"This is my first job," he cried. "Please don't kill me!"

Alana peered down, "I am not here to kill you."

Jimmy squirmed at her feet, holding his thigh. He began weeping. Given the skinny sandy-haired kid was younger than his coworker, it wasn't unexpected.

After much coaxing, Alana had Jimmy remove his clothes as Carl had done but allowed Jimmy to keep his undershirt wrapped around his leg to quell the blood.

She moved his clothing under the shack's desk and put his security belt on the mini fridge alongside Carl's.

Alana checked his ID, "Jimmy Clarkson. Now I know where you live. If you utter –"

"I won't tell nobody, I swear!"

Tears spilled down the kid's cheeks.

"Jimmy, stop crying."

The red-faced, teary-eyed guard reduced his sounds to a sniffle.

"Jimmy, if you share my description with anyone, I will find you and kill you. Understand?"

His sniffles grew to a low whine.

"Now stand up."

Jimmy took a moment to get to his feet.

Alana pointed to the unconscious Carl, "Come over here."

Jimmy sobbed, "Please don't shoot me again."

Fortunately, the whiny kid was already hunched over due to his injury.

She bashed him over the skull with her pistol.

Jimmy fell on top of Carl, and his crying finally stopped.

Alana adjusted the wrapping on Jimmy's wound and cinched it tighter. Next, she fished out a set of handcuff keys from one of the mini fridge belts and tossed them between Carl and Jimmy.

She grabbed her umbrella, wiped for prints, and left the two unconscious men in the small shack.

Meters away up a grassy embankment sat a larger building with lights emitting from the bottom floor. The three-level structure's exterior was constructed entirely of industrial glass. In one of those windows, there was movement.

Alana approached with the umbrella held tightly above her head. The building's glass doors also opened without the need for a key.

Inside were two extensive, wide corridors with entrances leading to interior offices and perimeter workspaces. One hallway went north but darkened the farther it ran until only the greenish glow of exit signs remained visible.

But the other hall ran easterly and held far more light.

Nearby, a bustling printer echoed, whirring out its documents.

Alana stepped down the hallway's tile floor.

She quietly placed her umbrella against a wall.

She found no one in the printing room but stacked office furniture, a coffee machine, and a dirty microwave.

She moved to the second office and found its door open and ceiling lights on. The inside held four tables with half a dozen chairs around each. A breakroom, she gathered.

In a far corner, she saw a man of some size and girth wearing the same guard uniform as Jimmy and Carl.

He stood facing the room's exterior window, watching the rain, and whistling to himself.

Alana entered.

The large male was about six-foot tall. In addition to the sidearm, handcuffs, and radio she'd seen on the beltline of the other two guards, he sported a round key ring with fifty or more sets.

He saw Alana's reflection in the window and turned toward her, "Didn't think anyone else was here. Working late?"

Alana said nothing.

"What's your name, pretty lady?" he smiled. "Mine's Everett."

Alana looked him over but remained quiet.

Everett glanced out the window again, "Got us a hell of a night outside. Raining like a sumbitch." He shook his balding head.

Alana closed the office door.

Everett turned, "Can I get you anything? Did you need something?"

She stared him in the eyes, "You are in charge of port yard, yes?"

"Yes, I'm chief yard manager." Everett nodded. "Say, that's an interesting accent you have. Swedish?"

"You are one who checks cargo going in and out of this area?"

Everett put a hand on his hip, and his expression curdled, "Ma'am, do you work here?"

Rain poured outside the windows as Alana fussed with something inside her purse.

"Ma'am, I need you to identify yourself."

Alana yanked out the Lebedev.

"Woah. Woah, okay." Everett raised his arms. "Whatever this is, there's no need for that."

"Shut up, fuck."

Even as his hands were high in surrender, Everett chuckled. "I think you mean 'shut the fuck up,' pretty lady."

Alana discharged a round into Everett's shin.

He fell to the ground and screamed.

"I meant what I said."

"Fuck, fuck! Okay!" Everett shrieked.

"You are one who checks cargo going in and out of this yard? You make sure individual containers are on specific trucks?"

He moaned, "Yes, yes! But the fucking crane guys put them on the ships and take them off. That's not me!"

Alana pointed the pistol, "I am more concerned with transports in and out of this place."

Everett held his shin tightly as blood oozed from the fabric of his pants, "Fuck!"

"You did not guard freighter properly when ship came in months ago, and the fiasco started. Do you recall this?"

"Oh, Christ! This hurts!"

"Do you remember the name of that freighter?"

"I'm bleeding badly! Why, why are you doing this?"

"Do you remember the name of that freighter?"

"Yes, dammit! The *Malusnavi*! But we had another fucking ship coming in that night that I had to –"

Alana stiffened her shoulders, "There were drugs on that cargo vessel."

"No shit!" Everett shouted. "There're drugs on a lot of these fucking ships out here! And who the fuck are you? Some dealer's bimbo? If you're missing your shit, talk to the damn drivers. I just move them out!"

Alana closed her eyes.

"Did you hear me? Talk to the drivers!"

Her eyes opened and she aimed the weapon at his head, "It is your employer who does not like excuses."

"Who?" Everett froze. "Oh, Jesus!"

Alana stared down at him, "Yes. Jesus is waiting to judge you for the deadly substance you transported."

Three flashes sent as many bullets into Everett's temple.

How does he break into a prison?

There was one constant Brack understood about people. Strangers instantly judged others on how they spoke and how they dressed. Those two factors decided how seriously a person was taken or how quickly they were labeled and stereotyped.

To garner the most unsaid admiration, there was one disguise that never failed. In the past, such an ensemble had secured everything from the casual elevator cornering of a CEO to cold meeting invites from company underlings to present his ideas to investors.

In Brack's frenzied wardrobe, he found a stain-free collared dress shirt, black slacks, a red paisley tie, lace-up cap-toe black dress shoes, and a matching black jacket.

Not surprisingly, the pushups he'd added in the morning, his jogging to and from Dax's office, and better eating were having unintended consequences on his wardrobe. Since he'd bought the pawnshop clothing in his last known size, the garments now felt baggy on his slender frame. The shirt didn't quite cling to his torso, and the pants required a belt set on the tightest notch.

Hair wax slicked his side part, and a quick shave erased the stubble. He'd scoured the pawn store's oxford gray briefcase with a washcloth to clear the scuff marks.

Brack eyed his outfit in the room's mirror. He looked every part the sophisticated businessman.

He redialed Nikki, and she answered on the first ring.

"Heya, I'm outside. You ready?"

"Heya back," he said. "Do you have an umbrella? I'm –"

"Of course. I'll meet you in the lobby."

When Brack arrived downstairs, Nikki looked him over and smiled, "Not too shabby."

She wore an oversized gray raincoat and matching fedora to protect her long blonde hair from the rain. She'd also brought two umbrellas.

Charlie rounded the desk, "Looking sharp, Mister David."

A pile of pressurized 4x4 wood sat neatly stacked in a corner, along with other large beams. Charlie was serious about that gazebo.

Brack approached the two at the front desk.

"Mister David, tomorrow afternoon, with your permission, I need to do a couple of hours of work in your suite if that's okay? Fixings and all."

"No problem."

Charlie smiled, "Very good. Stay dry out there, and best of luck with your meeting."

"Thank you."

Charlie's complement was spot on. That was, after all, the exact look Brack was shooting for.

"Shall we?" Nikki asked.

Brack smirked, "We shall."

The two hustled through the rain to Nikki's Sportwagon. She insisted he sit in the rear and took his umbrella once Brack was comfortably inside.

He and Nikki fastened their respective seatbelts, "Thanks for being available."

"No problem. Though, it's a nasty late afternoon."

Nasty, true. But this weather would work to Brack's advantage. "You know where we're headed, right?"

Nikki patted the Sportwagon's dash, "Already in the nav."

He hadn't told Nikki what this was all about. He only said he needed a ride immediately to an area outside the port to the warehouse. The fact was he didn't really know her well, and his story was darkly complicated. He wasn't sure he was prepared to answer her questions.

Though, during the drive, he did decide it would be a good idea to feel her out as a person.

"Do you like driving people around?" In retrospect, it was a stupid question, but he had to start somewhere.

"Don't mind it," Nikki said as the windshield wipers fought the rain. "I used to waitress. But after the pandemic, the place shut down and never reopened."

Brack knew this sadly happened to a lot of businesses.

"The restaurant owner's wife used to watch Curtis during my shifts for free. But now I gotta pay a neighbor to babysit and daycare. Still, I can keep my own hours."

He offered empathy, "I hear you. That's tough."

However, Nikki's next words were upbeat, "Next year, Curtis can attend pre-school. Then I can go back to the learning center. Get a certification."

"Certification?"

"Yeah. Classes are free there. I want to do something in the computer field. Not sure. Something remote, with flex hours, so I can take care of Curt. I like graphic design. Maybe start out building sites and see where it takes me? The learning center also loans out laptops."

"Sounds like a solid plan."

"Yeah. But they don't have many computers. So, you gotta get pretty lucky."

Brack frowned. Was she relying on luck to get a computer?

"Guess if it doesn't work out, I'll go into home health care or something. Got a cousin that's an RN, she says the hours are crazy, but it pays well. Of course, spending time with Curtis would be tougher."

Usually, Brack's radar would have gone up. He'd have considered her story a prelude to a con. A ploy for a larger tip. Living in a big city had caused that jadedness. He'd heard the hard-luck tales and seen the street people begging for more drug money.

But these months on the run had caused a change. He'd had ample time to think about his past and deeply evaluate who he once was, who he became, and how he'd wound up in so much turmoil.

Nikki was sincere—and Brack couldn't believe her entire career path was hinging on securing a computer—a device almost everyone he knew had. But with caring for her child and working jobs where she could manage her hours, the poor girl's dreams seemed an ever-retreating grasp out of reach.

He'd tip her another hundred for the ride just because it felt right.

They turned onto a road far north of the harbor and found the entrance to the warehouse's compound.

Brack instructed her where to park, then secured his umbrella and briefcase. But before he left the vehicle, he knew for her safety, he had to confess his motive for being at the warehouse—just in case things went sideways.

"Look," Brack eyed her through the Sportwagon's rearview. "What I'm doing here isn't precisely on the up and up."

She glanced at his reflection, "Figured that. Anything I can do?"

Her unflinching attitude surprised him again, "No, but I need you to wait here. Watch for me." He pointed in the distance to the warehouse's main entry. "If I don't return in thirty minutes, you take off. Got me?"

"Sounds exciting."

Yes, to a twenty-something, it would seem that way.

But Brack was praying nobody would shoot him.

"Thirty minutes, okay?"

"No worries. And I'll leave the rear hatch open. If you come running, you can dolphin-dive into the hatchback as I rip donuts in the parking lot to confuse them." She laughed loudly.

Brack gnashed his upper lip.

He considered Nikki's dolphin-dive escape idea not to be too terrible.

CHAPTER 26

Bloody rich people.

Rain clouds churned the evening sky as the two crept from the roadway, through the drops, down a sandy beach path toward the rolling waves. They rounded a meadow of bending cordgrass and stepped through a patch of wild panicum budding through the wet sands. The men scurried to a large natural berm, parallel to Rick Melton's enormous house, and hunkered behind it.

Bennett peered over the sand ridge and whispered, "Four-car garage at the beach. Damn, this dude's loaded."

Kendrick's place on Amelia was ten blocks from the water. Rent ate most of the military pension he received from the Kingdom each month. Food and necessities came from his savings and whatever earnings he made along the way. Breaking into Melton's place would be the closest he'd ever get to a home with an ocean view.

Rick Melton lived in this beachfront, seven-bedroom, two-level, detached Mediterranean villa. The home's rear had five sets of tall double sliding doors, and each opened to a giant balcony with an incredible panorama of Louisiana's coastline.

All this from minor league injury law?

Bullshit.

Bennett and Kendrick snuck under the massive home's beach balcony, where they could also avoid most of the rain.

140

"Want me to go around front?"

Kendrick shook his head, "I think he's alone in there. I say we stay low and together."

Bennett nodded.

"Once inside, you sweep left, and I'll go right. Then we'll head upstairs if he's not below."

"Copy." Bennett motioned to the home's beach access door and glazed inset window. "Who breaks the glass? You or me?"

Kendrick whispered, "Neither."

"What?"

"We're on the Gulf shore." Kendrick pointed to the door. "That's impact-resistant, laminated hurricane glass. It won't break. And we'll make noise for nothing and give ourselves away if we try."

Bennett turned.

"Do a lot of these B&Es, do you?"

Kendrick shrugged, "Fair amount."

"Ex-wife still has my golfclubs. We should visit her next."

Kendrick examined the door's deadbolt, "If your ex-wife has your golf clubs, how do you still have the putter?"

Bennett flexed his jaw muscles, "A good Marine never leaves his putter behind."

Kendrick snickered, then reached into his pocket and pulled out a set of lean wiry tools. "If an alarm sounds, you run upstairs. I'll take lower. Make sure he doesn't call the cops."

Bennett pulled out his weapon and checked the slide, "Got it."

Kendrick worked the door's deadbolt, which turned after less than a minute. He slipped the tools into his pocket and gripped his SIG 9mm, "Alright, here we go."

He turned the doorknob.

To their surprise, no alarm triggered.

Both men stepped inside quickly and closed the door behind them.

Most of the lights in the lower level were off, but they could hear music coming from somewhere inside the house.

Bennett whispered, "Upstairs?"

Kendrick nodded.

They crept across a large dark room, past the massive kitchen, toward a shimmer of brightness stemming from a north hall.

The wide half-spiral staircase led to a massive U-shaped interior balcony at the top level. Both men quietly ascended the steps with weapons at the ready.

Bennett whispered, "Hear that?"

Kendrick had.

A rustling.

There was someone in the other room.

Kendrick raised a closed fist, and he and Bennett halted at the stairway's top stoop.

Several seconds passed.

Kendrick pointed down the foyer, and they continued their quiet trek through Melton's second level. Outside the doorway, they halted in front of what appeared to be an office. Kendrick raised his SIG, and Bennett did the same with his Desert Eagle.

Kendrick signaled three fingers, then two, and both men charged down the upper hall toward the music.

A man in red polka dot pajamas turned and screamed, "What the hell is going on!"

Kendrick recognized him at once.

"Hands up!" Bennett shouted. "In the air! Now!"

Polka dot arms raised at once.

Bennett performed a quick pat down of Melton's pajamaed frame. The lawyer quivered at Bennett's touch, and he turned pale.

He cried sheepishly, "What do you want from me?" Then turned to Kendrick. "Wait, don't I know you?"

Kendrick snagged a mobile phone from a nightstand and scanned the area for weapons. "We're here to talk."

The man's hands remained in the air, but a small wet patch grew in his crotch area.

Chapter

27

Brack clutched the umbrella and briefcase and sloshed carefully to the side entrance he'd seen on the street-level map. From the discarded wet cigarette butts on the ground, he knew where the security crew took their breaks.

Despite a keyless entry panel, the gate door was propped open with a small piece of wood, and he stepped inside.

Brack had seen from the computer satellite images that the building was three levels with scattered windows aligning only the first. The structure was thousands of feet in square footage, with a loading dock and double-door entrance around its adjacent side.

On its exterior perimeter ran the stone walkway he was currently negotiating, but with no plants or unnecessary embellishments. This warehouse was all business.

Now, it was a matter of making his way around the front of the building in the pouring rain to the main entrance, looking the part, and not being stopped, questioned, or shot.

He cautiously rounded the building.

An armed, uniformed security guard stood near the entry doors.

Shit.

Brack trudged forward, straightened his back, clutched the umbrella, and held his chin high.

When he reached the building's awning, he shook the umbrella, folded it in, snapped it shut, and tucked it under an armpit. He tugged at his tie and supplied the guard a quick nod.

The guard pointed to the sky, "Cats and dogs, jeez."

"Always like this?" Brack asked confidently.

The guard patted his beltline, "Regular summer storm. But it's them damn electric bolts that spook me the most. They say those can contain a billion volts."

Brack stood near and watched the distant flashes through the rain, "You know, they say a lot of people struck by lightning are wet first. Swimmers, and whatnot." He'd heard this on a television show once, late at night.

"Didn't know that," the guard said, surprised. "I'm sure staying my ass out of the pool when that rumbling comes now."

Then, to Brack's amazement, the guard opened one of the entry doors for him.

Brack passed with a nod, "Appreciate it. Damn inventory got me running everywhere, I tell you."

"Try to stay dry," the large man tipped his hat.

"I'll do that," Brack smiled.

The guard remained outside as the door closed.

A large, unmanned reception desk with several glowing computer monitors was in the tight lobby. Whoever worked this zone must've been in another area, probably the restroom.

Brack counted himself fortunate again and walked briskly past the desk to a set of heavy rubber loading doors leading to the facility's central section.

He took a deep breath and held it in for a second.

Then he gripped the briefcase, ran a palm through his hair, and walked through the gray rubber entrance.

The warehouse was enormous. Industrial shelves soared thirty or more feet in the air, accessible only by forklift, holding pallets stacked with goods. It looked like one of the big-chain home improvement outlets but at twice the size. Beeps from the electric haulers sounded in every direction, and the steady hum from gigantic fans and air machines filled his ears.

Luckily, no one had seen him enter. The personnel inside the more significant part of this structure were busy moving and stacking elsewhere.

Brack found an empty aisle on the west side, set the briefcase and umbrella down, took out a small notepad he'd swiped from the Big B, and started examining the goods at ground level.

He was careful to keep a serious expression, almost a frown. He also didn't want to be caught bending or reaching at the palleted boxes too much. A stuffed-shirt inventory manager would never do that.

From his periphery, workers came and went, but nobody crossed into his aisle.

He moved down the row, scribbling in his notepad in case someone was shadowing him on the surveillance cameras.

He'd nod and scowl on occasion as he 'worked,' trying to convey with body language that even being inside this place displeased him.

Why am I forced to be among these filthy workers? I should be at a fancy restaurant enjoying a martini and sushi.

He switched to the other side of the row and continued scanning. But he wasn't finding anything to help Dax reclaim the merchandise. Was he wasting his time? Risking his safety for nothing?

Nevertheless, he moved to the next aisle and continued his hem-and-haw routine. After a bit, the beeps of the warehouse's electric forklifts grew fainter, and he found himself rummaging through packages in a far corner. This area appeared forgotten—almost abandoned—and several overhead lights in the vicinity were either not working, or someone had switched them off. He brought out his mobile and used its flashlight to read the package labels.

By some miracle, he spotted something.

An entire eye-level pallet was labeled with Margaret George's name and company. Shit, what were the odds?

Brack snapped a quick photo of the label. He could use it, proving the goods were inside this facility, caught in a weird limbo after their deceased owner had failed to retrieve them.

He searched a few more items, took more snaps, and found five other pallets of Margaret's goods. It was more than enough for Dax to take claim-processing action.

He was about to leave when a peculiar bunch of flat rectangular boxes caught his eye. They sat next to Margaret's goods but were covered in dust.

Curiously, he approached the stack.

A torn invoice revealed the pallet had been sitting in this warehouse for almost nine years. Was it unclaimed freight? Lost like Margaret's goods?

One of the large square boxes on the pallet stack had suffered damage on its corner end.

Brack pulled back its cardboard wrapping.

It was a large oil painting—about five feet by the same. From what Brack could see, it was nothing remarkable, a cheap attempt at floral still-life. He also didn't recognize the artist's name.

He opened two more boxes. They contained similar paintings. Some by the same artist as the first but, again, no recognizable names.

All paintings were original oil works. But none of the artwork was especially good—in fact, it was drab. Tedious subject matter and poor shading. The type of canvas one might see in a doctor's waiting room or hung on the wall at the department of motor vehicles. It was all shit.

Brack thought for a moment and did a quick count.

Twelve pallets of this stuff.

There had to be at least two hundred packages, maybe more, of artwork in these boxes.

He scanned the date of each pallet's invoice. Eight years old. Seven years old. Eleven years old. All parcels were unclaimed.

The boxes were of varying sizes, but all noted the same recipient on their label.

Melton Oliver & Associates, LLC.

Brack bobbed his head. Yeah, he should've guessed they'd done something like this.

He aimed his mobile's camera at the pallet's tag for a quick photo when a sudden jingle of keys startled him.

"Excuse me?"

The deep voice came from behind.

"I need to see your identification."

CHAPTER

28

Bennett ordered Rick Melton to sit in one of the bedroom's high-back burgundy chairs. Nearby was a stack of papers on a side table, with a small, silver thumb drive sitting on the topside. The lawyer was using this space as a small work area.

A subdued Melton peered up at Kendrick, "You're not a real detective, are you?"

Rick Melton's master suite was a vast living space on the second level. The oversized area included dual open wardrobe closets, a king-sized bed, and a substantial chamber room next to the sleeping quarters.

A 75-inch flatscreen hung above a fireplace, surrounded by a couched seating area. The suite's entire southern wall was framed with floor-to-ceiling glass sliders. Each opened to the dwelling's southern balcony, which offered an unobstructed 180-degree view of the coastline.

Kendrick had only seen villas like this inside magazines.

"You lied to me," Kendrick scowled. "You didn't drive. You flew to Key Largo, didn't you?"

Melton's eye line shifted to the floor.

"Who are you working for?" Bennett barked. "We want their names."

Melton squirmed in the seat.

Bennett aimed his weapon and cocked its slide.

"I don't fucking know!" Melton cowered. "Do you think I'm told anything? I only keep inventory of what moves in and out. From the ships to the trucks. One place to another."

"Alright, then." Kendrick circled him. "Perhaps another question. One you can answer. The drugs at the freeport. The opium in those shipping containers. Where was it headed?"

After a sigh, Melton lifted his head. "Here... the drugs end up here."

Bennett kept his pistol aimed at Melton's chest. "The states?"

Melton bobbed his head. "They've got stash houses all over the place. They move the opium to one of those and cut it. I don't know anything more than that. It's not my business. That's only what I overheard. I'm not the guy you want."

A mysterious, soft hum came from beneath the stack of papers on the side table next to Melton.

Bennett moved to the room's doorway to keep a lookout.

"They?" Kendrick said. "Who are your partners?"

Melton shook his head.

"You said they cut the opium we found at the docks?" Kendrick said. "Cut it with what?"

"Look, you two should just go," Melton pleaded. "These are dangerous people, and they're everywhere."

"Who's dangerous?" Kendrick re-aimed the SIG, "We need answers. Who are your partners?"

Melton panicked, "They might be listening to us now! Got eyes everywhere, and they'll come for us!"

"Damn it! Answer me!" Kendrick shouted. "Cut the drugs with what?"

Melton lowered his head. "With the stuff."

"What stuff?" Kendrick tapped the SIG against Melton's chest.

The lawyer shook, then replied quietly, "The stuff they trade to China for the minerals."

An eerie chill filled Kendrick. Trade to China? Did he hear that correctly? Is that how they were doing it? It would answer two of his most pressing questions: where the minerals were going and why the opium was coming north.

Bennett stepped from the doorway, balled a fist, and readied to strike Melton in the face. "What' stuff?" he yelled.

Melton recoiled, "The synthetic. They transport bricks of it. The new stuff, xylazine, too."

Kendrick wasn't as surprised as he was incensed.

"Use it to up the potency," Melton muttered. "Raise the value. But I'm not sure how it all works—I'm only on the shipping end."

"Shipping?" Kendrick glared down at him. "Explain to me exactly what your role is."

Melton's head sunk again, and his voice grew meek. "I hide the goods. Fake the weights. Get the cargo in and out of the country on the right vessels. Make sure nothing is flagged."

"And you're exporting these drugs?"

"No," Melton shook his head. "They're distributed through channels here. But other things come and go from the port."

Kendrick knew what the other things were and didn't bother asking. He leaned over Melton, "And you do this without knowing who anybody is?"

Melton silently shook his head.

Kendrick tried a different angle, "Why did you lie to me and tell me you drove to Key Largo when you flew down there?"

Melton squirmed, "Why does that matter?"

Bennett shouted from the doorway, "Because he thinks you're full of shit, and I've never known the man to be wrong."

"Driving gave you an alibi, but why did you need it?" Kendrick gazed down at him. "Did you have anything to do with Gary's death?"

"It's not what you think." Rick Melton sobbed then quietly said, "Gary did the books. Moved money from account to account. Bounced cash all over the place, hundreds of millions."

Kendrick was getting the picture. Melton scheduled shipments and managed the inventory, but Gary Oliver was the money man. It did make sense, given their backgrounds. But who was directing it all?

"Who are you working for?" Kendrick asked calmly.

But Melton shouted, "Someone killed Gary! And things got all fucked up! They thought I knew how to access the funds, but I don't know, dammit! Gary never told me anything!"

Then, strangely, Melton glanced at the small, silver device on top of the side table's document stack.

Kendrick noticed the suspicious eye movement, stepped to the table, and picked up the thumb-sized gadget. But the device was attached to a black wire. A wire that ran underneath the pile of documents it rested on.

Kendrick detached the tiny silver device and examined it.

"I don't know… I don't know the codes," Melton cried. "And they'll kill me if I don't… if I can't…" he trailed off.

The whirring under the paper stack grew louder.

That also seemed to be where the black wire led.

Kendrick lifted the documents.

Beneath was a laptop computer.

"What's this?" his eyes narrowed.

Rick Melton sank into the chair.

"Answer me," Kendrick demanded.

Melton's hands shook.

Kendrick read the initials etched into the computer's casing, "G-A-O?" He shot a glance toward Bennett, then back to Melton. "Gary Allan Oliver? The man who 'tagged' everything, including his coffee cup."

"Wait, wait…" Melton exclaimed.

"How did you get Gary Oliver's computer?" Kendrick loomed above him.

Melton sobbed.

"You heartless fuck!" Bennett shouted. "You killed your partner, didn't you?"

"No, no, no!" Melton closed his eyes and wept. "Gary was my best friend. We… we came up together. I would never do anything like that. But something happened."

"What happened?" Kendrick lowered his gun. Melton's anxiety had reached the level where threatening the man was no longer necessary. He just wanted to atone.

"A ship," Melton exhaled. "One of the freighters that came in, the *Malusnavi*. There was trouble. I was on vacation down south. Unreachable. Gary tried to handle things. And, and…" he trailed off.

A chill struck Kendrick's shoulders. He knew the rest.

Months prior, his team had infiltrated that freighter, rescued the two hostages they'd kidnapped aboard, killed the South African, and dragged a barely breathing Russian named Yuri from the area. During those events is also when Sergeant Catalina Rosales sadly lost her life.

But before authorities could get through all the bureaucratic red tape and enter the ship's restricted port trade zone, the freighter and its cargo left the harbor, jammed its tracking signal, and vanished into the Gulf of Mexico.

"They killed Gary," Melton wept. "I still don't know why. Maybe they thought he was involved? Thought he tipped someone off? None of the ships had ever been breached like that. Not one. In years. But Gary didn't sell them out." He sobbed. "I… I don't know what happened."

Then Kendrick had a thought and put another piece together. "That weekend Gary was murdered, you flew back up here before authorities discovered his body, didn't you?"

Melton held his eyes shut.

"Somebody told you to return, didn't they?" Kendrick knelt in front of Melton. "And the mess in your office—the tossed boxes and documents—was your doing, wasn't it?"

Melton slowly bobbed his head.

"You were looking for Oliver's codes, weren't you?"

Melton's voice went weary and low, "They thought I knew Gary's passwords. Thought I could clear out the money. Ten months of revenue floating in Gary's tangle of accounts that hadn't registered in their ledgers. But I don't know, and I can't access anything on his laptop or his personal ledger. I've tried everything, and nothing works. And now they're getting impatient."

Kendrick stared him in the eyes, "And you don't have a name for me? Not one?"

The sullen Melton replied, "They'll kill me."

Bennett signaled Kendrick. The two stepped aside for a private conversation.

"Shit, the *Malusnavi*?" Bennett whispered. "Our rescue? We did this? We set this off? That's what got Oliver killed?"

"Unfortunate happenstance," Kendrick frowned. "But what concerns me is that we don't have anything beyond Melton here. We need a bloody name, or the trail stops."

"Yeah," Bennett glanced toward Melton. "But I say we snag the computer and see if your buddy Adler can access it. That might lead us somewhere."

"Right," Kendrick turned toward the sobbing Melton. "But I want to press him."

"Ask what he knows about the other shipment?" Bennett said.

Kendrick nodded, "I think we've got him where we want him now."

Then Bennett added, "Amigo, there's a lot of shady shit going down here. I mean these freighters in and out, the illegal cargo, and the other. It's a fucking empire of criminality."

"Runs deep," Kendrick said. "But if I get him to –"

Something cracked.

Not a shatter.

More of a split.

High-pitched, like glass.

For an instant, Kendrick thought he saw a female outside in the rainy darkness. However, the silhouette vanished as soon as he'd made out half a shape.

He rushed toward the balcony's sliding door.

The glass panel showed a tiny round hole to his left.

Kendrick readied his pistol and flung the slider open.

The dark, drizzling night breeze ruffled his shirt.

There was no one in sight.

"Oh shit," Bennett called from inside.

Kendrick turned.

The Marine gazed in horror at the high-back chair.

Blood oozed from a dime-sized hole in the center of Rick Melton's forehead.

CHAPTER

29

An imposing security guard stood at the side of the aisle, tapping his fingers on the edge of his revolver.

Brack slid his phone swiftly into his shirt pocket.

He was fucked. He'd purposely left the Smith & Wesson back at the hotel in case there were metal detectors. His only weapon now was to play the part and keep talking.

He approached the man with an open palm, "Yes, good evening."

The security guard didn't move either hand from his waist. Extremely broad-shouldered, the big man was six foot three or taller and looked like he could snap Brack like a toothpick.

Brack let his proposed hand greeting slowly fall to his side, "Lewis Goodman. Checking on freight for one of our clients. A Margaret George. And fortunately, I've found it."

The guard didn't take his eyes off Brack.

Brack kept in character and pointed to a section of pallets, "Your staff keeps excellent inventory. It didn't take me long to locate it amid all this." He outstretched his arms to mimic the size of the giant warehouse. "You've got a terrific system here. I'm putting that in my report."

The guard looked down at him, "Sir, your ID?"

The nametag on the giant man's uniform read Myers.

Brack's real ID was in the hotel, and it was the only one he had. But it read David Brack.

Should he pop onto the grid because someone ran it, then Gezzle's men would know he was here. If this guard detained and fingerprinted him, he was screwed. His only move was to stall for time until he could figure a way out of this.

"Right. It's in my brief one aisle over. Sorry, it's easy to wander around in this ginormous place."

Myers tongued a cheek, then took a step to the side for Brack to pass.

It was like navigating around an oak tree.

"Excellent inventory system, really," Brack said tensely. "Your crew should be proud."

Big Myers followed behind him but said nothing.

Inside the brief were tax files from Dax's place, but nothing even close to the badge the security guard hovering behind him was wearing. When he reached the briefcase, he placed it on a ledge, opened it, and ruffled at its insides. "Gotta be here somewhere, darn it. I just had it when I entered."

Myers hovered behind him.

Brack needed to buy more time and turned to the large man, "You know it's possible I dropped it when I came through the compound's gate."

Myers looked down at him, then thumbed the radio mic hooked on his uniform, "Conner." He released the mic button and stared at Brack.

Brack's heart was beating out of his chest.

"Conner. Yo," came the radioed reply.

"Yeah, Con. I gotta guy here with no ID in the back stacks. Says his name is…"

"Goodman. Lewis Goodman," Brack said as confidently as possible. "Corporate sent me."

"Says his name's Goodman, Lewis," Myers examined him head to toe. "Supposed to be from corporate."

"Bring him to reception, and we'll check it out."

Myers' stare held on Brack, "Copy that."

Steadily, Brack closed the briefcase, kept his posture stiff, and picked up his umbrella.

Myers walked him out the way he'd snuck in.

They had him for trespassing. Easy. But this facility was a foreign trade area, and he might have violated other laws. For all he knew, Dax was right, and this property might be like an embassy on foreign soil. They might beat the shit out of him, break his legs, or suffocate him with industrial cling wrap like a mummy. After that, they'd pack his body in a long box and stack it on one of the warehouse's high shelves to let it decompose.

He tried to remain calm and focused on his breathing.

They reached the outer area. The man behind the security desk was even larger than Myers. "Goodman," he said, looking Brack over. "Not showing any Goodman on the entry list."

Brack cleared his throat, "Have you checked the corporate schedule? I was instructed to visit this facility to obtain the whereabouts of merchandise for a crucial shipping client. A Margaret George. Perhaps this is under her name?"

Time was all he was buying.

A pair of handcuffs dangled from the backside of Myers' belt. He'd soon be wearing those.

The guard behind the desk tapped on his keyboard and scanned his screen.

The main entry door squeaked open. It was the same entry the guard had held for him after their lightning discussion.

Brack didn't turn around. It was clear the third guard had entered. He wondered which one of these three monster-sized men would punch him in the gut, which one would break his legs, and which one would fetch the cling wrap for his mummification.

But instead of a clattering security belt, a woman shouted, "Sir! Sir!"

Brack turned.

Nikki rushed toward him. Her gray raincoat and fedora were wet from the rain.

"Sir, it's bad." She caught a breath. "HQ called. Said layoffs are coming. Quarterly profits have tanked. I need to get you out of here and on a plane, pronto. The board is pulling an all-nighter." She put a hand on her chest and caught another quick breath. "Janet was hysterical."

"Janet?"

"She was crying, sir. Uncontrollably."

Brack lifted a brow, "Oh, no, not Janet."

Myers and the other guard locked eyes with one another.

"Mr. Goodman," Myers cleared his throat. "We don't need to hold you up any longer. Just doing our jobs, you understand?"

Brack raised his chin, "Yes, yes. Of course. Myers, is it?"

The big man straightened his back, "Vic Myers, yes, sir."

"And Conner Simps, sir." The second guard behind the desk stood.

"Myers and Simps." Brack nodded with authority. "Thank you. I'm afraid I must run. But I'll remember your names."

Brack turned to Nikki.

"Myers and Simps. I'll note them in your scheduler, Mr. Goodman."

Brack picked up his briefcase, "Excellent. Well, good evening, gentlemen."

The armed men actually waved goodbye.

Once outside, Nikki and Brack scurried back to the Sportwagon through the drops. She revved up the car, and they sped from the lot.

Brack buckled himself in, "Who the hell's Janet?"

"Sounded office-like. The name just came to me." Nikki giggled. "Man, that was so much fun!"

Brack laughed aloud, "Maybe for you it was."

Nikki had just saved his ass in a way she'd never understand, and Brack sighed with gratefulness.

CHAPTER
30

Alana sprang from the balcony into the sand.

She sprinted through the rain barefoot along the home's east side. Her pulse soared, and her entire body tingled. She crouched low in the shadows when she hit the beach access stairs.

A strange man appeared on the side of Rick Melton's balcony for a moment but disappeared.

She ascended the stairs quickly, galloped over the neighbor's bushes, and hustled down the dark wet street to the Escalade. She jumped in, eyed the vehicle's rearview, and checked the rounds in her pistol.

There were two others inside that room.

She didn't know who they were or how the lawyer knew them, but she wouldn't kill them unless she had to. Especially if they were police. She prayed neither would try to follow her. She didn't want to take innocent lives. Too many had already been hooked by this deadly turmoil.

Rick Melton, though, had been intimately involved. He coordinated the comings and goings of transports that brought in the drugs, that…

Alana closed her eyes and started the car.

Quickly she sped from the area, glancing in the rearview for any tailing headlights. But there were none.

Her breathing came under control, and her pulse slowed. She now had a decision to make.

The time neared 10pm.

She couldn't get a flight north for a day or two. Also, no airline would allow her to board with an unregistered handgun, especially since she did not have a concealed carry license. The drive, though, would be a long one. Still, it would supply her time to think, to rest.

Though there was a significant hurdle, she'd yet to cross.

Now was that time.

She reached into her bag and brought out her mobile phone.

So far, Alana had done everything he'd asked.

But her reasons for doing were much different than his.

Alexei wanted to sweep up. To find and eliminate anyone he thought betrayed him. To tie those 'loose ends,' he'd said.

But this was Alana's last assignment.

She was expected to return to Alexei at once.

And he'd know if she'd left the area.

Holding the wheel, she fingered the mobile phone's flip side. After a bit of picking, the back panel came loose.

She set the two pieces next to her in the console, stared out at the rainy roadway, and listened to the steady back and forth of the wipers.

She eyed the phone.

If she continued, it meant risk to her own life.

This was a moment of no return.

He'd either believe her or kill her on site.

Alana blinked out at the pouring darkness as the Escalade kept a steady speed.

She reached a hand into the console.

She tugged at the mobile's battery first.

Her chest swelled before a long exhale.

The car raced along the interstate.

Alana rolled down her window.

A damp wind blew at the side of her face.

She hurled the battery from the car onto the roadway.

Then she removed the phone's tiny SIM card.

She bit down on the silicon circuit with her teeth, which cracked in two.

Alana turned her head and spat the tiny data chip into the wind.

Finally, after another mile, she flung the phone into the darkness and rolled up her window.

"Net puti nazad," she uttered.

There was only forward.

If Alexei didn't believe her, she'd face those consequences directly and soon.

But now, he could not track her.

However, he would know something was not right.

Alana only hoped the love he felt for her was robust enough to get past this.

Though, before that reckoning, there was still one more person, one more place she had to visit.

Another target to purge.

She steered the car east onto Interstate 10.

In 400 miles, she'd make the turn north up I-85.

After that, it was another 18 hours to Boston.

Brack could do 53 pushups without stopping now. After finishing his exercise, he showered, readied, and headed down to the hotel's lobby.

Charlie's 'text or call for service' sign sat on the counter's ledge.

The pile of wood in the lobby was noticeably smaller. He was working hard on that gazebo. Or he was off somewhere, potting a plant, painting a wall, or shampooing the resort.

The weather had cleared some, and Brack trotted along the shoreline. It was the best commute to any job he'd ever had.

As usual, Dax was slugging coffee and hunched over his desk at the office.

Brack approached, "I've got something for you."

Dax's hair was a tad wilder than yesterday, meaning he either hadn't slept or showered. Likely both.

Brack took out his phone, pressed its screen a few times, then handed the device to Dax, "Believe it or not, I located some of Margaret's shipments inside that warehouse."

The screen displayed a photo of one of the labels.

"Sweet shit." Dax's eyes widened. "And I'd half expected a call from Frank or a foreign embassy that you'd been arrested."

"Nearly was," Brack laughed. "That place is a stronghold."

Dax eyed him, "I won't ask how you got in."

"Please don't."

"But Clemson wins again." Dax gazed at the phone and nodded. "I gotta be honest, I didn't think you'd find anything. Not in that place." He returned the phone to Brack. "There's a recovery reward, you know. I think you deserve every dollar."

But Brack put up a hand. "Let's split it. You gave me the job and didn't have to."

"Alright," Dax grunted. "Mighty noble and decent of you."

Brack noticed a paperweight with a familiar horse and wagon insignia on Dax's desk. It read, 'Congratulations on Fifteen Years of Service.'

"Previous employer?" Brack pointed.

Dax picked up the paperweight and sighed. "This is a reminder."

"Reminder?" Brack asked.

Dax leaned back in his chair. "Government treats us like a number. We are what we earn for them during our lifetimes. A laboring, spinning taxpayer. We're debt slaves to it all." He gnashed his teeth. "Until it comes time to vote. Then, politicians get all chummy with John Q. Public for a few weeks. Make promises they never keep."

Brack nodded. He was learning Dax held a frustrated philosophy about many things in life—especially the government.

"And it's all bullshit," Dax continued. "Though with big corporations, it's even worse. We trade our lifetimes to them for a fee. Do their bidding. And we undersell ourselves every single time."

Brack stood by, unsure what to say.

Dax nodded to the heavy service award, "When I worked for that bank, there was an incentive to open accounts for clients. Checking, savings, credit cards, loans, and such. Each opening paid the bank employee a commission."

"But that's —" Brack started to say.

Dax raised a finger, "Without the customer's knowledge, that bank allowed its employees to open multiple accounts for clients who'd never signed up for them in the first place." He shook his head. "Falsified bank records. Fake accounts. Pure fraud at the expense of the customer. And management knew. But none of those bastards gave a shit."

"Did you confront them? Were you a whistleblower?"

Dax shook his head and rubbed his temple, "No, David. I was management."

Brack didn't understand.

Dax exhaled, "Well, I knew, but I didn't know. Rumors of misconduct, really, but not the totality. I refused to believe that anyone in my department was involved. I didn't even investigate, dammit."

"But they were?"

Dax nodded, "The bank's illegal practices ruined so much credit that folks couldn't get legitimate home and car loans. It was catastrophic for their lives. What ended it for me was a meeting during the aftermath. Senior leadership called the illegal incentive program 'an experiment that needed to be ironed out,' and the $3 billion fine they labeled as 'the cost of doing business in a competitive industry.'"

Brack shook his head.

"Fucking corporate robots. Would you believe I still got a bonus? A big one. Every red cent my 'team' earned from that fiasco."

"What happened?"

Dax cleared a cough, "Crisis of conscience. Leadership presented me with that damn award during the same 'cost of doing business' bullshit meeting." His head turned. "I quit a day later. Wouldn't sell those assholes anymore of my soul." He brought the crystal weight to eye level, then set it down. "Couldn't give the bonus money back. Not to the people the bank screwed over. So, I renewed my CPA license and used the funds to open this place."

"Oh," Brack offered.

"I dedicate myself to ensuring honest people don't get screwed by Uncle Sam."

Now it made sense. Dax's low fees for tax preparation. Helping Deena and others at the diner deduct their uniforms. The elderly man who'd come into the office unable to afford his wife's medical bills.

Working to help Margaret's kids by hunting down the missing inventory.

A strange feeling hit Brack's insides that he couldn't describe. "You're a good man," he ultimately said.

Dax nodded. "Try to be," and with that, he resumed working on his papers.

Brack left Dax at his desk and returned to the one he'd been using. He brought up his laptop and exhaled quietly for a moment. That story—a man walking away from his career on principle. Nobody Brack had ever known would ever do such a thing. It was all about the Benjamins and nothing else in his earlier world.

But he'd table his thoughts on that for now.

He could do a few more tax returns for Dax, and now that the recovery job on Margaret's company's property was solved, he had more time to focus on his primary goal. His reason for being in the area in the first place.

Melton Oliver & Associates.

They'd stolen from him.

He kept thinking about those packages—those oil paintings—he'd found in the warehouse. As far as he knew, the lawyers now mainly handled injury law. But he believed those packages represented an altogether distinctive line of business, one Brack was regrettably familiar with.

He looked outside. It was raining again.

If he left now, he'd have enough time to complete a promised chore for Charlie back at the Big B hotel before evening rolled in.

Then he'd visit the lawyer's offices tonight.

Only this time, he'd bring along the Smith & Wesson.

CHAPTER
32

Even the second cup of coffee didn't help.

Kendrick kept second-guessing what he'd seen outside Melton's sliding door. Was that a woman? It was too dark, and the rain.

Whoever it was had killed Melton. A professional hit, done with tact and skill. The unknown killer also held the advantage over Bennett and himself during the deed yet hadn't bothered with them. How long would it have taken to also zip a round into he and Bennett's heads? Seconds. But that didn't happen.

The killer's strike was surgical.

They were staying at an inexpensive motel right outside Covington, Louisiana. The Chrysler was parked directly outside.

The room was nothing fancy, though neither man cared for much more than a cot and blanket. But the space had two beds, fresh towels, and a tiny television with a million channels.

Bennett had restlessly flipped through each one last night. Watching shows for mere seconds before moving on to the next. Back and forth, back, and forth. And, as the exhausted Kendrick readied his SIG Sauer to shoot both the flatscreen and the man flicking through its stations, Bennett finally fell asleep.

Yesterday, Adler had them hook the laptop to the internet, remoted into the device, and transferred a complete copy of the locked hard drive. Adler also went into his usual over-explanation on precisely what he was trying to do. Kendrick absorbed about five percent of the second lieutenant's techno gobbledygook.

But they couldn't access the laptop's encrypted data without the password. However, Adler had software capable of replicating the data on its drive. He said he'd put that image on a 'staging area' where he would try to hack into it.

Along with the computer, Adler did the same with the data from the silver thumb-sized USB device Kendrick found wired to the laptop.

And that's where things stood as of this early afternoon.

The Marine finished his shower and wrapped himself with a towel. He stood and stretched his back, "Where to now, amigo?"

As good as Adler was, Kendrick knew even he might be unable to hack the devices. They may never know what data either gadget held. He tried not to let that consume him, but the possibility loomed, "We hold until we hear something."

"Hold, hold," Bennett repeated. "I don't like it, but I copy."

Bennett was getting restless. Like all good soldiers, he needed something to do. The motel room was driving him batty. For now, he retreated to the small bathroom to ready himself.

Melton had confirmed where the opium was headed, which Kendrick had half expected. The number of illegal drugs in the states was skyrocketing. That freighter was only one of several avenues they'd been trafficked. Human mules with pills, cartels and tunnels, fishing boats, speedboats, submarines, and aircraft. In fact, drug kings were inventing new methods and points of entry every day. It seemed America's decades-long drug war had only emboldened its opposition. Made them more innovative, more efficient, and more determined.

Melton never told them who he was working with. But what was most frustrating was that the soft, sobbing man was close to breaking. Kendrick could feel it.

However, the drugs at the port had only been a starting point. Kendrick had more important, crucial questions yet to ask.

Though now, those would never be answered.

They needed to understand the totality of cargo on that freighter. Each container. Who were the senders, and who were the receivers? Because contents varied, there was no way they'd been marked with accuracy on the shipping manifests. Not according to what Kendrick knew.

Bennett dressed in dark cargo pants, a yellow smiley-face t-shirt, and completed the questionable ensemble with a short-sleeve floral overshirt.

Kendrick had already showered and dressed. His outfit was much more conservative, opting for black slacks, a plain white undershirt, and a top with no blossoms.

Together, he and Bennett were a couple of aged, scruffy-looking crime fighters who couldn't catch their suspect because they kept running out of leads.

Though, there was one place they'd yet to explore. It would again require them to break in under cover of darkness.

Until then, there was nothing to do but wait.

The steady rain poured outside the motel window.

Kendrick's jaw shifted side to side as he gazed at the downpour. After a long moment, he retreated to his bed and thumbed through a magazine. It featured reviews on eating establishments in the area, which only made him hungry.

A long hour later, his mobile rang.

Bennett snatched the phone from a side table and put the call on speaker.

"Sir, Second Lieutenant Adler here."

Bennett smirked, "Never heard of him. Sounds like a scoundrel."

"Give me that." Kendrick grabbed the phone.

The Marine was going stir-crazy.

Kendrick couldn't blame him.

"What do you have for us, Adler?"

"Sir, on the laptop data, I don't have much, but –"

"We'll take anything you got." Kendrick eyed the punchy Bennett. "Were you able to break into the laptop's hard drive?"

"Some, sir. I got past the front-end security and could see the file directories. But everything, every type of file, is individually password protected."

Kendrick balled a fist. "Shit."

"Well, sir, stow that for a minute."

Bennett cackled. "Yeah, major, stow your shit."

Kendrick eyed the Marine.

"Go on, Adler."

"First, that USB drive in your possession isn't a USB drive. It's a cold wallet."

"A what?" Bennett said.

Adler continued, "Sirs, I know my explanations are sometimes tedious, but I need to give you some background here. I'll try to put this in the best terms I can."

"Alright," Kendrick said cautiously.

"You've both heard of something called the blockchain?"

Kendrick nodded, but Bennett looked skeptical.

"Crypto funny money bullshit," the Marine said.

"Not at all, sir. It's secure and decentralized."

"Decentralized?" Bennett said quizzically.

"Sir, decentralized because it takes traditional banks out of the equation—which is the whole point. Cryptocurrency can be sent to anyone, anywhere in the world, at any time. There's no need to route transactions through a central broker or bank. It also eliminates peer transmission costs—like service fees for wire transfers."

"Ahh," Bennett nodded, but glanced at Kendrick and rolled his eyes.

"And the more a crypto type is adapted, the stronger security gets," Adler continued. "Most surpasses even military grade."

Kendrick held the phone, "Explain that."

"Well, sirs, the blockchain is a distributed ledger. Think of it like how you once balanced a checkbook—or balance—if you still have one. The ledger, where you wrote in the deposits and debts. Only the blockchain records every transaction for everyone buying, selling, and holding cryptocurrency."

Bennett sat on the bed to redress, "I don't understand?"

"Sir, things in this world are complicated. But imagine if 100 people, who didn't know one another, all had a copy of your checkbook's deposits and withdrawals ledger. Over half of them would have to agree to the payments and takings before you could balance your checkbook. There'd be no fudging numbers."

Kendrick spoke this time, "Okay, so how does this work with crypto?"

"Using the same analogy, that crypto checkbook is built of scrambled data blocks. Each contains a transaction, and every transaction 'block' links to the one before and after itself. This chain of blocks is wrapped in a layer of complex cryptography and creates the checkbook ledger, sir. Not just for you, but for everyone trading in the currency."

"Everyone has a copy of this checkbook?"

"The ledger is publicly distributed. Yes, sir."

Bennett buckled his trousers, "Anyone can see it?"

"No, no, sir. The blocks are highly, highly encrypted."

Kendrick said, "Can someone hack into it or change it?"

"That's the genius of distributed blockchain technology, sir. Especially of this size. It's impossible."

The Marine chimed, "Nothing's impossible."

"This is, sir. The structure for every crypto type is unique. Bitcoin, for example, uses an entirely different mathematical hash arrangement than Ethereum coin, and so on. The more people using a particular crypto, the stronger the security gets. It's an adaptability defense."

"What do you mean?"

"Bitcoin is by far the largest crypto trading with the most users. It runs on distributed, non-centralized computing, sir. It's not just 100 people who have a copy of it. Hundreds of millions, maybe a billion, computers and devices hold that electronic public ledger. A hacker would have to gain control of over half of them to alter the ledger, sir. It's called a 51 percent attack. Only by overtaking most of the devices could a hacker alter things. And there's no way that could ever be done with something of Bitcoin's size."

Bennett pulled on his overshirt and nodded to himself, "Impossible."

"So, the larger the network, the harder it becomes to hack it," Kendrick asked Adler.

"Right. Smaller start-up cryptocurrencies are often attacked because they don't have that massive user base. They haven't been adopted widely yet. Anything in its infancy is at risk for this type of attack."

"Alright, what are we looking at, Adler?"

"Sir, as I said, that small device you have is called a cold wallet. If someone buys cryptocurrency, it's through an online exchange, like a bank. And the exchange holds that crypto after purchase. But that's a bad idea long-term. It's like if you go to a cashpoint, and –"

"A what?" Bennett asked.

Kendrick turned, "Cash machine, an ATM."

"Right," Adler said. "Leaving cryptocurrency on an exchange platform is like… well, you wouldn't process a withdrawal from an ATM and then just leave the money sitting in the slot, would you?"

Bennett uttered, "Hell no, I'd grab the cash and put it in my wallet."

"Exactly, sir. And in the crypto world, this is called a cold wallet. 'Cold' because the device stays offline until you need to use it. That wallet allows whoever knows the password to exchange the cryptocurrency. They can do this with anyone, anytime, anywhere in the world."

Kendrick understood that. Adler was getting better at framing his technical explanations.

"Sir, I can't see the key itself. But using tools here, I can see a data imprint of the cold wallet's structure. It mirrors the arrangement of the SHA256."

Bennett glanced at the mobile, "What?"

"Bitcoin, sir. That cold wallet in your possession holds Bitcoin."

Bennett slipped on his shoes, "How much? Are we rich?"

"I don't have the passcode to get into it, sir. It's a three-fail system that locks me out for 24 hours after those three attempts. Could take months, even years, to break."

Bennett looked at Kendrick, "Bummer."

Adler cleared his throat. "But, sirs, let's get back to the laptop itself. As I said, I can see the names of directories and files even though I can't access the data. And there are hundreds of spreadsheets."

"What does that tell us?"

"I found two things. First, I can see an encrypted directory of non-fungible tokens but not access."

"What the hell are those?" Bennett asked.

"NFTs, sir."

"NFTs?"

"Digital certificates, sir. Creators attached them to unique assets, virtual ones. But I can't view the elements. Not without hacking the passwords attached to each one, which would take a lot of time."

Adler, again, had veered into a technical mire that Kendrick found confusing. NFTs? Virtual? Unique asset? It was like an astrophysicist delivering a lecture to a block of granite. Thankfully, Adler switched topics.

"I'm not sure what they were using these NFTs for, but I found something else I think is even more interesting on the laptop's drive."

"Which is?" Kendrick said eagerly.

"Sir, do you recall that shipping container? The one tagged with the PELG stamp you broke into on Alexandra Island?"

"Pellgrin. Yes."

Bennett eyed Kendrick, "Broke into?"

"Well, sir, Pellgrin's name is all over these files on this laptop."

Kendrick didn't get excited because they'd hit this dead-end before, "What you're going to tell us now is that you still have almost no information on Pellgrin other than what's available publicly, right?"

"That's where there's been a change, sir."

"Change?"

"Sir, remember you had to break into the Louisiana PD because they were on a non-public network?"

Bennett patted Kendrick on the shoulder, "Another break-in? You're a regular second-story man."

Kendrick shrugged with a grin.

"Sir, I'd assumed all law enforcement agencies were like this. None of their internal systems were connected to the internet, and there was no physical way for me to penetrate their network."

"Right. Said you could never connect to something like that."

"But then, by accident, I got lucky, sir."

"Lucky?"

"If even one device connected to one of these non-public networks is also connected to the internet, I can get into their network."

"What does this mean?" Kendrick said.

Adler snickered. "Sir, there's a small police station in Massachusetts that plays a lot of Call of Duty online. And their internal servers had some bloody interesting stuff about Symon Pellgrin."

CHAPTER

33

Incessant rain continued outside the motel room as Kendrick and Bennett waited on Adler's information.

"First, sirs, before we get to Symon Pellgrin, let me share what I learned about his multiple organizations." Adler's keyboard clicked. "It's interesting and should help you understand how all of this works."

Kendrick raised the volume of his mobile's speaker.

"Pellgrin's container business is effectively separate from all its shipping vessels," Adler began. "The ships are all under Pellgrin International, but every container is currently under the possession of a different company."

"Kilgore Logistics?" Kendrick said.

"Affirmative. There's a labyrinth of layers between Pellgrin and Kilgore. I traced it through four offshores, three dummy corps, and six anonymous trusts. From what I uncovered, I found that Symon is the ultimate owner of both businesses."

Bennett turned with concern, "Pellgrin and Kilgore? How?"

"Pellgrin leases its half million shipping containers to Kilgore Logistics. It's a twenty-year deal. This is why, in Alexandria's port, you saw the ID number on the doors with the Kilgore designator but found the PELG owner code on top of the container when you crawled up there."

Bennett turned to Kendrick, "Crawling up shipping containers? Busting into places? Is your actual name Thomas Crowne?"

175

Kendrick smirked.

"Sirs, whoever relabeled the cargo boxes didn't change that identifier on top. Probably most were stacked, or they were in a hurry."

"But why?"

"Sir, he structured things like this in case of seizure."

"Seizure?" Bennett said, confused.

"If a freighter is caught at sea moving illicit cargo, the ship captain can immediately point the finger at the sender or receiver. Different ownership puts distance between the freighter itself and the cargo it carries. Authorities will remove the cargo and let the ship and its other goods move along."

Kendrick appeared unsure, "How do you know this?"

"Because, sir, Symon Pellgrin's done this before."

Bennett sounded surprised, "He has?"

"Yes, sir. Several times," came Adler's reply.

"How do we know this?" Kendrick asked.

"Sir, the ship's name was the Cupertino. It was en route from West Africa, headed to a port in South America. But it found itself caught in some serious swells in the Atlantic. A hurricane."

"Hurricane?" Bennett looked to Kendrick.

"Happens more often than you know," Kendrick said flatly.

"The Cupertino was fully loaded, but the storm crippled its motors and tore payload from its deck. They lost power to all the major systems, and the ship went into a dangerous list. Took her sideways pretty bad."

"Lose any crew?"

"No, sir. Not according to these records. But things do get curious."

Kendrick squinted, "Curious?"

"Seems the storm pushed the containership way off course to the northwest. But the vessel still hadn't crossed the maritime boundary."

"Into U.S. waters?"

"Right. These guys aboard had no control, sir. The Cupertino was drifting in the Atlantic, all 200,000 tons of her, in international waters. That storm was brutal. And they had over fourteen thousand containers aboard."

Bennett began, "The Navy did they —"

"Well, sir, for safety, in severe weather, service ships take to port in times of non-combat. And beyond radar sweeps, other service vessels don't patrol that far out unless an incident is called in."

"So, these guys were screwed?" the Marine said.

"Would've been properly, sir. But the Cupertino's crew panicked and radioed out a mayday."

Kendrick bobbed his head, "Coast Guard."

"Right. Rescue dispatched air and sea support. Took a couple of hours to find them. Someone aboard the freighter popped a flare, and the Jayhawk helicopter reached the listing Cupertino 250 nautical miles east of Miami. Lucky for them, the storm pushed the cargo ship closer toward the Florida coastline when they were found."

"Souls?"

"All accounted. Rescue swimmers found three in the water but fished them out to safety."

Bennett grinned, "Waterdogs."

"Except for some cargo loss and mechanical damage, the freighter was still afloat. But sirs, the Navy did send a ship out there," Adler exhaled. "And I don't know how, but the crew corrected the ballast and put the Cupertino under tow."

"You're shitting me?" Bennett said, astonished. "A freighter that gigantic?"

"Navy, sir. Tell them they can't, and those Squids will prove you wrong or die trying."

The two men glanced at one another, and Kendrick said, "Don't we know it."

Next, for some reason, Adler laughed for several seconds.

"What is it?" Kendrick demanded.

Adler stifled another chuckle, "Sorry, sir. According to this, they moved the personnel off the Cupertino onto the Navy ship. The exhausted crew gave handshakes and hugs to their rescuers. They received blankets, coffee, cocoa, and a hot meal in the mess."

Kendrick grimaced, "Where's the humor?"

"Gets better, sir. Because the Cupertino's captain accepted the Coast Guard's aid, he'd unknowingly authorized a complete ship inspection."

Then Kendrick smirked, "And the ship was foreign-flagged."

Adler snickered, "Correct. During the tow back to port, while its men filled their bellies, the ship received a lot of attention. Officials cited the maritime security law of 2004 and performed a seaworthiness assessment and a random check of several containers onboard."

"What'd they find?"

"This is where things go thorny, sir." Adler cleared his throat. "Officials discovered several containers of firearms. True combat weapons: grenade launchers, machine guns, and rifles with military flash suppressors. Munitions of high caliber and capacity that violated the UN's Arms Trade Treaty, as well as numerous embargos."

"Headed to South America?"

"They believed so." Adler paused. "But I think, I think it was going someplace else."

"Someplace else? Where?"

"Sir, given what you and I know because of recent events, I believe those weapons were headed for The Port of New Orleans. Where these unlawful items could be transferred to ground, and…" Adler stopped.

"And what?"

"Sir, this is speculation, my guess. But I think most weapons were headed to one of the larger ports in Los Angeles."

Kendrick rubbed his chin, "The west coast? Why?"

"To avoid the Panama Canal, sir. Since the withdrawal of the American military in 1999 to the local authority down there, it's increasingly difficult to smuggle goods through its locks."

Bennett stood from his bed, "Tighter security, I bet."

"No, sir. The opposite. Corruption can be so bad in Panama that the high bribes take a serious bite from smuggler profits. It's not worth it. However, if goods move to a northern freeport—like one of those in Port NOLA—they can be trucked west or east to another port without inspection. And Smugglers avoid the Panama Canal altogether."

For Kendrick, things were falling into place. Gezzle Lift & Haul— this is precisely what they were doing. And if Remo Gezzle was transporting guns in his vehicles, he was also moving minerals and drugs. In fact, anything they hauled in their trucks could be moved to any place. Domestic or otherwise.

Adler continued, "Customs officials seized the Cupertino. The skipper and his men were initially detained, but once lawyers got involved, blame was placed on Kilgore. That company then accused those who packed the container at its point of origin."

Kendrick said, "Shifted blame."

"Yup, and the Cupertino's captain and crew were let go within 24 hours."

Bennett watched the rain outside the window, "Who filled the illegal containers with those weapons?"

"A company called 'Hallon, LLC.' It was an overseas packing and sorting outfit."

Kendrick paced the room, "And your research found it was owned by Symon Pellgrin?"

"Bingo, sir. Hallon was fined, and then declared bankruptcy before they were forced to pay and dissolved. Meanwhile, I uncovered another anonymous LLC that Symon Pellgrin started up a week later to take its place."

"I see," Kendrick said.

"This is how Pellgrin does things, sir. It's a five-layered shell game on a pyramid of companies. Pellgrin owns the boats, Kilgore Logistics the containers, Sigma-Sea runs the freeport, and Gezzle Lift & Haul does the trucking. But these small come-and-go LLCs pack and ship illegal goods under their names. So, they are the ones authorities go after if any contraband is discovered."

Bennett turned from the window, "And this Symon fucker owns all of them?"

"Yes, sir. If Kilgore is ever caught, they can blame the packers. The packing company dissolves into bankruptcy, just as Hallon did, and Symon Pellgrin just starts up another."

"But what if Kilgore is caught red-handed?" Bennett asked.

"It's more work, sir, but the result is the same. Symon Pellgrin can recall the lease from Kilgore and take back possession of his containers. Then he'll lease them to a new company. One that he secretly owns, and the whole thing starts over. On paper, he stays at least one layer away from the activity. Pellgrin International Shipping, Symon's main company, is deniable at every turn."

"Damn smuggling empire." Bennett clenched his jaw. "The ships, containers, storage, and the companies that pack those illegal goods. Bastard Symon Pellgrin."

Kendrick nodded.

"But with Interpol, sirs, the gunrunning incident was a turning point. That's when agents began to secretly track Pellgrin's vessels. But because of the sheer volume, only a fraction of its company-owned containers were tagged."

"Ahh," Kendrick nodded.

"Interesting endnote to the Cupertino incident, though, sirs. Two months after the ship's hurricane rescue, police discovered the Cupertino's 49-year-old captain beside a garbage dumpster in Old San Juan—sporting enough holes in his chest that his corpse would whistle during the next gust of offshore wind."

"Christ," Bennett offered.

Kendrick rubbed his cheek. Was Pellgrin the type who didn't leave loose ends? With so much money at stake, that would make sense.

"I've worked up a dossier on Symon Pellgrin's background. It includes all the information I pulled from the local PDs servers once I breached their firewall. Publicly, his records are non-existent."

Kendrick slid the SIG into its holster, "But they had them?"

"Affirmative, and likely because they were too lazy to purge them. Or someone was keeping them for blackmail. Who knows? But when I began downloading the files, my box was initially attacked by a search-and-destroy Spybot. This program is designed to crawl the internet for personal information and demolish it on any public platform."

"How'd he –?"

Kendrick put a hand over the mic and grinned. "Don't ask. Kid's a tech wizard."

"I pieced things together and figured my merged report would make for better reading."

"Thanks, Adler."

"I'm sending my report to both of your mobile phones now. The password is capital 'PELG.'" Adler paused. "I'd stay on with you, but the Brigadier scheduled a late call with standing staff."

"Understood. Adler, thanks for the info."

"No problem. And good luck, sirs."

The call switched off.

Seconds later, Kendrick and Bennet's mobile phones pinged with the same incoming message.

And both started to read Adler's report on Symon Pellgrin.

CHAPTER

34

Symon Windell Pellgrin grew up the only child of Maude and Bernie Pellgrin. Pellgrin International Shipping wasn't nearly as significant as Denmark's Maersk or Germany's Hapag-Lloyd ventures, but Pellgrin was family-owned with no debt or outside investors.

High school sweethearts, the elder Pellgrin's started the company with a shoddy forklift and a less than seaworthy oil tanker—which they'd converted into a 300-foot cargo carrier using a high-interest second mortgage on their small family home.

Bernie ran the scheduling and logistics, and Maude hustled the contracts and payroll. Pellgrin Shipping blossomed to six vessels in four years, with regular routes to five countries and one hundred ports. Its employee count swelled to include more captains, freight managers, CDL drivers, heavy equipment operators, technicians, many deck and dock workers, and lawyers and accountants. Even the company name grew an adjective.

In thirty years of operation, Pellgrin's assets increased to 80 ships, including nine Neopanamax cargo freighters—sea vessels the length of city skyscrapers that could carry tens of thousands of containers.

Pellgrin's substantial profits afforded Maude and Bernie a comfortable life in Boston and London, with a massive vacation home in the Hamptons.

It also allowed their ingrate son to flunk out of three Ivy-League schools.

During Symon Pellgrin's pampered teens and collegiate relocations, he became well-known to authorities in Massachusetts and the surrounding states. Drugs, driving under the influence, more drugs, and finally, a charge of assault with a deadly weapon at his last university. Apparently, Symon tried to settle a dispute with a baseball bat when another student accused him of groping his girlfriend.

None of his crimes made much news, of course. Instead, each incident was silenced with cash or choreographed with fake rebuttal witnesses. And in the event neither of those methods worked, evidence mysteriously went missing, and a handsomely paid district attorney refused to prosecute the case.

After his third scholastic strike, Maude and Bernie planted 21-year-old Symon behind a desk at Pellgrin's Boston headquarters, put him in charge of nothing, and hoped to hell he'd mature and blossom into a responsible human being.

Symon thanked them by learning what he needed from the business, seizing space on one of the ships for his own use, and attempting to import six stolen, custom-made, carbon-fiber Lamborghini supercars from Italy.

Though, young Symon also made a ridiculous mistake. Standard rectangular, twenty-foot equivalent unit (TEU) containers can hold almost 1,200 cubic feet of goods. Instead of securing double-deck auto-transport types, Symon sought to avoid suspicion from inspectors and used three ordinary, single-level general-purpose containers for his crime.

The flunky severely miscalculated the size of his cargo. He'd used the Lamborghini's wheelbase instead of its overall length—leading him to believe he could jam two vehicles inside each of his three containers.

But the cars were too long.

At sunrise, he and his nitwit crew were left with a trio of undocumented, exotic metallic-red supercars sitting out in the open when Ravena's authorities showed up.

Pellgrin's lawyers and a suitcase of money arrived quickly.

Symon and his thieving friends were released within a couple of hours.

Symon's father suffered a fatal heart attack shortly after that fiasco, and a distraught Maude followed Bernie to his grave less than a year later.

Nefarious, felonious, and diploma-less, 23-year-old Symon inherited the family's $1.9 billion empire and took control of the family's fleet of freighter ships and the worldwide whereabouts and contents of 491,000 shipping containers.

Young, rich, and in command of critical supply chain goods worldwide, from raw materials to finished products, Symon could easily transport anything to any continent in the world… and he did just that.

According to IRS reports, Symon's profits exploded 900 percent in the first year of his takeover. And this was just his reported income.

In an industry where only five percent of cargo is ever inspected, suspicions grew that Symon was now dabbling in things beyond stolen cars, and his new customers—whomever they were—were paying top dollar for his shipping services.

Adler's report included a link to the Cupertino incident. Kendrick watched the video press conference on his mobile phone.

At its Boston headquarters, donning a jacket with tie and growing more egotistical with age, a dark-haired, groomed Symon Pellgrin stood before cameras and addressed the situation himself—denying he knew anything about the illegal cargo.

Symon grinned and nodded at the cameras from a podium embellished with his company's logo, "Regrettably, shipping companies such as Pellgrin are at times affected by trafficking issues. In this case, an unknown actor placed a prepaid blind shipment of five containers onboard." His hands cavorted above the podium, "This type of arrangement is normally done to protect the supplier from potential undercut by the purchaser. But in this case, this small shipment of intermodals included illegal firearms. That's five containers among the 12,000 on the ship." Symon raised a triumphant fist, "…and we caught them!"

Several members of the press clapped in delight.

When the camera clicks slowed, Symon's expression shifted to a frown, and the 30-something-year-old shipping tycoon leaned into the podium with concern.

"Pellgrin has a history of assisting U.S. federal law enforcement agencies and will work tirelessly to put an end to illegal smuggling on our vessels—as any principled container business must commit to doing."

PR-polished words combined with unblinking confidence he'd stolen from his dead father. Symon sold the lies to an adoring media and the public.

Then, with connections and currency, the cunning shitbag arranged for the release of his captain and crew. Maritime officials ceased their inspection of the Cupertino's containers but did cite the ship for minor watch-keeping and pollution infractions to satisfy public optics.

For the most part, the press ignored the helmsman's killing as no article in Adler's trove of data linked to it. Though another item did connect Kendrick to a Forbes magazine article about Symon. The puffiest of puff pieces.

The writer noted Symon as a car collector, a 'bashful' bachelor, and framed him as an enchanting, hardworking man saddled with the challenges of running his family's business. "I'm giving 110 percent and doing my best," the article quoted. "I hope my dear parents look proudly down on their son."

In closing, the article's author assured readers they were.

What a little fucker.

Kendrick knew one thing for sure from his contact at Interpol. Twenty months ago, a brave agent had managed to tag one hundred of those half-million Pellgrin-owned TEUs at an industrial freeport harbor in Louisiana.

They tracked them using electronic tags via satellite. Pellgrin's ships, like those of his competitors, traversed the global seaways and docked at every deep-water port in the world. However, forty-two of his company-owned containers seemed to bounce between Africa, South America, and China like clockwork. In fact, these same intermodals never once deviated from those routes in almost two years.

For months, agents watched the marked cargo bounce from port to port until thirteen containers and the Pellgrin ship carrying them mysteriously fell off the radar completely.

The freighter had passed the island of Cuba, just outside the Gulf of Mexico, and disappeared.

Interpol's astonishment turned to horror. The giant ship and its cargo vanished two hundred miles from the closest shoreline.

Distraught agents believed the freighter had sunk. They called in every favor they could, depleted the operation's shoestring budget repositioning satellites, and covertly arranged a flyover of the area. But there was no sign of the missing ship, its men, or its payload.

Until weeks later, 500 nautical miles northeast of its disappearance, and in the middle of the Atlantic Ocean, one of those missing tagged containers inexplicably began pinging a satellite again—as if suddenly appearing from a time portal.

It was on a different freighter, a smaller container ship, moving toward Florida's easternmost coastline.

After a refueling stop in Miami, the freighter chugged north once more.

Interpol got a fix on the ship's direction. It was heading directly for Alexandra Island.

Another favor was called in.

Agents desperately wanted to find out what was inside that tagged TEU.

An aside note in Adler's report read, "Sir, this is where you came in. This was the shipping container you investigated."

Adler was right.

That was the evening Kendrick discovered the pinging container resting inside Alexandra's secured seaport. It sat atop a trailer-bombcart, surrounded by three strange men, who picked its padlock and stole the weapons inside. After they left, all Kendrick found in the container was a dropped rifle magazine among crates of peculiar minerals.

Bennett exclaimed, "Oh, shit, this is our guy. I have no doubt." He stared excitedly at Kendrick. "Time for a trip to Massachusetts? This fucker knows exactly where that cargo with the –"

"Yeah, he does," Kendrick said bitterly.

"Weather's supposed to clear tomorrow morning or early afternoon." Bennett clapped. "Fire up the Riley. Get out of this cage."

Antsy Bennett was excited.

But Kendrick stared out at the rain, thinking.

CHAPTER

35

Rain showers slowed to a trickle when Bennett handed Kendrick a coffee. It was time to leave. Fly north and visit young Symon Pellgrin, the owner of Pellgrin International Shipping.

Bennett finished examining the map on his mobile, "Radar is clearing, and it looks like we're good to leave. Should touch down after dusk. His place is about a 40-minute car ride away after we land. Think it'll be nice and dark by then," Bennett said.

Kendrick nodded, "Perfect."

The men readied and checked out of the hotel.

They drove the Chrysler to Lakefront Municipal Airport, loaded their gear, and took off without incident.

The plane ride was much smoother. The clouds had dissipated, and Bennett offered to let Kendrick take the stick.

Kendrick shook his head, "Uh, no thanks. I'm good."

"C'mon, it'll be fun."

"Didn't turn out that way last time."

"Yeah, guess you got a point."

Both men chuckled.

The flight was a little over seven hours.

They'd stopped in Williamsburg to refuel, relieve, and grab more snacks. Bennett was particularly thrilled by mixing M&Ms into his Frito crisps. Pilot grub, Kendrick figured.

Within a few more hours, nighttime rolled in.

Bennett adjusted the radio to 122.8 MHz and chatted on CTAF. He called in his intention for approach.

"Orange Traffic, Red Riley twin Cessna, twenty miles northwest entering left downwind runway 32."

Another pilot answered his call, "Twin Cessna inbound Orange, I just landed. Be advised the AWOS is reporting a false ceiling. I broke out at 400 feet!"

Bennett shifted in the pilot seat, "Yuck, amigo. The clouds get lower up ahead, and I hate fog."

"We can land?"

"Oh, we'll land." Bennett leaned forward. "Be nice to do it on the runway, though."

Beneath them, a blanket of thick clouds came into view.

Bennett fussed with a knob on the cockpit dash, "Better check AWOS."

Kendrick held wide-eyed and stared out the air shield. "What's AWOS?"

"Automated weather observation from ground." Bennett turned a switch, and a mechanical voice came over the radio.

"Orange Municipal Airport. Automated advisory. Wind northeast at five knots, temperature one-nine Celsius, dewpoint one-six, altimeter three-zero-zero-two, density altitude two-seven-one-two. Low fog advisory."

"Now they tell us." Bennett adjusted something on the dash. "Switching us to IFR before things go CSS."

"CSS?"

"Can't see shit," Bennett grumbled. "This haze means we're changing to instrument flight rules. IFR shows altitude, direction, speed of climb and descent, and such. Keeps it so we don't become spatially disoriented and get 'the leans.'"

"The leans?"

"Fast answer? Our bodies have a sense of space, just like the primary senses of touch, taste, smell, and all that."

Kendrick felt uneasy.

"Our inner ear and internal organs orientate us to the ground," Bennett's eyes darted between the dark sky outside to the instrument dash. "But when moving in the air, within three-dimensional space, bodily senses can get all screwed up. Without visual references, like land or lights, we might think we're level when we're not. Or believe we're climbing when we're really in a bank and descend. The leans are deadly dangerous. Prominent theory is this is what got John Junior, his wife, and sister-in-law when they crashed flying into Martha's Vineyard in 99."

Kendrick scanned each of the panel's instruments but only understood what a few meant.

"When we're in the air, and inside milky white mess like this fog, we have to rely on our gauges and disregard what our body feels. Plus," Bennett raised a finger, "we gotta avoid those flying beasts from Boston-Logan International to our east."

Kendrick felt his insides tightening, "Avoid?"

"Yeah. Our little Riley would be a bird strike to a 900-passenger A380. They might not even feel it. We'd be a flaming mess, though."

Kendrick gasped, "What?"

"Relax, they're far from us. I'm just kidding."

The skies had their own language, and Bennett had his own humor. Kendrick really disliked the latter.

"Orange traffic, Red Riley twin Cessna, five miles northwest, inbound runway 32. Please advise of the ceilings."

No one responded to his request.

Kendrick released a low belch.

The rain calmed, but the aircraft's wiper blades fought to clear away the thick mist they were flying through.

Bennett called, "Hang on!"

They pitched downward into the clouds.

The Marine began muttering, "Where is she, dammit?"

Something was growing in the pit of Kendrick's stomach.

"Where the hell is she?"

Kendrick's heart raced, and his throat ballooned.

A faint line of lights shined ahead.

Bennett exhaled, "Orange traffic. Red Riley twin Cessna, short final runway 32."

A surge of relief came over Kendrick.

Despite the fog, the plane landed at Orange Municipal Airport, about 75 miles west of Boston. Kendrick let out a series of burps and was simply thankful when they touched down safely.

Bennett throttled the plane to a parking area between two other resting aircraft. Then he made a final call into the radio, "Red Riley twin Cessna, full stop."

He removed his headset, and Kendrick did the same.

It was pitch dark when they paid the landing fee and retrieved their rental. Another Chrysler Sebring, maroon or maybe brown, Kendrick couldn't tell in the heavy gray air.

They loaded their gear, left the airport, and Bennett steered them onto Route 202, heading south.

CHAPTER

36

The drive didn't take long and allowed Kendrick's stomach to settle.

Symon Pellgrin's primary residence was in ritzy Cambridge. A mansion with 11 rooms and even more bathrooms. Old money, bought by his deceased parents, no doubt.

According to Adler, though, the young shipping baron was currently spending time at his hillside country house outside Northampton.

Kendrick knew this confrontation would be their most significant. Symon Pellgrin was 33 years old and ran a massive shipping operation to ports worldwide. He had billions of dollars. Friends in high places and friends in low places. But Kendrick still didn't know much about the man himself. Though, if his youthful appetites were any sign, the young man might be more the unmanageable idiot Adler's report made him out to be.

Nevertheless, he and Bennett would work him as they had Melton. Kendrick would start with what he knew of the gunrunning and set a baseline for Pellgrin's truth-telling. Then, he'd move on to understand who was shipping what to whom. The guns, the drugs, and the minerals were one batch of ills, but there were more pressing issues beyond just those.

What still bothered him was Melton's killer. Had that person been hired by Pellgrin himself? Was he erasing anyone involved with the incident on the *Malusnavi*? Or did Kendrick have this all wrong?

He was thankful this part of his probe was playing out far from Louisiana and, hopefully, far from the killer.

Pellgrin was key. And this time, he'd keep his suspect more protected, away from large windows and such. No way would another bullet end their efforts before he and Bennett got the answers they were seeking.

The fog got heavier on the roadway. Bennett turned on the wipers to fight the heavy mist, but it didn't work very well. He switched to low beams and decreased their speed.

Traffic was sparse. The time was nearing 9pm when the Chrysler found the unnamed road. The property was surrounded by a gated fence in all directions. And, due to the fog, they couldn't tell how far Symon's place was up the long, hilly, tree-lined road.

Bennett spotted one camera, which he pointed out to Kendrick, and they both avoided it.

The men found a safe space to park up the road near a dirt service inlet. They left the vehicle under cover of darkness and set out on foot.

A large, black iron gate with the initials' SP' lay ahead.

Kendrick found a low spot in the wall not too far from the gate, and both men climbed over.

Bennett checked his weapon, and Kendrick did the same.

An amber light glowed through the fog about a half mile in the distance.

Visibility was less than fifty feet and growing worse as night settled in. Bennett and Kendrick held by a line of trees at the property's retaining wall. The wall was made of stacked railroad ties, over a body length high, but unfenced at its top to keep the home's valley view unobstructed. The barrier was tall enough to keep out critters and deter easy entry.

Bennett pointed, "Over here."

An unequal breach in the wall saw three of the railroad ties stick out at irregular angles. It seemed climbable.

Bennett placed a foot on the first rail with a grunt, hoisted his body up, and clung to the top before signaling Kendrick to join him.

Kendrick did the same, minus the grunt. Soon, the two were side by side, clung to the rear of the eight-foot barrier, scanning the foggy surroundings of Symon Pellgrin's estate.

"This place is huge," Bennett whispered. "It looks like a fucking fortress."

Stone shelled the home's two-level exterior from bottom to top. Wooden beams accented the windows and framed each of the roof's five enormous peaks, which seemed to disappear into the night's misty clouds at their highest point.

From what he'd uncovered, the 11,000 square foot home had nine bedrooms and as many baths, with most bedrooms upstairs, including the master.

Bennett motioned to his left, "Gotta be over there."

The eastern half of the giant dwelling sat dark, while several sections of the west were lit from the inside. Kendrick watched for movement, but it was difficult to make anything out through the thick haze at this distance. "We need to get closer."

Bennett spotted a small cleft large enough to fit the ball of his foot. He stepped into it and crawled up the wall as Kendrick followed.

Once topside, Kendrick touched Bennett's shoulder, "Stay low, go slow."

Bennett nodded.

The two traipsed across the grass toward the home's courtyard to a long crescent-shaped hedge line. Past the bushes rested a sizable rectangular in-ground swimming pool with tile decking. Half a dozen oversized cement pots—large enough for each man to hide behind—held manicured trees to accent the area.

Kendrick made his way to one of the pots, and Bennett hid behind another. They were less than fifty feet from the home's attached covered lanai.

"Christ, this little shit has an outdoor kitchen bigger than my apartment," Bennett whispered. "That grill could fit an entire swordfish, nose and all." He shook his head, "More money, more shit."

He was right. The outside entertainment area was gigantic and included a pool house on the east end.

To the right of the immense outdoor grill sat a woodpile of stacked cut stumps for the dwelling's four fireplaces.

Bennett pointed, "He's home."

A silhouette walked past a window at the uppermost level, inside the compound's far left. It was male-shaped, but there was no way to make out a face at this distance.

Two surveillance cameras were mounted about the home's courtyard, and what Kendrick surmised were motion detectors attached to LED lights. The cameras didn't concern him. He knew how to maneuver around those. But if the motion detectors were also connected to the home's alarm system, that could be a problem.

"How do we get past that shit?" Bennett pointed.

Kendrick had an idea, and the two men had a quick discussion. Kendrick reached over the concrete container and quietly snapped off a sizable branch from its shaped tree. He passed the stick to Bennett, and Kendrick steadily aimed the pistol's laser sight at the home's bullet camera to blind it.

Bennett hurled the branch at one of the motion detectors.

It struck the device, and the stick fell on top of the woodpile.

Kendrick commanded, "Go, go!"

The compound's LED lights blazed through the fog, lighting most of the courtyard.

Both men darted across the grounds, back to the retaining wall, clambered over its flip side, and returned to the forest of wild pine trees.

In the darkness, he and Bennett found an elevated position where they could see over the retaining wall. It wasn't a clear view, of course, but Kendrick saw the home's occupant open a set of French doors and scan the pool area.

The Marine whispered, "Is that the little son of a bitch?"

It was impossible to tell.

"So, what? We wait to see if the cops show?"

Kendrick nodded.

They lingered until sirens sounded from a nearby road. Kendrick looked at his watch, "Fourteen minutes."

"Will that be enough time?"

Kendrick ascended the mound, and he and Bennett moved farther away from the home's retaining wall.

A few more minutes passed until flashlight beams appeared in two sections of the grounds.

"Clear," one of the men said.

The other finished his scan of the yard, "Yap, same."

Shortly after, the flashlights left, and the courtyard's LED beams were extinguished.

"Now what?"

Kendrick glanced again at his watch, "We wait."

Precisely fifteen minutes passed before he and Bennett reclimbed the wall, snuck across the grounds, snapped off another branch, Kendrick blinded the camera, and Bennett tossed the stick at the same motion detector.

The men sprinted from the scene, back over the wall, and waited.

Twenty-three minutes passed.

Sirens rose in the distance.

Kendrick and Bennett surveyed from afar as two cops or security persons rechecked the grounds.

Kendrick muttered, "Again, the villagers came to his aid."

"What?" Bennett turned to him. "You Welsh are weird."

Two officers checked the perimeter. After five minutes, the officers left. The yard's LED lights extinguished, and the area went quiet again.

Fifteen minutes later, they repeated the routine. Only this time, it took a full thirty-one minutes until sirens were heard by the road, and only a single officer showed up to check the grounds.

As a bonus, the armed security guard and the home's occupant had a heated conversation before the yard's exterior lights turned off, and the two went their separate ways.

Bennett held in the tree line and turned to Kendrick, "Man, that security dude was pissed, wasn't he?"

Kendrick allowed himself half a smile, "Perfect."

CHAPTER

37

Again, they waited a quarter-hour.

This time, however, there was no need to toss a stick.

Bennett and Kendrick moved past the hedges to the pool, then ran toward the French doors, where Kendrick worked the mechanism open in seconds.

The motion detector sensed their presence.

The LEDs blasted the foggy yard with light.

The alarm cried wolf again.

He and Bennett had roughly 30 minutes, give or take. The authorities would be in no hurry to visit this residence a fourth time tonight.

Inside, a mounted panel alarm beeped with a high-pulsed pitch.

Kendrick pointed and whispered, "You check the upstairs."

Bennett snuck past a large dining room, down a corridor, to a winding staircase, leaving Kendrick to secure the downstairs.

The interior space was massive. Ceilings of at least twenty feet or more, squared with layers of crown molding and intricate custom millwork on each overhead surface.

A collection of antique furniture filled an enclaved reception area. It didn't match the modern fixtures in the other rooms he passed. Maybe this was a den of heirlooms?

Five Roman columns ensconced the entrance. Each ornate pillar rose an imposing two levels in the foyer. These and other fixtures bordered on grandiosity.

Did some of the ultra-wealthy see themselves as financial conquerors of the giant? The fancy? The impossible? Décor they believed rooted in bizarre ancient wisdom? Or maybe Symon, the shipping shithead, thought he was an emperor?

Kendrick explored the lower floor's halls.

He didn't know much about art but had studied some historical works. And what Symon Pellgrin displayed on the walls in this home puzzled him.

A mishmash of framed portraits—each a different period and style. Landscape, still life, impasto, baroque, impressionism. The paintings looked like a confusing mishmash, a barnyard collection, and didn't go together with any common theme.

Did Symon just see 'art' and buy it? Like a child reaching for a shiny object?

Kendrick shook his head.

Real works from talented artists held an effectual feeling on the viewer, emitting thought or emotion. He didn't understand how it all worked, but as the saying went, Kendrick knew good art when he saw it.

The better a piece was, the more people were drawn to it, like da Vinci's Mona Lisa or van Gogh's Starry Night. True art was enchanting.

But this stuff was utter shit.

The works were trite, devoid of inspiration, and not of any real quality. Many looked rushed, and others appeared to be knockoffs of knockoffs. None of these low-tier oil paintings belonged in a home like this, which Kendrick thought very odd.

The alarm's beeps stopped, and the home went silent.

Kendrick searched more of the area. Behind one door, he found a smaller room humming with electronics—three computers and a bank of monitors. This was the compound's security hub, and wires waterfalled from its drop ceiling into four digital video recorders. Although they'd blinded the exterior camera with the gun's lasers, cameras inside this dwelling had recorded their entry and likely every move they'd made since.

Kendrick removed each recorder's memory card. There were no coaxial or cat5 ports on the recorders, which meant it was a closed system and not communicating with the internet. That saved him a call to Adler.

Next, Kendrick carefully crept from room to room—pointing the SIG at every opening and turn—but nobody seemed to be on this level. Quietly he made his way up the winding staircase into a long, lighted corridor where more strange paintings hung. Bennett was someplace, as was the person they'd seen meandering inside.

Shouting came from a connecting hallway.

Kendrick hid against a wall.

Then, ten meters down the long corridor, a hand strangely waved him forward.

Kendrick tiptoed into the hall.

The striking ceilings were high-pitched with exposed beams—like those in a gothic church. Someone had spent millions designing and building this place.

Bennett waited inside the archway, and Kendrick joined him.

The space was like a secondary keeping room. Light from the connected corridor was enough to make out a bookshelf on the far wall. But this was no library. A tall, dark sculpture stood in a far corner, and a grand piano took up space in another. An oversized Persian carpet covered most of the area's oak floor, with couches and a long, low table filled with crystal decanters and glasses in its center.

More money, more shit.

Bennett whispered, "Listen."

Down the hall, an irate Symon shouted, "No, no! How could this be my fault? Why would you charge me for the visits? You guys installed this shit!"

Kendrick almost chuckled. The man was worried about incurring fees for false alarms when, according to everything he'd seen so far, he spent as haphazardly as the immature idiot he was.

"Gotta be him," Bennett whispered.

Kendrick nodded.

"Do we?"

Kendrick shook his head, "We'll wait a full minute after he's done with his call."

"Why the minute?" Bennett asked.

"If there's someone in there with him, we should hear another voice within that time."

Down the hall, Symon's hollers hit a crescendo, "Well, I don't know what's going on either! But screw your company if you think I'm paying anything extra! You can fuck right off!" A smash broke the air, and a thousand dollars of busted smartphone hit the wood floor. "Fucking shitheads!"

Symon grumbled other obscenities for a few seconds.

But no one else spoke.

He was alone.

After the minute, Kendrick and Bennett exited the piano room, through the archway, and into the hall. They passed a row of closed doors until Bennett grabbed Kendrick's wrist to halt him.

Symon's office lay ahead. From this concealed angle, it looked more like a library. Books on built-in shelves lined every surface they could see. Another giant throw rug, a leather chair, and a decorative globe stood beside a fireplace.

Deeper inside the room, where they could not see, was Symon.

Bennett checked his handgun, "I'll go first."

Kendrick nodded.

They couldn't wait for Symon to exit. Security, although almost certainly in no rush, was on its way here, and they needed to interrogate their target before that arrival.

Kendrick readied his own pistol, "On your six."

Bennett darted down the corridor and into the room with Kendrick close behind.

The Marine sprinted through the doorway.

A brief struggle ensued.

Bennett subdued Symon with a single punch to the jaw.

The 33-year-old fell to the ground.

Symon cried, "What the fuck?"

"Stay down!" Bennett commanded.

Symon squirmed at his feet.

"Is anyone else in the house?"

Symon massaged his jaw, "Fuck you."

Kendrick pressed the pistol to Symon's head, "Is anyone else in the house?"

"No, no, no," Symon cried, spreading both hands in surrender.

"Get up," Kendrick demanded.

Symon rose slowly.

Short black hair, like in his photo. But his clothing was a strange contrast. A casual t-shirt touting someplace in Saint Barts but with baggy dark britches hanging low around his waist, showing half the man's underwear. An extra-large watch, probably worth more than Kendrick would make in a lifetime, was strapped to his wrist. A trio of gold chains swung from young Pellgrin's slender neck.

Symon looked like a skinny hoodlum ready to roam the tubes. Or a wannabe rapper desperate to force his music on anyone that would listen.

Though, this boyo-pretender was neither of those. While the attire was odd, it was the dichotic fashion in which modern young moguls dressed. Whether their 'hustle' was online or in international smuggling.

According to what Kendrick had learned from Interpol and his own investigation, 33-year-old Symon used his ships and containers to move black market goods all over the planet—from China to the Caribbean islands silkscreened on his shirt. He'd commissioned the assassination of at least two captains when they'd been caught. Symon handled failure like a street gangster: the dead didn't snitch.

Bennett gave him a pat down.

"I don't have any damn weapons," the young mogul cried. "I don't believe in them."

Bennett finished his search, "Pull up your fucking pants, kid."

The office had a single, large ornate wooden desk with a closed laptop on its surface. Each wall held a built-in bookshelf stuffed with novels. An older collection of pioneer works sat tucked into an enclave. Camus, Salinger, Nietzsche, and others. They seemed out of place among the pop culture and modern crime fiction they rested next to. At least a thousand books or more.

Kendrick scanned the older section, slid out a volume, and eyed its cover. Dicken's Copperfield. He frowned, replaced the book, and turned to Symon, "Read any of these?"

Symon chided, "Enough to know what a plebian is."

Kendrick signaled Bennett.

The Marine positioned himself in the doorway to watch the hall.

"My security will be here in minutes. You morons are fucked. My lawyers will sue the shit out of you! And if you ever get out of jail, I'll make sure someone beats your ass every day until they find you face down in a puddle of your own piss!"

"Boy, you really are an unlikeable shit," Bennett said.

Symon barked, "You dickheads after money? Well, guess what, dumbass? There's none in the house."

Kendrick turned the handgun to Symon's gut, "That's not why we're here."

Symon scoffed. "Then what? My artwork? Good luck fencing any of that old shit."

"Do yourself a favor and shut the fuck up, kid," Bennett snarled from the doorway.

Symon jeered, "You assholes are on camera. Even if you get away, I'll hunt you down myself."

Kendrick eyed the smaller man, "Stop speaking."

"What do you chumps want from me?"

Bennett raised a finger, "Probably not the best idea to piss the guy off who's got a weapon on you."

Kendrick leered at Symon, "Let's start with the firearms."

"I don't know what you're talking about."

"Tell me who's involved."

"Fuck you."

Bennett pointed, "Shoot him in the leg. That way, he can still talk."

Kendrick aimed the pistol's laser at Symon's thigh.

Symon raised his hands, "Alright, fuck, fuck!"

Kendrick checked his watch.

They had nineteen minutes.

CHAPTER

38

Symon's demeanor was uppity and arrogant.

"Everyone's looking in the other direction."

Bennett glanced at Kendrick, "What the hell is he talking about?"

Symon rubbed his jaw and wiped the blood from his lip.

Bennett looked at Kendrick, "Want I should give him another?"

Kendrick raised a palm.

"Shipping and freight movement isn't sexy," Symon blurted. "Not on its surface. It's loud, dirty, boring work most of the time. But remember nothing moves in any country without people like me. We are the unseen backbone of every business, supply depot, grocery store, and mom-and-pop retailer worldwide. We handle it all in bulk sizes you could never imagine. And we do it every day, all day."

Kendrick pointed, "Enough with the self-congratulatory bullocks. Tell us about the weapons."

"Ah. An Englishman?"

"Welsh." Kendrick stared, unblinking.

Bennett shouted, "A Welshman who'll kick your ass, so you better start talking."

Symon took a deep breath, exhaled, and rubbed his skinny chin. "They're all complicit, you know."

"Specifics?" Kendrick tilted his head.

205

Symon pointed to his wooden desk, "If you wanna have this conversation, then I need to sit."

Kendrick held the pistol but gave a nod.

Bennett stood by, watching the doorway.

Symon lumbered behind the desk to its chair and promptly opened a drawer.

"Stop!" Kendrick shouted.

Symon raised a hand but gradually pulled out a Kleenex with the other. He dabbed his mouth with the tissue.

"Another move like that, and I'll shoot you."

Symon chuckled as he pulled a tiny brown snuff bottle from the drawer. He removed its cap and sprinkled a powdered line on the desk.

"What the fuck?" Bennett called.

"Gotta get the mind right." Symon examined the small heap of cocaine, then leaned in for a snort.

Let them drink it, smoke it, sniff it, or shoot it. Kendrick had seen it all before. Whatever gets you chatty, asshole.

Symon's head sprung up, and his eyes went wide, "Fucking good sting!" He wiped his nose with the napkin and smiled.

"Now that you've had your shit, no more stalling," Kendrick aimed the SIG. "Where are those shipments going? Who's behind this?"

Symon raised his eyebrows, "My shipments go lots of places. Ports all over the world."

Bennett stepped forward, "I'm gonna pound the hell out of this twerp, I swear it."

"Weapons," Kendrick began. "Small arms, the automatics, the stingers."

Symon wiped a nostril, "The one's from Africa?"

"Africa?" Kendrick said, surprised.

"Handbags to handguns," Symon laughed.

"Fakes?"

"Near identicals. Need only the right connections, and you can get whatever you want. Made by the hardworking hands of 'who the fuck cares' for next to nothing. Whatever you want. But it's still the crap."

This confused Kendrick, "The crap?"

Symon raised a palm, "Guns work, for a while at least. But like all counterfeits, they fail. Substandard alloys melt under repeated firing heat. Mill a fraction or two in the wrong direction, and rounds jam in the clip. No quality control on the sights." Symon wet a finger and wiped a shadow of white dust from the desktop. "Shoddy junk." He smeared the residue on his tongue and swished it around with saliva.

"Junk? Then why ship it? Why the risk?"

Symon shrugged, "Money's the same. And then there's what's happening at the other end."

"The other end?"

Symon laughed. "You guys… you guys don't know shit about shit, do you?"

Bennett sneered, "I'm about to beat it out of you."

Symon raised his hands in excitement, "Secondary wars. Stockpiling. Every fucker wants weapons. Turkey, Vietnam, the Kurds in Syria."

Bennett looked confused, "Who the hell's sending weapons to Vietnam?"

Kendrick didn't take his eyes off Symon, "Uncle Sam. It's a deterrent to Beijing."

"Thought we were done with that place," Bennett uttered.

"Now, most militaries transport their own munitions." Symon mimed an airborne carrier with his hands. "Fly them into whatever region. Real military-grade firearms. Missiles, and what have you."

"Ukraine?"

Symon mocked, "Duh." Then, he curiously placed a finger on his chin. "Though that's been a hard one for sure."

"Hard?"

Symon shouted, "Everything! Everything's been so fast over there. Damn weapons come in—and I mean by huge transports, buzzing about, one after the other. Crates and crates. We can't even get them into the depots for the swap before half are stolen. Those bastards are quick as rabbits over there."

"What do you mean swap?"

Symon chuckled brashly. "Forgot you didn't know shit. Before we can replace the munitions with the junk weapons from Africa."

Bennett shouted, "What?"

"Oh, big boy, it's a huge business. But those bastards swipe the guns right off the runway before we get our hands on them. It's such a damn mess."

"Why this swap? I'm not understanding?"

Symon dumped a heap of powder on the desk and arranged it with a pinky. "Yeah. We put most of the stamped stuff into our trucks and move that shit out, man."

Bennett scoffed, "He's not your man."

"Stamped? Does that mean you're boosting the genuine weapons and replacing them with counterfeits?"

Symon dipped for another snort. "Bingo."

"Black-market bullshit," Bennett said from the doorway.

Symon smiled, "Profitable black-market bullshit." He raised his arms and turned half a circle in the chair. "And business is good, good!"

Bennett shook his head, "What the hell is wrong with you?"

"Most authentic stuff doesn't even make it into the stockpile," Symon nodded. "Crates put right back into containers to be sold to the highest bidder."

"Wait, what?" Bennett said.

Symon chided, "Business, dumbass. Are you paying attention at all?"

Bennett pointed, "Call me dumbass one more time, and I'll make sure every one of your meals is fed to you through a straw."

Kendrick shook his head at Symon. This arrangement didn't surprise him as much as it infuriated him. Looters often took advantage of wars and conflicts, but he'd never heard of something on this scale before. And this man-child Symon Pellgrin didn't have a care in the world beyond profit. In fact, it seemed he thought the entire thing was funny.

"Stay on point here, or I'll turn the big man loose on you."

Symon peered down at the desk and grinned to himself, "Alright. The crap weapons from Africa go to 'the cause'—whatever the crooks don't steal is swapped out. The real stuff from the states goes on the open market."

"Who's buying?"

The shipping mogul smiled, "Everyone. Hell, even the Russians."

Bennett cried, "You gotta be fucking kidding me?"

Symon ranted, "It's a free for all, man. The 'other' fog of war."

Bennett marched from the doorway, gritting his teeth.

Though Kendrick would do the honors. He clinched a fist, lunged forward, and blasted Symon across the jaw.

The 33-year-old tumbled from the chair onto the ground in pain.

"Fuck!" Symon shrieked, holding his chin. "What was that for?"

Kendrick glared, "I don't like you, either."

CHAPTER
39

"The minerals," Kendrick hovered over Symon. "The ones you're stealing from Venezuela. Who's the buyer?"

Symon reseated himself, rubbed his jaw, shook his head, and mumbled, "Fuck you."

Kendrick readied a fist.

Symon's hands shot up in defense, "Alright, dammit!" He paused and gazed at Kendrick curiously. "You guys," he half-chuckled. "You guys were the ones on the *Malusnavi*, weren't you? Caused all that chaos?"

Kendrick flexed his cheek muscles. Yes, they were on the *Malusnavi* freighter. They saw the illegal mines and knew of Yuri Melnyk's overseeing the exports. He was also smuggling guns along with the ore. Landing things at the freeport and trafficking them with no customs inspection.

Kendrick knew the guns were headed west to various countries, but many to Ukraine. Although Yuri was Russian, he was a gunrunner at heart. He went wherever the business took him. Further, his actions were probably sanctioned by a party, if not the full support of the country's foreign intelligence leaders. Another proxy war between Russia and the U.S.—a fiasco costing human lives with murky roots, playing itself out on the world stage. Bullets and bombs launched with the stroke of opposing biros.

They'd also found drugs at the freeport, undoubtedly shipped by Symon's freighters. Kendrick wanted to get to the bottom of that, too, but there was an even more pressing matter he needed to resolve first, "None of that matters right now..." Kendrick scolded.

Symon gave a fiendish grin, "Made a fucking mess, you did. Still cleaning that one up."

The SIG aimed at his head, "Tell us where those minerals are going."

"Well," Symon began. "First, I'm not 'stealing' anything. My company arranges and manages shipments for customers. Simple logistics. What they need us to transport varies."

"Bullshit. This is like trying to get frozen ketchup from a bottle. Let me work him up a bit?"

Kendrick waved Bennett off, "Who wants the minerals?"

Symon's eyes closed, and he went oddly poetic, "Icarian hubris colliding with the wrath of nature."

Symon had unusual mannerisms. His tone now was smug and steady. This wasn't the same idiot from minutes ago. It was hard to know if he was saying too much or too little. And these obscure references were a new development.

Symon Pellgrin had received a smattering of education in several American universities and abroad. However, his overseas learnings were more to hide him from his troubles at home. Still, it became clear to Kendrick that the deceptive little son of a bitch had cracked open at least a few of these books.

Kendrick raised the pistol, "Details?"

"Carbon monoxide."

Kendrick shook his head, "Climate change?

Symon nodded.

"What do those illegal mines have to do with that?"

"You're not seeing the picture."

The pistol steadied, "Then paint it for me."

Symon gazed at the barrel. "Decades of fighting have only led to waning public trust. They finally understand this oil war is a war they will never win."

"They? You're not being –"

"We're getting to that," Symon interrupted. "The lapdog media has done a tremendous job ramming fear into the population. Deep into the social fabric." He raised a finger. "But the real genius was the young… once you have the youth, you have passion and rage. Protesters in the streets, believing themselves saviors, inciting the push to 'green' energy as a moral imperative to humankind."

"What does any of this have to do with global warming?"

"Still not connecting those dots?" Symon said.

"You'd better link them before my finger twitches."

The tycoon's hands rested on the desk, "Big business and politicians are they. And they can't compete with the oil industry. They've lost that battle, too many battles, in fact. And the middle east has them by the balls."

"Oil prices. No surprise. But what does your company have to do with it?"

Symon grinned, "Right in the middle of things."

Bennett growled from the doorway, "Just one punch. I'll be quick."

Kendrick raised the SIG, "I've got a full clip and no time for puzzling rubbish."

Symon raised a palm. "This eco-hysteria. It's manufactured."

Kendrick was leery, "Are you saying climate change isn't real?"

"Who cares if it's real?" Symon said. "That's not the fucking point!"

"Then what is?"

"Money, control. It's what they're after. The powers that be can't profit from oil. They've tried it."

The asshole was right. When U.S. domestic oil production was booming during the last administration, the price went down to $21 a barrel because, at the same time, OPEC flooded the market with more of its product. It was a war of attrition to drive U.S. profits down. Now, the U.S. wasn't producing anywhere near total capacity, and crude was trading at $128 a barrel and rising.

Symon cracked his neck to one side, "Oil companies in the states are fighting a losing battle, working harder for less. And saving the planet? It isn't about that, not to them. Yes, they shut down pipelines and restricted and canceled drilling leases to appease the eco-mob. Yet, what they're doing is driving the price up." He chuckled. "On purpose."

"You're all over the place. Where does your company come in? What's happening?"

"True capitalistic power. The ability to make anyone rich."

"Who?"

Symon plucked another Kleenex from the drawer, "The most corrupt crime in American politics is lobbying." Symon dabbed at his lip. "Paid influencers funneling cash to legislators for favors. But it goes much deeper than that. And they've found an easier and more lucrative way to funnel money to their backers." Symon massaged his lip with his tongue. "Scumbags behind the scenes can channel tens of millions to anyone they want without raising suspicion."

"How?"

Bennett stepped forward, "C'mon. Just let me rabbit-punch him in the gut."

Kendrick halted him and stared down at Symon.

The 33-year-old cleared his throat and closed his eyes. His jaw shifted side to side, "It's right in front of you, in front of all of us."

"What is?"

"They're touting green initiatives while invested in oil. Captains of the crude industry, politicians, and other elites."

Kendrick's neck stiffened, "Invested, as the price rises. You're talking about market manipulation."

Symon nodded, "Now you're getting it. And they've done it under the guise of green energy."

Sadly, this made sense. Oil would always be around—lubricants, plastics, the roads—widespread uses that would never phase out. And right now, alternate fuel vehicles make up less than one percent of cars on the road. Oil wasn't going anywhere, not for decades. But there had to be more.

Symon continued, "Is CO2 really a threat? The sleeping volcano, the invisible dragon of our time? None of that matters to them. But if climate variations were truly out of control, would any of them fly in private jets? Live in coastal areas? Drive giant SUVs? Nope. They'd demand all cities abandon private transportation in favor of the public. Push for clean natural gas and nuclear energy. Limit air travel, and such." He glared at Kendrick. "You don't see any of that happening, do you?"

"And the minerals?"

Symon leaned forward and smirked, "Rare earths for batteries. Where do you think they invest the other half of their money?"

Kendrick furrowed his brows.

Symon leaned back in his chair, "It's a new energy source. Though, unlike oil, this one is under their control. The batteries are made overseas, but the real money is in powering and recharging them. That's how they divide up the energy world, man."

Bennett stepped to Kendrick's side, "No, no, no. These assholes are playing both sides?"

"Now you understand. The 'assholes' are loading up on stocks while at the same time they grant these chosen companies exemptions and subsidies for producing electric vehicles. They're picking winners. All they need to do is hold as the switch occurs. Align themselves in this 'green new order.' Keep pushing this agenda. Force the migration. All the while collecting a profit on both ends and laughing in the face of the public."

Kendrick shook his head, "They can't all be in on it."

"A faction of the career ones, for sure. Both sides. The rest of the revolving door political idiots see themselves as fighting for the greater good, protecting the planet for future generations, or whatever the current hype. They even boldly state that the pain people feel at rising prices is the 'cost of transition.'"

"Sounds like conspiracy theory bullshit," Bennett said.

Symon laughed loudly, "A derogatory term made-up to quash debate but most times to dismiss an uncomfortable truth." Symon leaned forward. "Why do you think the price of used cars has risen so dramatically? They want people to abandon those vehicles in favor of electric."

Bennett shook his head, "No, the price rise is due to a chip shortage."

Symon's eyes narrowed, "Do you really believe the supply chain slowdown is accidental?"

Kendrick's eyes widened.

Symon's finger rose, "None of the public realizes this entire thing is an orchestration to wrestle the next medium of energy away from foreign influences. To bring it under domestic corporate control, where electric energy producers can set whatever price they want, forever."

"But if they can set the cost domestically…" Kendrick started to say but stopped.

Arrogant Symon mocked, "You were going to tell me they'll make it cheaper? Are you that naïve? They'll use it to throttle the pocketbook of the middle class and keep them in check. But the poor, well, they'll never get off their knees." His head bobbed. "They're already manipulating the power grid. Full-on deregulation is next. The same commoditized shit they pulled out west, but it'll be everywhere."

Bennett turned in disgust, "Jesus Christ."

"Not even he can stop this," Symon concluded.

Kendrick vaguely recalled the western electricity crisis in 2000, when greedy companies restricted the market and shut down power plants to limit energy to customers. The price per kilowatt shot up 800 percent almost overnight.

If Symon was to be believed, the ultimate goal was to move consumers to a new energy source. One manipulated nationally, using the same artificial restrictions OPEC had—but on its own population. Squeezing more and more money from unsuspecting Americans at the flip of a switch.

It was unconscionable, reprehensible greed. But if Symon was right, it was coming. Auto manufacturers either knew or were so terrified of missing out on the changeover from gas to electric that they feared they'd lose out if they didn't act quick enough and seize their share of the new green order. They didn't give a shit where the source materials came from for those batteries.

But now it was time to change subjects.

Despite the cry-wolf strategy on the alarm, they had only a few more minutes before the police showed up.

And there was more pressing cargo aboard that freighter beyond the guns, the minerals, and the drugs he found at the freeport.

Freight that Symon's company shipped for someone.

Cargo which cost Sergeant Catalina Rosales her life.

Chapter

40

Alana sped by a maroon Chrysler on the dirt lane road and past a set of tall iron gates with initials on them. Around the enclosed estate, a tiny red light blinked, and she made out a surveillance camera.

The night air was thick with moisture. Tall trees and overgrown grass flanked the property's fence line. Even if the evening were clear of fog, the barrier of thick trees obscured any view of what lay beyond them.

Alana drove another hundred yards, picked an area far to the west, parked, crossed the road, and climbed the fence.

The air's wetness dampened the dirt road, and her flat sandals skidded in the light slosh. She found a trail through the heavy forest of trees which paralleled the dirt road, leading to the home—about half a mile up an incline.

Alana pulled back the Lebedev 9mm's slide, which clicked a round into the chamber.

She took a calming breath.

There was wicked up this path.

Something she had to destroy.

This one would be special, though.

She probably wouldn't need to use the gun beyond getting the small, wiry man to comply.

She'd met Symon Pellgrin before at one of Alexei's gatherings. Parties Alexei arranged with friends and associates at his portside business after

217

hours. Drinks, drugs, cigar smoke, business dealings, card games.

Alana's role was as a hostess among a handful of other shapely women under Alexei's employ. Get them stoned, keep them stoned, and let them spend their money.

Alana and the other girls were his leisure harem and had to adhere to Alexei's rule: available but never attainable.

Symon Pellgrin had attended Alexei's smoke-filled soirée once. The little bastard wouldn't stop talking, yammering on and on about some car he bought, his pretentious homes, and how he was wealthier than anybody else around them.

He was also handsy. More so than most of Alexei's associates. As with the others, she served him drinks, pocketed his outrageous cash tips, and tried not to let his groping get past second base.

Alana recalled Symon's obnoxious attitude, and the question he repeated several times, "Do you know who I am?"

Mostly, the small man was harmless, except for his mouth.

However, when Alana rose to refill his drink at one point, plastered Symon restrained her in a bearhug.

She could smell the whiskey and pot on his breath.

Symon tugged at her hair, "How much, baby?"

She tried to laugh it off as anger filled her insides.

But slimy Symon wouldn't let go.

He crushed her narrow ribcage.

She fought him. He fought back.

His hand moved to her chest and squeezed hard.

Out of reflex, Alana dug her nails into his crotch.

Symon yelped, "Ouch, ouch. Oh baby."

Her nails clawed, stabbed, and squeezed.

Symon released her at once.

He played things off with those around the table, "Sexy and feisty, I love it!"

If not for Alexei's dealings with the man, she'd have slit the little fucker's throat on the spot.

She never saw Symon again after that, but she knew Alexei and Symon remained close business partners.

However, to Alexei, she'd also been other things—more than one of his mere teasing hostesses. She was exceptional, he'd told her.

Crimean by birth, Alana left with Alexei when the invaders came. Russia took over the region's seaways, and Alexei smuggled her into America.

The two became lovers.

At the time, Alana was only 17.

She thought she loved him, too. He let her stay at his place, gave her money for new clothes and other things, brought her flowers, and made her feel like she mattered to him. Alexei was so good to her.

But one thing tugged at her heart, which mattered above anything else. "My mother and sister. They are still there, Alexei."

The man who'd become her entire world in this new place of America pulled her close. "I will get them. But after this, you are mine."

Alana was unsure what that meant at the time but agreed without any reluctance. She'd feared the worst for her only family in the war-torn region, but if Alexei could help her, she'd do anything he wanted.

Alana's father, an electrician, had died of liver failure before her eleventh birthday. Despite his drinking, he was always good to his girls. The volatility of the nation, the insecurity of his job as the primary breadwinner, and fear for his family's safety drove him to the liquor.

After he passed, the three women became exceptionally close.

As a seamstress, Alana's mother worked every day of the week to support her two girls. Even after hard days, she'd ask them about theirs while fixing fritters, borscht, or potato pancakes.

Katia was five years younger than Alana and wanted to be a piano player, an artist, a botanist, a model, a hair stylist, and an astronaut. At twelve-years-old, she had it all figured out.

Over the following months, Alexei repeatedly promised to smuggle her family into the states. Less than a year passed before he made good on his pledge.

Alexei placed Alana with her mother and sister in a small apartment he rented for them. He'd provided them nice beds, linens, furniture, and more kitchen supplies than the three women had ever seen. He gave them everything they needed.

But now Alana was deep in Alexei's debt.

As years went by, Alana's duties increased.

Alexei was distrustful of many and confided more and more in her. He understood she'd do anything to keep her mother and sister safe.

Alana began spying for him.

Alexei's gatherings brought all manner of business associates, and as the night progressed, the men's lips loosened. Who might be skimming his shipments? Who may be talking with authorities? Was there anyone weak, sloppy, greedy, and who may ultimately betray the man?

She'd report any overheard wrongdoings to Alexei at once.

Things further progressed, and she became his quiet enforcer. Someone that could get close to targets without being suspected and take them out. Traitors to his organization, competitors, or enemies. Alana did his bidding. Poison, execution, compromised strangulation—whatever it took to keep her family safe.

And she remained devoted to Alexei, even as his eye wandered.

Alana's mother found work with a local tailor who paid her cash. Katia grew up beautiful and went to university but sadly did not finish.

Up the foggy road, Alana saw Pellgrin's house lights.

The enormous home embodied the little man. It sat on the crest of a hill where its windows could look down at those in the valley.

She climbed the home's back wall.

Once on the lawn, she removed her sandals.

She was far quicker barefoot.

In a second-level window, she saw shadows.

CHAPTER

41

Kendrick eyed more books on Symon Pellgrin's shelves.

All this knowledge of the past and no humanity.

Lots of things Kendrick kept to himself. He and Bennett had their banter, he trusted the man with his life, and the friendship was solid. But even Bennett was unaware of the depth of loss he felt for their friend Catalina Rosales.

Because inside, he suffered profound anger that ran thick. And it wasn't only that her death had invoked the same feelings of powerlessness that he'd felt losing Bethany.

Kendrick closed his eyes.

A tightness grew in his chest.

When Adler later showed him the video from Rosales's smartglasses of their incursion months ago, it crushed him. The recording made him so ill he'd even thrown up.

Kendrick and a brave civilian named Aldous Phinn trailed the *Malusnavi* from South America, through the Gulf of Mexico, into Port New Orleans.

That night, Bennett, Nelson, and their asset suffered injuries when their jet skidded off the runway at Dauphin Island. Nevertheless, Kendrick and Phinn secretly boarded the freighter as it made its long trip from the Gulf of Mexico up the channel to the port.

Two souls onboard, both doctors, were kidnapped from that illegal mine in South America. Yuri, the Russian, and his South African counterpart held them hostage.

Sergeant Catalina Rosales, a young would-be Green Beret, had snuck aboard the freighter when it left Columbia. She was hiding among the cargo in the ship's midsection.

During the voyage, somehow, someway, within those thousands of containers, Rosales found a suspicious intermodal while the ship was in transit to the states.

What she discovered inside was astonishing and horrifying.

But before she could affect a rescue, a shitty little man gunned her down.

Rosales fell from the stack, five stories to her death.

Kendrick found her on her back, gasping.

He rushed to her side.

Her hand squeezed his, but there was nothing he could do.

And now her death haunted him.

Still, he hadn't understood the totality of the situation. Not until weeks later, when he saw the recordings of Rosales's smartglasses, did he fully realize why she'd scaled those shipping containers in the first place.

That night, the eyewear's grainy video showed the ascent as the *Malusnavi* freighter sloshed in the stormy ocean waves. Its 15,000 containers creaked and groaned while Rosales grappled hand over hand up the corrugated stack.

The exhausted Rosales halted her ascent, dangling fifty-foot in the air, and worked open the intermodal's elevated doors.

Revealing the black insides of the shipping container.

And the scared faces trapped inside.

Young girls reaching out in the darkness.

Sobbing for help.

Frantic for rescue.

But Rosales had perished in Kendrick's arms before she could tell him.

And Kendrick never saw the horror unfolding directly overhead. The stormy events aboard the *Malusnavi* freighter were too chaotic, too loud, and too demanding.

He'd walked away from twenty-nine lives in that container stack above and hadn't realized it for weeks—a horrifying mistake that haunted and enraged him.

Pellgrin and his partners were shipping goods around the world to the highest bidders—drugs, weapons, minerals. They weren't the only company doing this, and Kendrick would be a fool believing he could stop it all.

With the guns, he was up against rogue actors, oligarchs, and dubious officials profiting from a decentralized mess. The 'other' fog of war, as Symon had put things.

With the drugs, it was the cartels. A chaotic business led by cash-rich criminals, whose leadership often changed with the spray of bullets. Yet, as countless skirmishes and wars have shown, cartel soldiers are as loyal to profits as customers are to their products. Not even governments can slow that enterprise.

However, the illegally mined minerals were different.

In South America, the men were forced day and night to mine the coltan and gold at gunpoint. Kendrick and his team had ended that brutality in that mine. Yes, there were other illegal mines in many parts of the world, but he'd affected at least one.

And this was where his boundary was. That 'thing' he was willing to give his life for. His personal redline.

Human trafficking and smuggling were an edge of wickedness that struck him deeply. A callous, unconscionable disregard and lack of compassion. Leashing one human under another—the audacity of someone willing to do that to any person was beyond his understanding.

Still, throughout history, bondage has been near ritual.

A bizarre byproduct of the social ladder system.

Exploiting those demoted to its lowest rungs.

The division seems harmless at first, splitting by political belief, age, gender, race, ethnicity, religion, national origin, or physique. Economic poor, labor, wealthy class. Strong, weak. Black, Brown, White. Old, young. Abled, disabled.

But then comes the ridicule.

Stereotypes to erase empathy.

Lazy, misogynist, racist, denier, commie, privileged, millennial, boomer, animal, fascist, deplorable, retard—terms to dehumanize and divide.

The favored tactic of sociopaths and dictators, whose foolish followers parrot the slur with a bizarre sense of superiority, reducing enemies to a single, shameful word.

Absent compassion, the enemy segment can easily be enslaved or destroyed.

And every civilization, race, and religion has practiced this brutal tyranny, from the Sumerians and Egyptians to the West Africans who sold slaves to the Europeans. Its cycle repeats as far back as the Mesopotamians.

The monetization of savagery, mistreatment, and misuse. Targeting and vilifying the ostracized. Turning helpless persons into cheap labor or exploiting the vulnerable for sexual gratification.

Most see slavery as humanity's regretful past.

Something disgraceful, never to be repeated.

But Thomas Kendrick knew a terrible truth.

Even this day, there were more living in servitude throughout the world than at any time in human history. Serfdom, sweatshop workers, forced and bonded labor, child brides, and sexual captivity. Humans who would never know any true measure of freedom in their lifetimes.

He squeezed the SIG tightly and peered down at Symon Pellgrin with rage.

This man was part of that barbarity.

It took everything inside Kendrick not to pull the trigger and end this miserable fuckhead Symon the druggie's life.

But there was more he needed to understand first.

How many were involved?

Who kidnapped these poor girls?

How deep did this network go?

And who were the buyers?

Would cutting off the snake's head make a difference? Or would the dead serpent only spawn more sycophants, like mushrooms around an outhouse shitter, as Bennett had said?

There were so many pieces and layers. The mix of companies, crooked lawyers, illicit cargo, and Kendrick still wasn't sure how it all came together.

But Symon Pellgrin would answer for his part.

Kendrick would crack his criminal world and act decisively on those answers. He could shut this dreadful part of Pellgrin's wicked empire down.

And, as Sergeant Catalina Rosales had brilliantly put things: 'Scrape off some evil because there's a lot of it.'

"Enough!" Kendrick held the pistol's laser on Symon Pellgrin's forehead, "What about the girls?"

Symon blinked, "Girls?"

"The ones your company smuggled inside those shipping containers."

Symon shifted in the chair, tilted his head, and glanced at the open drawer and its box of Kleenex. "My ships move half a million containers around the world. My company cannot inspect every single box of freight. We must rely on our customers to properly name their cargo."

Bennett stepped forward, "He knows, he fucking knows."

"Perhaps if you have a container number, I could check?"

Kendrick clenched his jaw. Adler had the same idea, but since Rosales's video only captured the bottom half of the container's right door when she'd picked it open, they never saw the vessel's ISO identifier.

Symon reached into the open drawer and fussed with the Kleenex box. "Without a number, there's little I can do for you," he said bitterly.

Bennett balled his fists, "Let me beat the shit out of him, c'mon!"

Symon dug for another tissue. He'd been almost eager to give up what he knew of the minerals. Moreover, there was arrogant pride in his explanations. It was much the same with the weapons, a cavalier cunningness the young shipping baron was thrilled to boast about.

If Symon did own the company that 'packed' the container, as he did with Hallon, then he knew everything. It was a matter of getting him talking until the cokehead became sloppy, lippy, and rattled off what he knew. Symon was, at his core, braggadocious, unfiltered, and cocky.

But even if the container was shipped by a true third-party, Symon still had something. A shipper's name, a receiver's address, and perhaps more.

The key was to push him, but not too hard.

Symon liked being in control. Thinking he was steering things and that Bennett and himself were at the mercy of the young tycoon's shrewd will.

"Where are the records for that freighter?"

Symon sneered, "My company owns almost 70 ships. This'll take a minute." He pecked at his laptop.

Bennett repeated the ship's name aloud, "The *Malusnavi*."

"One of our largest, but I'll need a container number."

Kendrick and Bennett looked at one another, "We don't have one."

Symon stopped and smirked, "Then I cannot help you."

An impasse. Though instead of spouting quirky references, Symon's answers became abrupt and less obscure. He sounded like a bored post agent who couldn't track a missing package.

He was lying.

Kendrick would remain diplomatic for another question or two, but time was running out, "How about the list of shippers? We can start there."

Symon looked down at his computer and laughed. "There were 14,612 containers on that freighter. A little over 1,100 separate shippers. Would you like me to print you a list? We could put it into a nice binder. I must have a three-hole punch around here somewhere," he taunted.

"I'll punch three holes in you," Bennett called.

Symon grinned, "I'd like to help, really."

Kendrick wanted to shoot the bastard, but tried another tact, "We know the container originated from South America, so we can start there. How many –"

But Symon cut Kendrick off, "Ninety percent of these containers originated from that port," he clicked away at his keyboard. "Still going to need that three-hole punch."

Bennett mumbled, "Fucker," and then turned to Kendrick. "The little son-of-a-bitch is toying with us, amigo. Stalling."

Bennett was right. Symon had to know far more than he was telling them. The men on that ship were neither captain nor crew. The Russian. Symon was either working with them or knew who was.

Symon snorted the last of the brown bottle's contents, leaned back, and cleared his nasal passages. "Afraid without a container to track, you two are s-c-r-e-w-e-d." The coked-up 33-year-old snickered.

Bennett dashed past Kendrick.

He lunged at the desk.

A right fist swung for Symon's head.

But Bennett missed.

A quicker Symon swiveled from the counter and drew a black pistol from the Kleenex drawer.

The barrel smashed Bennet's forehead.

"Stop!" Kendrick shouted.

Symon and Bennett were face-to-face. One in the chair, the other belly-down on the desk with a weapon pressed to his head.

"Drop the weapon, or you die," Symon said.

Bennett released the Desert Eagle.

The .44 caliber fell to the ground.

Kendrick's pulse drummed. But he aimed the SIG's laser sight at Symon's head and said coolly, "I can turn you off like a switch."

Symon's gaze rose slowly to Kendrick, "And my muscles will instantly tighten. You must know this. Those in the hands especially. Not even my doing. Involuntary. But enough to end your partner's life in that same moment."

Bennet's breathing got heavier, but he held still.

One of them would die, maybe both.

"You two believed you could break into my house and get me to tell you about my most precious cargo?" Symon's stare didn't break from Kendrick. "My most important clients, and you thought I'd just give them up?"

Kendrick tried to focus and think of a way to end this without getting his friend killed. Though if Symon was right and firing did cause him to pull his trigger… the horror was unimaginable.

Symon bolted from the chair and growled low into Bennett's ear, "You have no idea what's going on here. Neither of you. This is a world of powerful, savage people. You'd be nothing to them. Their latest annoyance." His furious gaze rose to Kendrick, "And your end would come with utter agony."

Kendrick's only hope was for Symon to make a mistake, to take his aim off Bennett's skull for a fraction of a second. In that instant, Kendrick would pull the trigger and drop this bloody fucker.

Vicious Symon rammed the barrel into Bennett's temple, "Your man's death now would be merciful in –"

But another voice came from outside the doorway.

It startled Symon and baffled Kendrick.

"You have three seconds to drop weapons."

A woman took aim at the trio.

"Or I kill you all."

Chapter
43

The unusually attractive woman kept her muzzled pistol steady.

Symon glanced toward the door and inched the gun from Bennet's head, "Alright."

"Unchamber and toss here," she demanded.

Symon complied.

Then, the woman stared Kendrick's way.

Mid-twenties, long brown hair, bronze skin, and naturally beautiful. Her blue stretch skirt and sleeveless white tank top were soaked from the rain, and her feet were bare.

Kendrick lowered the SIG and placed it at his feet.

Bennett rose from the desk with his hands in the air and turned to Kendrick. "Sorry, partner."

Kendrick grimaced. It wasn't Bennett's fault, and time was not so long-ago Kendrick would've lunged at the little bastard himself. It was also Kendrick's failing for not checking Symon's area for weapons.

"You two, over there," the woman instructed.

Bennett and Kendrick took several steps from Symon's desk.

Symon ogled her body, "You do know who I am, right? I'm a rich man. An important man. I could change your life. We can –"

"Shut up, fuck!"

"Plucky," Symon remarked. "But so beautiful."

With her bare foot, the woman slid Kendrick's gun across the floor toward Symon's in the doorway. She turned, eyed the two men, and then marched over to the side of Symon Pellgrin's desk.

Symon grabbed the tiny brown bottle and tapped it on the bureau's surface. Cocaine dust fell onto the office table, and he wet a finger, swiped it up, and licked it with his tongue.

Kendrick and Bennett stood feet from the woman in the large office. Bennett looked like he was calculating the distance between himself and the two weapons on the floor.

Kendrick put a hand on the Marine's wrist and shook his head before releasing his grasp.

The woman held her weapon on Symon and cleared a strand of hair from her face, "My name is Alana Kerkovich. And it is time you now found out who I am."

Symon looked up at her, "Hey, wait, wait. I think I know you. Did we meet in New York last year and go at it?"

She swung the pistol and popped Symon directly in the eye.

"Fucking bitch!" he screamed.

Bennett and Kendrick turned to one another, and Bennett raised his eyebrows.

"I am not here for your disrespecting," she shouted. "You filthy little man."

The ridge of Symon's eye was bleeding, and he cupped it with a hand.

"My sister Katia is…"

Symon jeered, "Is that the one I screwed around with?"

This time the gun struck him square in the forehead. The sickening crack was a direct hit.

"Oh, oh, you bitch!"

A faint siren sounded outside. The home's security service was inbound.

"Any more comments like that, and I will put a bullet in you." Alana aimed the pistol at his head.

A bloodied Symon cupped a hand to his wound and nodded, "Okay, okay."

"My sister, mother, and I were very close," she said softly. "But you changed all of that."

Symon looked up, "Me? What the fuck did I do?"

Alana's expression softened, "While my mother worked, I took care of Katia. Raised her, brushed her hair, and readied her for school. She was…" Her head lowered.

"Look," Symon gestured. "I don't know your sister. Whatever this is, you don't know who you're dealing with." He picked up the tiny brown bottle and shook it, but nothing came out. "I'm not someone who you –"

Alana took a deep breath and exhaled. "I do not wish to hear anything you have to say."

Symon examined the blood from the cut on his forehead, dabbed it with a Kleenex, and then fussed with the tiny brown bottle.

Kendrick glanced at more books on the man-child's shelves. Bennett stood next to him, eyes on Alana.

"There is a bond between sisters. Between women. We came to the country not knowing anyone, not knowing the language. Most of the time, all we had was each other in a small place."

Blood trickled from Symon's head wound, but he peered toward Kendrick and Bennett, and the little shit rolled his eyes.

Kendrick wanted Alana to pistol whip him again.

Alana glared at Symon with disgust, "You are not listening."

Symon steepled his fingers, "Like I told these assholes, I don't have any money in the house. If that's what you want from me, you're shit out of luck."

"No," Alana exclaimed. "I am here to return something to you." She fished a hand into her cleavage, pulled out a tiny plastic bag filled with a white powdery substance, and tossed it onto the desk in front of Symon.

"Did I lose this?" He picked up the baggie, eyed its contents with excitement, and tossed the tiny brown bottle aside. "Hells-to-the-yeah!

This is more like it!" Symon broke open the bag and dumped a pile of powder on the desk.

Alana backed away.

A glassy sorrow filled her eyes.

"Looks like good shit!" Symon said eagerly.

"What the fuck?" Bennett mouthed.

Kendrick watched with caution.

"At university, Katia received top marks," Alana resumed. "Our mother was so proud."

Elated, Symon busied himself arranging the powder.

"A great, kind person who gave everything to her daughters so we could have a better life one day."

Symon cleared both nostrils with an index finger. He gazed at the powder with a broad smile, then leaned in for a snort.

Then Alana uttered a disturbing phrase that sent a chill through Kendrick.

"Your banquet of consequences," she spoke softly.

Bennett shot a quizzical glance at Kendrick.

Neither man moved.

The siren outside grew louder.

After a long sniff, Symon's head sprung up and he shouted, "Wow! What a sting!"

Alana watched, expressionless.

"Woah!" Breathless, Symon pounded his fist on his desk. "Where the fuck did you get this?"

Alana lowered her weapon, stared at Symon, and said calmly, "Your boats, your men."

"Damn!" He pinched his nose and chattered his teeth. "This is some of the best shit that I —"

Unexpectedly, the veins in Symon's neck goosed, redness overtook his face, and his expression changed to horror.

Alana's eyes deadened, "It is same substance you fed to my sister," she said grimly. "And you will apologize when you see her."

Symon's quivering lips turned deep blue.

The muscles in his skinny arms tensed.

A hand clutched his chest, and his eyes bulged.

Symon dropped to the ground and shrieked.

Alana trained the pistol his way but did not fire.

Symon's breathing shallowed.

Milky bile seeped from his mouth.

Bennett rushed forward, "Fuck, he can't die! We need to –"

But Alana turned the gun Bennett's way, and he halted.

Symon's body shuddered and convulsed.

"Don't go near him, don't touch him!" Kendrick commanded.

Alana and he shared a dire glance.

Kendrick pointed at the powder on the desk.

"That's pure fentanyl."

A ghastly gurgle, a final thrash, and the man on the floor exhaled for the last time.

Symon Pellgrin was dead.

CHAPTER

44

A siren blared outside.

Alana turned to Bennett and Kendrick.

The woman had ended Symon's life. But that little cokehead was their only lead to the human smuggling, and now they'd never know what secrets Pellgrin held about who and what the operation was all about.

If they'd gotten there sooner, maybe? If Bennett hadn't lunged, if Kendrick had checked the area, if…

He looked down at Symon's body.

Now, they'd never know.

Alana turned suddenly, "You are the police?"

Bennett gave a slow nod.

If the sirens speeding up Symon's dirt road made her believe they had called in backup, she'd have to let them go. But again, she was a killer and may not want to leave any witnesses.

"He was nasty man," she swept a strand of hair from her face. "His shipping allowed many illegal goods."

Kendrick nodded, "We know."

"Of drugs?"

"And much more than that," he frowned.

Alana stared down at the motionless Symon.

Bennett anxiously turned to Kendrick and gnashed his lips.

If she was going to go, she'd better do it soon. And that exit had to leave enough for Kendrick and Bennett to escape. If they left before she did, she'd know they weren't who they'd claimed to be.

Alana snatched Symon's water bottle and poured it over the plastic bag and powder on his desk.

"What the fuck?" Bennett whispered.

"Fingerprints," Kendrick replied.

Alana didn't touch the substance, but the liquid spilled over the surface onto the ground. She then wiped her prints from the bottle using her shirt and dropped the container next to Symon's body.

The sirens outside slowed.

"This was his doing," she bowed strangely.

Kendrick's hands remained at his midsection, "We understand."

A doorbell chimed.

Kendrick turned to Alana, "How did you get in?"

"Rear entry was open," she said without looking up.

That was good and would supply them with three or four minutes for the security agent to figure out the point of entry and clear the downstairs, but maybe less.

Alana tilted her head, "You are not police, are you?"

"No," Kendrick confessed. "We were here because this man was smuggling girls inside his ships, which we wanted to stop."

She lowered her weapon, paced around Symon's body, stopped, and closed her eyes.

Bennett stepped to the guns on the floor and cautiously picked up his .44 and Kendrick's SIG.

Alana didn't stop him.

"Uh, partner," Bennett called. "I think they might be inside the house."

A faint call came from downstairs.

"Mister Pellgrin, hello? Hello?"

Bennett gave Kendrick the SIG, which he tucked into his backside.

"We gotta go, amigo," he insisted.

Alana stared down at the dead Symon for a long moment until her gaze slowly rose to Kendrick.

"There is a woman," her voice softened. "At the port. New Orleans."

The guard downstairs trudged room to room, calling out occasionally for the dead Pellgrin.

"A woman?" Kendrick sensed sorrow in Alana's eyes.

She nodded, "It is not just freighter. They are taking girls from many places."

Wait, did she know about the smuggling?

"Partner?" Bennett's tone was urgent.

Kendrick grabbed Alana by the wrist, "We need to go right now."

Bennett led them down a hall to a back staircase as Kendrick clutched Alana. Quietly they descended.

A voice called from the outer hall, "Mister Pellgrin, is that you?"

The hushed trio crept across the home's lower level.

Kendrick whispered to Alana, "Where do they take the girls?"

"I… I do not know," she said silently.

He held her firmly by the wrist.

He had to find out what she knew.

Bennett led them through the large, dark room and out the rear into Pellgrin's backyard pool area. They scurried through the fog, around the outdoor kitchen, and toward the back wall.

The three scaled down the barrier as quick as they could.

Someone shouted through the fog, "Halt!"

But the three kept their pace, sprinting to the trees and into the heavy brush away from the home. Once out of sight, Bennett slowed their pace to a quick walk.

"Where is this woman?" Kendrick huffed.

Alana caught her breath, "They knew."

"Who knew?"

"The lawyers," she pulled her wrist from Kendrick's grasp. "The one who made the shipments." Her anxious eyes glared into his. "He had records and addresses."

She was talking about Rick Melton.

Bennett pointed to the trees behind them, "I think they're at the wall, coming this way."

The three restarted their race through the woods.

Several meters later, Alana began to veer in another direction.

But Kendrick caught up to her.

"Who is this woman?" he demanded.

She halted, and so did he and Bennett.

"Woman, she is not what you think," Alana placed her hands on her hips, gasping. "She was good to my family."

Behind them, a distant holler came, "Is anybody out here?"

Then a second shouted, "This is private property!!"

There were two security guards.

And they were getting closer.

Alana's breathing slowed, "Seek out this woman. You must find her. She is called 'Nia.'"

"Nia?" a winded Kendrick replied.

Her tired head bobbed.

"What's her surname?"

Alana put a hand up, "Nia is what they allowed us to call her."

Kendrick took a deep breath, "Who?"

But she either didn't know or refused to answer that question. Instead, she replied, "They take her to ports when shipments get to the area. That is what I know."

Kendrick was puzzled. Who was this unknown woman Alana was speaking of, and what did she know of the kidnapped girls?

"That up there," Alana motioned toward Pellgrin's hillside house. "I have killed the delivery man. Now I return to origin."

Her words confused Kendrick.

"Do not get in my way again," she said firmly.

And with that, Alana turned and disappeared into the fog.

"C'mon, amigo," Bennett urged. "We need to haul ass out of here."

CHAPTER

45

They found the Chrysler, and Bennett sped them through the dense night south of the area.

Kendrick checked the rearview to be sure they weren't followed before they came to the connection for Route 202.

No headlights were visible in either direction.

Time was nearing midnight.

So much had happened with Symon Pellgrin. The knowledge about the bogus weapons and the reason for the minerals.

Ultimately, the importation of drugs and a woman's family destroyed by those dealings had brought Symon down.

But Alana was still a mystery.

She'd called Symon Pellgrin the delivery man. In a way, he was. Shipping anything to anyone, legal or otherwise, with his freighters.

But who was she? How had she been part of all this? Was she kidnapped along with so many others, as she'd alluded to? Had she been sold into this life?

Though how had Alana come for revenge? Was she a trafficking victim? Did she escape? And furthermore, how did she get a weapon and travel to Boston? Did this mean she was special in some way? He wanted to ask many questions but knew he'd likely never see the mysterious Alana again.

However, her words had put them on a new trail.

239

A shadowy woman dubbed Nia was somewhere. How was she involved in this strange scenario? Alana had said this person had been good to her. But who was she? If the kidnapped girls had been brought to Nia, did it mean she was a victim or villain? None of it was making any sense.

They'd head back to New Orleans in the morning once the fog lifted.

Adler had replicated the hard drive from Gary Oliver's computer, but they needed passwords because none of the files were accessible. It wasn't quite a dead end, but things had stalled.

Then Kendrick recalled the words of Rick Melton about his partner Gary Oliver. The man who labeled everything. Wrote things down.

Could the information they needed be recorded someplace? Did Oliver have a notebook somewhere in his office that Melton himself had missed?

A search could take a long time, given the mess he'd seen in their offices. There were cabinets and random cardboard boxes everywhere, and he didn't really understand what he was looking for.

Bennett drove them down the dark road in silence.

At least they'd made a clean getaway from Pellgrin's. As Kendrick thought about this, they'd left no trail beyond the dew in the dead man's backyard. The security team would discover Symon on the floor, an overdose victim. Just another unfortunate soul in an extensive list of well-to-do celebrities and regular folks who'd stumbled onto a bad batch of drugs that ended their lives. Kendrick doubted there would be much of an investigation.

He and Bennett decided against getting a place for the night, as it was better to keep a low profile after what occurred at Symon's.

Bennett steered them to the terminal, "We'll take off in the morning. Get some rest in the Riley."

They returned the rental and headed to the plane across the quiet, foggy runway. Once inside, Bennett supplied each with a blanket and a full-sized pillow.

An exhausted Kendrick took the offerings, "Plush accommodations, thank you."

Bennett supplied a tired smile, "Nothing but the best here on Riley Airlines."

The two slept for a handful of hours in the rear seats of the parked plane before Kendrick awoke to the loud sounds of Bennett chatting with someone over the radio and the plane's props whirling for takeoff.

The fog was gone.

Bennett tossed him a wireless headset, "Morning, amigo. Clearing us for takeoff."

Kendrick adjusted the wireless cans onto his ears. He'd had some time to rest and think. The woman Alana was still a mystery, but at least now they understood her motive. She was taking out anyone involved with the operation's drug arm—which, while important—was not where he and Bennett were focusing their pursuit.

Regarding their next move, there was only one place they hadn't investigated yet, and of course, it would require another break-in.

Kendrick remained seated with his blanket and pillow in the passenger space, and the ride south back to Louisiana was much smoother than it'd been on their arrival.

CHAPTER
46

The following evening, Nikki was talking with Charlie at the front desk when Brack appeared wearing the same suit as before but with a blue paisley tie.

"Aren't we looking dapper again, Mister David."

Brack noticed the entire stack of boards from the lobby was now gone, and no trace they'd even been on the carpet remained.

"Just David, Charlie. You make me sound like a magician or something."

"Well, you are. And again, thank you for all your work on the software. I feel much better about those rate tables now." Charlie turned to Nikki. "My brother-in-law, bless him, had set things up originally in the program, but there were many errors. Mister David cleared them all up for the cost of two iced teas. Can you believe that?"

Nikki nodded, "He's been good to me, too."

Charlie turned to Brack with a nod, "Sometimes we find ourselves surrounded by better people than we think we deserve, don't we, Ms. Nikki?"

Nikki agreed.

"Oh, and that reminds me," Charlie raised his hands with excitement. "The Big B is planning a get-together for all guests and their plus ones. It's this Saturday. A groundbreaking for the new gazebo around the pool area. I'll pencil you both in, and it should be enchanting."

Brack looked at him in disbelief, "You finished it?"

"Just gotta apply the stain and hang the lights, but yes, she's ready."

Brack was astonished. "Sounds like a good time."

"Oh, it will be," Charlie grinned. "Well, I won't hold you two up any longer. Gotta make those rounds. Have yourselves a good evening and stay dry out there."

Charlie left the area carrying a small toolbox.

Nikki turned to Brack, "I like him."

Brack patted a bulge near his ribcage, "Yeah, a real upbeat guy."

"Ready when you are."

She and Brack sped off in the Sportwagon over I-10's 'N'Awlins' Frank Davis Bridge.

The navigation system took them north, across rail tracks, to an outdated strip mall with a high, neon pink-orange sign that blinked 'Wrner Paza.'"

Once they entered the zone, Nikki uttered, "What the hell?"

Most of the overhead streetlamps weren't functioning. As they turned into the center's dark, wet parking lot, they saw two gatherings of homeless people huddled under the plaza's awnings.

"I think you might have overdressed for this one, Mr. Goodman."

Nearby was the storefront of Melton Oliver & Associates. Nikki found an inconspicuous spot and parked the Sportwagon.

They'd not talked about what he was doing there, but Brack knew she was wise to his activity.

Nikki shot him a glance in the rearview and casually asked, "Bustin in again?"

Brack eyed the area nervously, "Yeah. These guys have the information I need, files, and —"

Nikki's mirrored stare locked on Brack, "Ever busted into a place like this before?"

Brack shook his head.

"Know how to pick a lock?"

"They didn't exactly teach that at University." He motioned to the storefront, "I figured I'd break a window."

Nikki gave a half-laugh and pointed to the vehicle headlights moving on the nearby frontage road, "We'll you can't do that. I know it's raining, but there's too many cars and wanderers around. You have to go in through the back."

He'd honestly been so focused on the strange packages in the warehouse, Gary Oliver's killing, and that they'd stolen from him that he hadn't considered the small steps. Nikki was right. He didn't think this through enough.

However, she reached under her seat and pulled up a crowbar. "Take this, Mr. Bond. The back entrance is a fire door—which means it opens outward. Pry at the gap between the handle and the frame, away from the door. It's the weakest point. If it doesn't budge, come and get me. We'll bust off the handle and work the insides until it unlocks."

"How do you know how to do this?"

Nikki sighed. "Curtis's father was a thief... is a thief," she corrected. "My son spent his first three years waving to his dad from behind bars."

"Where's his father now?"

"Louisiana State, and not the University."

"I'm sorry."

"I'm not. The shithead wasn't out for a month before his umpteenth arrest for robbery and arson. And that proved to me the man had more interest in himself than our son." She put up a hand. "I stripped him of visitation rights and have full custody of Curtis now." She smiled at Brack through the rearview, then handed him the crowbar.

"Thank you."

Nikki nodded.

"If an alarm goes off, hustle your ass back here. I'll spring the hatch open for that awesome dolphin dive getaway I know you can't wait to do. Then we'll take off before the fuzz gets us."

"Thanks, Nikki. But promise you'll stay in the car. No matter what this time?"

She nodded.

Brack opened the Sportwagon's rear door.

"Good luck, 007."

Brack strode quickly through the drops across the lot. He'd left the briefcase and umbrella in the car but tucked the crowbar under an arm to hide it from view.

None of the destitute folks under the awning even looked his way.

He snuck around back and, opposite a pair of sizeable commercial garbage dumpsters, found the rear entrance to Melton Oliver.

He worked the bar into a crack and pulled.

In seconds, the handle creaked and snapped.

The door opened.

Brack jumped behind one of the dumpsters.

No alarm had sounded, but he held in case any wandering individuals out front got curious and decided to investigate.

A full minute passed.

Carefully, Brack stepped from the shadows toward the door.

He gripped the crowbar tight and stepped inside.

Chapter
47

No alarm. Brack knew the lawyers could be lazy, sloppy that way. Melton had likely forgotten to turn it on.

He closed the backdoor, but it would no longer latch.

Inside, the place was completely dark, save for a dim light in one of two offices at the rear. However, Brack knew the best area to start digging was in the files in a third room just ahead in the narrow hallway.

He entered and found a light switch.

The lawyer's case cabinets were all pale lemon-colored and stood uniformly at eye level. In a far corner, though, sat one shorter black cabinet.

He searched the yellow ones first. Standard injury cases, some files thicker than others. Brack pulled up several manilla folders, read the tabs, thumbed through a few pages, then replaced them in the same space he'd pulled. More drawers, more thumbing and replacing.

After the third cabinet, he decided to move to the far corner. Though, unlike the others, the black cabinet in front of him was locked.

Brack made quick work with the crowbar.

Inside he found filings on tax clients, divorces, and many folders marked 'special' or unlabeled. Out of curiosity, he searched for his divorce case with Vella but didn't find it. The thieving lawyers had probably tossed it out years ago after they screwed him out of his cash for that damn boat.

Still, he opened the ebony cabinet's lower drawers.

One file instantly caught his eye.

Gezzle Lift & Haul.

The records in the file included monthly tonnage reports for the organization's gross loads with a company called Kilgore Logistics.

Bizarrely, the printouts revealed two columns—one actual tonnage, but the other showed an inflated value.

Brack examined the numbers and frowned.

Shipping and logistics timing is straightforward. A professor at Clemson had pounded the scheduling and capacity variables into his head: cargo ability to given destinations, factoring in speed, supplies time.

Brack decided to rough things out.

Including box trucks, semitrucks, and miscellaneous transports, Gezzle owned 63 vehicles.

The median vehicle capacity was around 1,984 cubic feet, give or take.

If all 63 vehicles were moving cargo simultaneously, they could carry a maximum of 124,992 cubic feet.

Simple enough. Of course, because physical goods come in all shapes and sizes—and not perfect little cubic foot squares—the fleet would never be able to move at 100 percent CF capacity.

But he'd go the ideal route and say they did, for now.

According to the 11/10 Hours-of-Service Rule, a truck driver cannot drive more than 11 hours in a single shift before they must take a ten-hour break.

He rethought this.

He'd pretend Gezzle's drivers drove in two-man teams, disregarded the HOS rule, and all 63 vehicles went for 24 straight hours.

The rough average yearly distance for a single long-haul tractor-trailer is 125,000 miles. He'd double that and add five percent since the vehicles in his phantom scenario were running 24 hours a day. Next, he'd divide by four to split the distance into fiscal quarters.

With all 63 vehicles on the road, at 100 percent CF cargo capacity, traveling 100 percent of the time, the average speed was…

Something was wrong.

The math wasn't working.

Brack found a pen and sheet of paper and rechecked his equations.

His jaw dropped.

The math was correct.

Even if all Gezzle's vehicles were functioning perfectly, hit no traffic delays, had no breakdowns, never stopped for refueling, and ran 24 hours during the quarter's 91.25 days. All 63 hauled at a perfect 100 percent capacity to deliver the amount of cargo these entries were showing… each transport would have to be moving at an average speed of 174.3 miles per hour.

Oh shit.

Melton Oliver & Associates wasn't just a law firm—they were falsifying Gezzle's books and wildly overinflating his cargo shipments.

And neither man knew what the fuck he was doing.

But the activity's scale was more massive than Brack's shady dealings for Remo Gezzle. Cleaning cash through small businesses was nothing compared to the triangle of transactions between Melton Oliver, Gezzle Lift & Haul, and Kilgore Logistics.

As best he could decipher, for the last ten years, Kilgore brought all manner of goods ashore—both legitimate cargo and contraband. Gezzle Lift & Haul hid the illegal cargo by upwardly falsifying the weight of their kosher payloads. This allowed Melton Oliver & Associates to record higher revenue and disguise the profits from the drugs, weapons, and other prohibited merchandise they moved.

And they were laundering millions—much more than Brack ever had for Remo Gezzle alone.

Though, what he really needed were bank records. Where was all the money going? Who had control of it? Without that knowledge, he'd never recoup the $2 million they'd scammed from him. And there had to be hundreds of millions parked somewhere.

He left the file room and searched each office in the back. Melton's door was unlocked, but he didn't discover anything despite a search of the shelves, the desk, and a small chest of drawers.

Crime scene tape adorned Oliver's workspace.

Brack carefully removed the strips, just enough so he could enter. This door was also unlocked.

He searched the shelves and found Gary Oliver's scheduling log, which included a list of all appointments for his clients. Interestingly, many of the appointments were marked 'canceled.' In fact, there were pages and pages of canceled meetings. Then he read some of the canceled client names. Steven Doles, Justin Pile, Noah Buddy.

Brack was stunned.

These weren't clients. These were codes.

A sound came from the hallway.

He turned off the light, seized the crowbar, and ducked under Oliver's desk.

Footsteps.

Vagrants outside had broken in.

He'd remain hidden here.

Hopefully, they'd take what they needed and leave.

Seconds passed.

Beneath the desk, he touched what felt like a flat packet taped under Oliver's keyboard tray. Quietly, he worked its innards and pulled out a folded sheet of paper.

Using the glow from his mobile phone as a light, he unfurled the paper to reveal a lengthy list of client names and passwords.

The footsteps came closer.

Brack switched off the mobile phone's light and crouched under the desk with his knees tucked to his chest.

Someone entered the doorway.

He held his breath.

The room's lights switched on.

A pistol cocked a round into place, and a gruff voice called out, "Get up now before I shoot you."

Brack's heart raced.

He'd changed his appearance and kept himself off the grid for months. Every possession he'd had was either sold or sacrificed. And he'd hidden in a two-star hotel, in a small nowhere town, using a fake name.

But despite all that, Gezzle's men had found him.

Brack came slowly to his feet.

Two men, weapons drawn, stood in the doorway.

One had his hand clutched tightly around Nikki's elbow.

CHAPTER
48

Frightened eyes stared into his.

"I'm sorry," Nikki mouthed.

All David Brack could do was sigh.

The men were older but looked ex-military. Hired guns from whoever held the reigns now at Gezzle's criminal organization. These two were probably watching the lawyer's office for any unusual activity, and Brack had fallen into their trap.

He was cornered. The Smith & Wesson was tucked into his beltline underneath his jacket. Though, if he tried to pull it out, they'd shoot him before he could even take aim.

He also had nothing to offer to clear his debt with Gezzle, which, conservatively, was somewhere near $300,000.

Worst of all, though, he wasn't alone. Nikki was now entangled in his latest mess through his stupidity or bad luck. A young single mother whose only job was driving him around quickly became a trusted, loyal friend. She kept his secrets and had unbelievably saved his ass during his misdeeds in the warehouse when she could've simply driven away.

Brack shot another glance at Nikki. He made himself a promise. Whatever these men wanted, whatever they planned to do with him, he would first make sure Nikki was safe—even if it meant trading his own life to do it.

He took a quiet, deep breath and brushed a hand over the bulge in his jacket—mentally aligning the pistol's grip for a fast draw. He'd never fired a weapon in his life and prayed if things did escalate, he wouldn't strike Nikki by mistake.

One of the two—a fit man with salt and pepper hair—stepped forward.

"What are you doing here?" he stared unblinking.

Brack nodded toward Nikki. "Let her go. She's not part of this."

The man with brown hair glanced at his associate, but his grasp on Nikki's elbow did not break.

"My mate and I aren't releasing anyone yet," salt and pepper said. "Not until we understand these goings on." He motioned to the outer office area, "Breaking and entering is a very serious crime, you see."

The older man's accent and choice of words puzzled Brack. He knew how tight Gezzle's organization was, and there was no way he, or anyone associated with him, would hire a foreigner for something like this. Deranged mercenaries, felons, and white trash psychotics—all day long. But a mature, clean-cut outsider? No way.

There was also the fact that neither of these two seemed to know who he was. Yet they could solve that by snapping Brack's photo and sending it to Gezzle's henchman headquarters for identification.

But Brack thought more about things.

He was able to root around through the files for several long minutes before they showed up. If these two were Gezzle's men and watching the building, they'd have been on him in seconds. But they weren't.

And the man had said, 'Breaking and entering is a very serious crime...'

Brack's breathing quickened.

Holy shit, were these guys cops?

Did he set off a silent alarm when he'd busted in here?

He had to know for sure and motioned to the older guy, "Officer, can I see some identification?"

Salt and pepper man pulled out a leather fold and, sure enough, inside was a badge.

David Brack swallowed.

Salt and pepper slipped the fold back into his pocket. "I'll ask again, what are you doing here?"

"These men," Brack shook his head and exhaled. "These lawyers—they stole from me, officer."

The man raised his chin, "Stole from you?"

Although Brack was relieved these two weren't Gezzle's lackeys, there was probably no way he'd ever get out of this.

Perhaps, though, if he offered to cut these officers in if he found any cash? Yeah, but that was bribery. And if they didn't go for it, they'd tack on years to his burglary charge.

Wait, fuck.

The bulge in his jacket. The Smith & Wesson. They'd also find his fingerprints on the crowbar.

Oh, Christ.

The charge was armed robbery.

Remo Gezzle's underlings would find him now, probably shiv him in the county lockup before he saw trial.

Brack closed his eyes. He was hopelessly screwed.

The man holding Nikki spoke, "What'd they steal from you?" His accent was American.

Brack eyed Nikki. He didn't want things to get worse and decided telling the truth wouldn't get him in any more trouble than he was already in. The men might even testify he'd been helpful to their investigation.

So, he tried to convey everything he could in an abbreviated story. His divorce. The sale of a boat. The last dozen years of his miserable life trying to recover from the loss these bastard attorneys had suckered him into. Finally, he concluded with, "These guys are laundering money."

The two men looked at one another, and the one with Nikki bobbed his head.

"Laundering money, you say?" the older one repeated. "These lawyers? How?"

Then Brack had an idea. He'd try to assert some control.

"I want a deal if I talk anymore." He pointed to Nikki, "The woman doesn't do any jail time. Neither do I. None. That's non-negotiable." If it came down to it, though, Brack would go to prison if they agreed to his demand for Nikki's freedom. She didn't deserve to be tangled up in this mess in the first place.

Again, the two men glanced at one another.

"I'm okay with that deal if you are, Detective Crowne."

The older man smiled and bobbed his head, "Agreed."

"Alright." Brack held out an open palm and slowly reached under his jacket. "I'm taking out my cell to record this conversation."

Detective Crowne motioned to Brack's midsection, "Before you do, please lay your weapon down on the table."

Right, shit. The weapons charge for an unregistered handgun. Brack would have to add that to the deal.

"Yes, alright, okay." He fished out the Smith & Wesson by the handle and carefully placed it on Oliver's desk along with the folded sheet of passwords he'd found.

The man holding Nikki said, "Start talking."

Brack removed his mobile phone, found the app he was looking for, and set the device to record.

"First, your names, in your voices," he said.

"Detective Crowne," the first declared.

"Detective Riley," the second added.

Brack then put into words, as best he could, the deal they'd agreed to for his cooperation, also adding that the Smith & Wesson was 'given' to him by a friend, but he hadn't time to register its serial number under his name.

To Brack's surprise, neither detective seemed to care about the gun, and both supplied verbal consent without hesitation.

"Alright. According to what I could find out, the lawyers were working with a container company called Kilgore and another ground business named Gezzle Lift & Haul, and –"

Detective Crowne raised a brow, "And Sigma-Sea?"

This surprised Brack, and he nodded.

"What'd you find?"

Riley lowered his pistol.

"They're hiding money for these companies. Inflating shipments, falsifying weights, and other things."

"What other things?"

"Umm, I can't fully prove it yet, but there was merchandise I found in a warehouse that might be part of all this."

"What kind of merchandise?"

"Paintings, I think."

"Paintings?"

Brack took a deep breath, "Artwork is a laundering staple. It's a unique asset."

"Forgeries?" Crowne asked.

"No. The worth of any artwork is subjective. Whatever price someone is willing to pay sets its value. If experts say a given piece is of a million-dollar value, and one or two others agree, that's where bidding starts. This has been done for ages."

Riley shook his head, "I don't get it."

"If someone wants to launder cash," Brack explained, "they can pay three experts to overvalue any piece of art. When it goes to sale or auction, the anonymous purchaser outbids everyone, pays cash, and the artist receives the money. The genius is the artist doesn't even pay capital gains on the transaction. And now, whatever deal was worked out behind the scenes between the artist and the anonymous purchaser can be played out. When the bidder pays the artist, dirty money becomes clean, and nobody's the wiser."

"Shit, and that works?" Riley said.

Brack nodded. "I found what I believe was a bunch of packaged paintings inside a restricted warehouse –"

"Sigma-Sea's freeport?" Crowne said.

Brack was surprised. "Yes, exactly." These guys were obviously on the trail, too. "That warehouse is like a fortress. Kind of like a giant safe. It's patrolled 24/7 by armed guards."

"How'd you get in?"

Brack and Nikki shared a look.

"I have my ways." He didn't want to be charged with another crime by copping to one he'd gotten out of with the aid of a 'wouldn't stay in the car' twenty-something woman.

"So, the paintings are not forgeries, and someone lied about their value?" Bennett uttered.

Brack nodded, "Artwork is a singular asset, unique."

Crowne's eyebrows raised and he stepped forward. "What do you know about NFTs?"

"Non-fungibles?" Brack knew the basics of the electronic certificates, but because the technology was new, he'd never really understood their appeal or value.

But then something clicked.

"Wait," Brack exclaimed. "Shit!"

"What?" Riley said.

Brack laughed. "Those clever sons of bitches!"

Crowne eyed him closely.

"We can forget the auction and the experts. Hell, we can forget the physical painting," Brack nodded to himself. Now he understood why the artwork in the warehouse had sat collecting dust for so long. They weren't using that method anymore.

"If you could give us a clue, that'd be good," Crowne said.

"Alright, I totally get it." Brack raised his hands. "The old way was the physical artwork. But with NFTs, they represent a unique digital asset, and remain virtual."

Crowne frowned.

"It's basically digital artwork, one-of-a-kind stuff," Brack continued. "The NFT part is nothing more than an ownership signature enveloping a digital graphic. In the future, something like this might be used to prevent unauthorized duplication of copyright, allowing the owner to find anyone online using the piece without paying the rights to do so. The way music and movie companies search websites for digital footprints to their copyrighted materials and go after pirates." Brack shook his head. "But that's not what they were doing."

"Melton and Oliver? Enlighten us. What were they doing?"

"Selling crap," Brack chuckled. "The same substandard artwork I found in the warehouse, only using the NFT method, things became virtual. There was no physical painting, only a digital one. There's no longer any need to store anything in a warehouse. Once the NFT is bought, it resides on a computer hard drive someplace."

"What does all of it mean?"

"It means someone can create a graphic from nothing. Anything, really, provided it's in digital format. They can upload that to the blockchain, which is this encrypted –"

Crowne held up a hand. "We know what the blockchain is."

"Okay. Once the graphic is minted on the blockchain, the owner can charge whatever they want." Brack shrugged. "And Melton and Oliver can launder hordes of cash by its purchase."

"Just like they did with the actual paintings?"

"Better. Because no expert needs to evaluate it, and there's no storage. Dirty money buys the piece, the seller cuts the buyer in on the profit, and the cash comes out clean. Happens in seconds."

"Un-fucking-believable," Riley said.

"The technology of our times," Crowne nodded.

"More virtual bullshit," Riley chided. "But you know what I don't get? If these guys were laundering all that cash and doing well for themselves, what's with this office? The place is a fucking wreck."

Brack smiled. "It's cover. In the laundering game, keeping the same location is important to avoid any red flags that can lead to an audit."

Riley's brows furrowed, "But each of these guys owns a mansion on the beach. I'd say that's a huge fucking red flag."

Brack shook his head, "Not necessarily. Personal finances and the firm's revenue are separated by corporate decree. An uptick in Melton or Oliver's personal wealth can be explained through investments and other means. Even dubious ones. The IRS doesn't care where income comes from, only that people declare and pay the proper taxes on it." Brack nodded to himself. "But businesses, like law firms, have paper trails. Clients, settlements, books to keep."

Riley squinted, "So they kept the lowbrow business?"

"They had to," Brack shrugged. "It was their false front to funneling all the money."

"And all this money is where? Which bank?"

"No idea," Brack exhaled and shook his head. "I can't find anything, no institution, no instrument." He bit his lower lip. "I'm at a total loss."

"Alright," Crowne looked Brack over. "What'd you come across in this office?"

Brack shot an accidental glance at the sheet of paper on the desk. "Nothing," he lied.

Crowne tilted his head, "Let me see that."

Reluctantly, Brack handed him the paper he'd found under the desk.

Crowne scanned the sheet for a few seconds, then held it to where his partner could see it.

"What's your name?"

"David Brann—I mean Brack. David Brack."

At this point, he was just trying to keep his deal and not add charges.

"Got any ID?"

Brack pulled out his license and handed it over.

"Jacksonville?" Crowne seemed surprised. "A long way from home, aren't we?"

Brack shrugged.

Weirdly, the detective returned his ID.

"Set your phone to take a photo," Crowne instructed.

"Photo?" Brack said, stunned.

Crowne held the sheet, "We're going to keep the original as evidence."

Brack was confused but would do what he'd been asked. He snapped three quick photos with his mobile before Detective Crowne refolded and tucked the sheet into his overshirt.

The other detective let go of Nikki's arm and said, "If you're lying, we know where you live."

Brack nodded—though he'd probably never return there. But the detectives didn't need to know that. He held eye contact with Crowne and concluded, "That's everything I know, I swear it."

Again, the two officers shared a glance.

Crowne took a small device from his pocket and tossed it on the desk next to the Smith & Wesson, "This might be of use to you."

Brack eyed the silver object but wasn't sure what to say.

Crowne pointed, "One of those passwords on that list might help."

Then, the two detectives left Oliver's office, vanished down the corridor, and out the back door.

Nikki rushed to Brack's side, "What the fuck was that all about?"

"No idea. But I don't think those two were cops."

"What do you mean?"

He pointed and raised his eyebrows, "Unregistered handgun and neither seemed to give a shit."

Nikki lowered her head, "I'm sorry I didn't stay in the car."

Brack seized the gun, the silver device, and the crowbar from Oliver's desk. "I kind of knew you wouldn't," he grinned slightly. "But I'm thinking right now we get the hell out of here."

Chapter

49

They'd not spoken in two days.

Alana steered the Escalade south on I-95 through the early morning mist. If she kept up this pace, the interstate would cross to I-75 and finally I-10 around 6pm this evening—and that's when she'd know for sure.

There was something horrifyingly unique about this country. Both beautiful and blue. There was a forgottenness of the burdens existing with freedom, especially in the youth. To decide what to do with the future without the state dictating its will.

But with such independence comes the obligation of living with comparison and judgment. In the most basic sense, many people here were lost in this mire of social climbing and treated each other as commodities, not individuals.

In America, there was inequality and materialism. She felt the dichotomy of coming from a country where the communal benefit was practiced—often at the expense of self—to a country overrun with celebrated self-interest.

A mother teaches one set of values, and this society rewards the opposite.

University, no doubt, was overwhelming.

Schooling had to be putting tremendous pressure on Katia. She was expected to perform, fit in, and succeed without genuine support. Their mother, a seamstress, had no higher education. And Alana had only those teachings from general school with no individual disciplines, coupled with precarious learnings from this underworld she'd become a part of.

It all had to be confusing for her younger sister. Being self-steward of her own destiny perhaps presented Katia with too many choices. She was beautiful but inexperienced, just as Alana had once been. But for Katia, this strange world may have come at her too fast. Trying to fit in and be part of a society where popularity and worth hinged on how much money and class one had been born into. Or how much potential an individual held for the same.

Is this why she had turned to drugs? Were they an escape from the pressures Alana and her mother put on her when she'd been accepted to university? Was it the countless choices? Or was it that Alana simply wasn't there for her?

She steered the Escalade down the road and cleared a tear from her cheek.

All the things Katia once wanted in her life. Piano player, artist, botanist, model, hair stylist, astronaut. Now she'd become none of them. Her light doused far too soon in this country of excess and pursued wealth.

Maybe she'd also never really gotten over the death of their father. This was undoubtedly true for Alana, as he'd been her only positive male role model.

She recalled how Pavel always made time for them, even when he was working. Whether to read her to sleep or take them out on Sundays for a simple meal.

But what made Alana exceedingly sad was that the two, her father and Katia, were once unabashed idealists. Father the artisan, Katia the everything. And all of this despite the callousness of the world around them, the one that crushed them both.

However, unlike her father, Katia's undoing was not her own. These criminal drug runners had done it to her. And that required Alana to make them pay with their lives.

And it was worth it if she could save just one idealist—someone's brother, sister, somebody—from suffering the same fate as her sister.

Alexei would have to understand.

She would make sure of it.

CHAPTER

50

In the morning, David Brack brought out his laptop and tried to plug the small device he'd received from the mystery men into a USB drive.

But after opening the tiny silver apparatus, there was no mating connection.

Instead, it held a tiny female USB type-C oval, the same one he used for his mobile phone. And that seemed the only input.

Brack dug out the cable from his bag and plugged it into the small silver drive. Then, he connected the larger USB pinout to the laptop.

Immediately, the computer asked to install a browser extension—which he did.

A prompt appeared asking for a security PIN.

Brack retrieved his mobile phone and zoomed in on the photo he'd taken of the password sheet under Gary Oliver's desk—whose original those two 'detectives' had taken from him.

Names, numbers, and an array of figures with enumerated hashtags. He found a six-digit number with no pound sign on the sheet's lower half.

024601.

Brack entered the figures into the laptop.

He gasped, rose from the bed, and paced the room. He gazed at the ocean from the sliding window and took a cleansing breath.

Charlie still needed chairs for his guests. Nevertheless, a couple stood by the water's edge, holding hands, and enjoying the morning waves.

Brack opened the sliding door and walked out onto the balcony. The sun warmed his cheeks and a genuine smile grew on his face. Now he understood what Rick Melton and Gary Oliver were doing.

The money came in through different avenues. Businesses that were otherwise legitimate created paper transactions to conceal the origin of the criminal funds. False invoices, the purchase of questionable artwork, and so on. Even Melton and Oliver's firm was in on the action, placing appointments on their books for legal consultations and then canceling them—issuing a full refund of the client's retainer, which was never paid in the first place.

The mix of trades all basically worked the same way, where dealings appeared legitimate as currency changed hands. In reality, invoiced services were never performed, purchased merchandise did not exist, and all artwork was worthless. Nevertheless, money on the backend came out clean.

Next, funds were moved into shell companies in low, incremental amounts to avoid taxes. Not too much money at any one time—which would raise eyebrows. Instead, a network of false LLCs was used to spread the activity around, making the origin of deposits impossible to trace. Any copious amounts were transferred under the guise of reinvestments or improvements, which also hampered tracking.

But the final piece—integrating the money back into circulation— is where the real genius took shape.

Melton and Oliver didn't channel the ill-gotten gains into the banking system. They must've understood that this is how most laundering operations are caught—because criminals need to trust the bank not to report large cash deposits, as doing so would alert authorities... authorities with the power to seize all funds.

And the lawyers didn't park these assets in some offshore account, either. They were smarter than that.

Instead, Melton and Oliver had funneled millions into cryptocurrency using an overseas exchange. A financial vehicle that both kept cash off balance sheets and away from the IRS. The money was ported onto cold wallets. From there, as long as the currency remained digital, they could transfer assets to anyone in the world tax-free.

Rick Melton and Gary Oliver acted as both bagmen and distributors for these millions.

Brack retreated to the bathroom and splashed sink water on the backside of his neck. In the mirror's reflection, he noticed that Charlie had removed the fiberglass shower and installed white tile with towel and washcloth holders. Pieces of blue tape were still stuck to small white pieces to hold them in place as they dried.

He closed his eyes.

There was always a big chance this would never work. That chasing after the money was futile and would amount to nothing but a colossal waste of time. He'd find himself stuck wherever he was with only the memories of his envious salad days to mull over as he had for the past decade.

But the slim possibility he'd uncover something kept him going. Maybe it was strange desperation or his unwillingness to accept that his life would never be as fruitful as it once was. That he'd never get that second chance.

Brack returned to the bed and glanced at the computer screen.

The number read 186.77.

He suddenly realized he'd kept this fantasy alive so long that he'd overlooked other things. Who he once was, what he wanted, and where he was now. He didn't know precisely who the old him and the new him were. The two had become strangely divided, one dominated by the chase, but the other…

Brack nodded to himself.

This was a unique crossroads.

New decisions would need to be made.

One-hundred-eighty-six point seven-seven.

With the latest close of Bitcoin, this device given to him by the strange duo in Oliver's office held a little over $4.4 million in converted U.S. currency.

It was undoubtedly only a fraction of the felonious millions Melton and Oliver likely laundered, but it was significant to Brack.

It was enough money for him to move back to Miami.

To restart his business.

To recapture everything taken from him years ago.

He could get an office. Nothing fancy, but in the good part of the city. The nest egg was also sufficient for a decorator. That's what really mattered. Things inside the office had to look modern—like he was on the up and up. Appearance was everything.

New clothes were also needed. While casual wear was all the rage in corporate settings, finance had its rules. Suits and ties earned respect and commanded attention. This wasn't Silicon Valley—no intelligent person would invest millions with a fleshy, t-shirted, unkempt wunderkind.

He'd also need a car. While he was once partial to the Porsche, he'd have to see what the others in the business were driving. Perhaps he could still get the sportscar as a weekend ride, but maybe something more conservative to motor about town and take clients to lunch, golf, and after-hours parties?

And shoes, those were easy. Expensive Bally and Berluti, black and brown in both to start. Made for the business and for his feet.

He returned to the window and gazed out at the waves.

David Brack could do it all, but for one slight problem.

CHAPTER
51

Jelena and Pavel met in secondary school and immediately took to one another. He wanted to be a sculptor. She just wanted to be with him.

They'd married quickly during grade ten, left school, and found a small apartment to begin their life together. Pavel worked construction and crafted his projects on the weekends. Jelena tried her hand at crochet and designed a marital bed throw.

She discovered she enjoyed working with her hands and started stitching odds and ends together for practice. When Pavel left for the day, she offered her needlework services around their small village and began making a little money of her own.

Instead of being a traditionalist, Pavel was thrilled. He could see how much joy Jelena got from her work and looked to support his wife in any way he could. In the apartment's common room, Pavel cleared his clays and tools from half of it and insisted Jelena use the other half for her ventures. They lived happily in that apartment until a Spring surprise triggered the need for a larger space.

Alana had been a skinny baby, her mother said. So fussy, she ate only vegetables and loathed anything with meat or meat-like sauce. Jelena and Pavel changed their diets as she got older to adjust to their choosy daughter. Though, Alana recalled her father sneaking off to the butcher for bacon strips and pork chops when they went to market... and the curious smoke that arose from the family's grill once they returned home.

Back then, the only thing that scared Alana was thunder. That huge rumble echoed when the air was warm and dark clouds circled the skies. She'd run to her room, close the door, and place a blanket over her face until the flashes and the booms stopped.

But one night, the storm was more severe than ever. The cracks and bangs drew closer after each flash, and Pavel rushed to his daughter's bed inside her room.

"Everything will be alright, my little one. I promise." His strong arms hugged her close. "It is only the hot and cold heavens reaching out to one another. A powerful greeting. Everything will be okay, my little one."

She felt protected inside the impenetrable bubble of his embrace. They chatted between the rumbles, and he stroked her hair until the thundering ended, and she fell asleep in his arms.

Most mornings, Pavel grabbed the brown bag lunch Jelena had prepared for him the night before, kissed his girls on the head, and left for work. Jelena readied Alana for school, and the two hugged before her mother spent the day sewing and seaming.

Katia came in the Summer. Also thin, but growing up, the young girl didn't share the same dietary affinities as Alana.

A vision she often recalled was the first time Katia held their father's hand, and the two traipsed happily into his favorite butcher shop. On Sunday afternoons, her little sister smelled of the same porky smoke as her father. And lumps of BBQ sauce always squared the sides of her cheerful lips.

But shortly after Alana's eighth birthday, she noticed a strange, steady decline with the family when Pavel lost his job.

January's merriments brought fewer presents during the celebration. She hadn't complained, though her younger sister did make a fuss when a doll she'd begged for didn't arrive. And, the following season, instead of taking food to the neighborhood celebration, the family stood in a lengthy line for whatever traditional trimmings came their way.

Pavel had changed. He spent more time at home, and his once vibrant smile was reduced to a tiny grimace. The crinkle of his brown bag lunch became a sound young Alana never heard again. It was instead replaced by her father's untwist and pour habit.

Jelena attempted to tackle the family's financial load by taking on more extended hours and stitching. But it was never quite enough. They gave up their four-bedroom apartment, and Alana and Katia were forced to share a room.

Pavel traded his sculptures for whatever he could get for them and sold his tools. Whatever was happening to her father tore apart her mother.

Alana tried to help by doing dishes, bathing, and readying her sister—anything to ease the burdens.

Her father may not be working now, but it would be okay. Daddy would come out of it and return to them. Everything would be alright.

But on the night of Jelena's horrible scream, that all changed.

The broken woman shrieked inside her parent's bedroom, draped over the only man she'd ever loved with all her heart.

Jelena cursed the Gods using language Alana had never heard her speak before. They'd taken her better half, the one who'd watched over her and the girls his entire life. The man who'd worked so hard for their happiness remembered their birthdays, tucked them in, snuck off to grill meat on Sundays with Katia, and comforted Alana when the thunder came.

Now he was gone. The happy bubble burst, ripped apart by the pressures of a declining world he no longer had the strength to keep outside their home.

Her mother's wailing continued through the night until Alana found her puffy-eyed, delirious, and exhausted the following day. Somehow, young Alana aided her from her dead father's side into her bedroom, where she could rest.

The Autumn funeral saw Pavel's three girls weep over him in despair.

There were things Alana had not understood about life, emotion, and loss, well into her teens and twenties. Looking back, her mother, Jelena, had remained incredibly strong, trying to hold the family together once Pavel passed. But the woman had lost a part of her soul that she would never recover from, and it aged her quickly.

Shortly after, Alana left school to help support the family. She found a menial wage job in a shipping facility after a lengthy search, but when she had trouble keeping her long-flowing auburn hair in its net, the plant moved her from packing to receiving, which is when she met Alexei.

He was kind and charming, the way her father had been. He always asked about her day and if she needed anything. He visited her station more and more. A smile, a laugh. But the attention he supplied was somehow different than any she'd known before.

Alexei took her to lunch, then dinner. He told her stories of America and how he could take her there.

They soon shared a kiss.

He was one of the plant's bosses, and she was a nobody working in a cubicle.

At first, she'd thought it was love.

A fairytale.

The path her parents had once embarked on.

But it was not.

CHAPTER
52

Before the evening, Brack squeezed off several rounds in the outdoor range with the Smith & Wesson. The first shots were jarring, and the .38's recoil stung his wrists and biceps.

However, he'd become used to the recoil by the tenth or twelfth shot. He was getting the hang of all the weapon's power—and it felt cleansing.

Vella wasn't where he'd left her. She'd moved on long, long ago. She had the job she wanted for ten years and would wed the man she'd probably been seeking for some time.

Brack had romanticized that relationship. Time massages the mistakes and the troubles. He recalled how he'd become too self-satisfied with her—as if she was some sort of prize—and she'd become complacent shopping and neglecting her once lofty goals of education. Looking back, they weren't good for one another.

Besides, deep feelings of genuine love had never really been part of the picture between them. He knew it was probably his fault for making the relationship as transactional as it once was. Focusing on himself and his dreams without urging Vella along with hers. A lack of support, he'd been too egocentric to understand at the time.

Those wild horses his father had told him to tame. Throughout college, he'd pushed them off and set them aside until he became rich. Then they came loose at the wrong time. He was supposed to have matured, ready to settle down and focus long-term. But with success

271

came options he'd never had in his life before. Tons of money, no barriers, and freedom to indulge in everything without moderation. He now knew that bringing Vella into his outrageous life at that time was a huge, huge mistake. He'd not learned to tame himself yet.

Though Brack was happy for her. Vella had found someone more on her level and gotten the job she'd always wanted. She was sharing her life with someone Brack understood to be a good, honest man in the doctor.

Brack also couldn't help thinking he was trying to run to the familiar. The last time he felt safe, secure, and thought he was content was the time he spent when Vella was in his life. But he now understood it was an illusion. He'd bolstered something in his mind and put it on a gratifying level to which he longed to return.

That, however, would be going backward.

Vella had moved on, and so should he.

This got him thinking about his former profession.

Financial counseling in the greater Miami area. He was good at it, but the trappings of that successful life had ruined him. There were too many alternatives and pitfalls for a man who—as his father had put— never tamed his wild horses.

Being from a small town, he'd consumed himself with becoming wealthy. In fact, that was his singular goal the entire fucking time he was in college. He'd hooked up now and again but never seriously dated during those formative years. This is perhaps where his sense of priorities went askew.

Money first, always money first.

He'd constantly remained detached from his clients. If they made money, great—if they lost it, it didn't matter. As a CFA, he profited either way. Brack did work to steer his clients to the proper stocks and whatnot, though his priority was always to keep them hooked and coming back.

And he'd never seriously thought about anything, or anybody, beyond the money. Not that this precisely paralleled Dax's business or the things he'd gone through.

What scared him now was that he'd seen the future with Dax, or maybe it was his past. The older guy had been sucked into the same world, where profits over people were the goal. And it didn't matter how or from who the money was squeezed. In Dax's case, unsuspecting account holders at his giant bank. In Brack's, pilfering discretionary savings from investors.

And the fact was what Brack did as a counselor was more dumb luck than skill. When that dumb luck ran out, everything came tumbling and crumbling down in a hurry. Looking back, he was fortunate none of his less astute investors had killed him for his inability to see what was coming with the market—as the wiser investors should've been his clue.

But Dax talked about not selling any more of his soul to it.

Dax was living with a quiet torment now, though it looked like the man was doing okay. Nevertheless, being involved in a situation where he'd caused harm to his customers had unnerved Dax, and, as the more Brack thought about it, his previous career had unsettled him, too.

Though Dax had turned his anguish into generosity. He was the most charitable man Brack had ever met in his entire life. Walking away from a job like that out of pure principle.

That was a nobility which Brack admired greatly.

Though of all people, it was Charlie—the owner of the Big B Hotel—who'd put the thought in his head. He'd made a comment to Nikki that stuck with Brack.

Sometimes we find ourselves surrounded by better people than we think we deserve, Charlie had said.

We do, indeed, Charlie. We do, indeed.

He squeezed off the remaining rounds and checked his target. Many misses but a few in the center. Not bad for a man who never owned or fired a gun in his life.

As Nikki recommended, he bought a holster before packing his gear and heading back to The Big B.

CHAPTER

53

The time was 6:15pm. Alexei said he would meet her at his villa, which was good because they'd be alone.

Her story of the missing phone must've worked, saying it'd been damaged during the break-in and execution of the lawyer. It took much time to find a replacement which is why she hadn't called earlier to report her progress. It would not be the first time she lied to him, but hopefully the last.

Still, there was a risk.

If Alexei felt she'd betrayed his trust, he would've come after her, hunted her. There would have been no talk, no pleading, no pause.

Alexei would've killed her for what she had done.

But now was her time to rectify all of that.

At the gates to his home, she entered her code. Relief washed over her when they rattled open, and she drove through unimpeded.

Alexei had to be excited. They'd not seen one another in weeks and hadn't been alone together for far longer.

The home was opulent, befitting of a man sucked into the self-interest lifestyle of the country he'd adopted for his own. A large driveway encircling a five-tier fountain, lush with landscape and space.

Alana parked in the vacant area and went up to the double-door entry. No other cars meant they'd be isolated with only each other this time, and that eased her nerves. She was tired and had no energy to entertain more than one.

The door was unlocked, and she entered.

Alexei had the home lit low for the evening, and soft music played throughout the manor—something he often did to set the mood for parties and her visits. She gazed about its entrance but did not see the man himself until a voice atop the entry's vaulted stairway called to her, "My love, it is magnificent you have returned."

Alana smiled, but her eyes did not.

Despite his drinking and other excesses, Alexei was fit for his 40 years. Handsome, tall, dark-haired, with broad shoulders she'd once considered safe.

"I have missed you so very much. We have the home to ourselves tonight, and I have set up drinks on the veranda outside below."

Alexei, wearing a casual dark suit and red tie, bounded down the round staircase, arms wide and smiling.

The two hugged and kissed deeply.

The dark scruff on his face was exactly right, not so much it curled but not so little to appear patchy. In the past, it'd reminded Alana of her father. The spiky feel of security when her father kissed her cheek and tucked her into bed.

She'd made good on everything but for the one extra stop up north. Though it needed to be done. Alexei would soon understand what she'd affected was out of her love for her family.

He led the two out to the elevated veranda. The beautiful, secluded view lit by the setting sun and yard's lights showed the manicured lawn space and his luxurious pool, whose splashing deck jets echoed peacefully through the grounds, arching into the pool like a Roman bath.

Alexei prepared two wine glasses and poured a white.

Alana reached into her purse.

The first bullet struck him in the left shoulder.

Alexei's smile vanished quickly.

In her country, there was the sacrifice of the self. She'd known no other way. And when it came to leaving the war-torn region, she'd used the only commodity her upbringing had taught her. Fortunately, she'd been born beautiful and tried to use this to her advantage. Alexei was drawn to her looks, and this was the trade-off.

At first, it was purely transactional. Despite Alexei's roughness and his cheating, she'd become bonded to the man because of what he'd done for her family by taking her mother and younger sister from the area to America, where they could start a new life.

But there was more she needed. Again, fortunately, the older she became, the more Alexei wanted her.

Alana's curvaceous good looks and classic long flowing hair made her his favorite. He said she reminded her of a beautiful sculpture created by a God.

But she'd used him, and he'd used her.

Katia's schooling was not cheap.

Alana remained in Alexei's employ for her mother and sister, doing anything he'd asked, even killing. Though they spent less time together as Alexei's wealth accumulated.

Then she saw him for what he indeed was.

When she'd told him of her sister's death, he did not say he was sorry, as was the custom. He did not try to console her, not really. No, Alexei dismissed himself, saying he had critical business to attend to, handed her some cash, and was gone.

Alana had whored herself to Alexei for years, all so that her mother and sister could live a better life. She paid for her sister's college. Her body paid for the small place in which they lived. But the man who'd told her he loved her had dismissed her in her time of need. It became clear what she was to him, a plaything like all the others.

The second and third bullets struck Alexei in his chest, and he fell to the veranda's travertine tile.

However, the man was still conscious.

Alana stood over him with the Lebedev 9mm.

He stared up at her in terror and uttered, "Why?"

Alana did not answer.

Instead, she stepped away.

Everything he'd asked, she'd done—but not for the reasons he'd set her out with—but for those of her own. Individuals directly involved, every person she killed, was engaged in the illegal smuggling of drugs.

The boasting captain that knew of every forbidden piece of cargo on his ship. The head guard at the port who'd kept the illicit activities secret and moved the yard's merchandise on those trucks. The lawyer who hid the illegal shipments, the other who hid the ill-gotten profits, and the man who owned and ran those ships. Each one had to answer for her sister's death.

But it had come to more than that.

It was Alexei himself who had coordinated the tragedy.

Alana lifted the glass of wine. Cold spirits ran down her throat as she gazed at the dying Russian on the ground.

The only connection she'd truly experienced with Alexei were those of usury, where she had to give all of herself to get anything. Her asset was her body. Her place was as a servant. Alexei took and took and molded her into this device that served both his pleasure and bidding. He'd turned her into both a callus lover and a cold-hearted killer.

She'd stayed with him because she had no choice. Her family depended on his care, much like they had on her father. Though Alexei wielded things to his strict advantage. Still, she could manage the unfairness as long as her family was safe.

But his takings had gone too far.

Alexei's blood pooled on the floor's tile under his backside. He breathed and coughed, then moaned and squirmed.

Alana felt nothing.

In fact, she felt less than nothing for the man she believed she once loved. The one who'd made her promises, but only ones that came with intimate payments.

Alana lowered her head, "Katia."

Alexei glanced at her in fear.

"My sister. Your men, your drugs. Poisoning those without care to consequence."

Alexei's breathing labored.

"Her death took part of my soul. Katia was my father's jewel and my mother's youngest joy."

The blood vessels in Alexei's eyes darkened.

"And your focus has been on all this." Alana outstretched an arm. "Your home of plenty. This country of no limit to selfishness or wealth. These are the appetites that obliterated her."

Alexei whispered. "No, please…"

Alana sipped her drink and shook her head, "But it was the next death that took the rest of my soul."

Alexei squirmed.

"My mother endured my father's decline. Kept us clothed and fed. She never thought of herself and protected us. When we lost father, she never wavered in her devotion to family."

Alexei gasped, "I do not know –"

Alana cut him off, "I sacrificed everything I could for Katia. She was the one who would have the best life in this new country. My mother knew it, and I knew it."

"No, no," he moaned.

"Katia's death broke my mother," she said calmly. "A good, kind woman. She sank into sadness, and her health failed."

Alexei tried to reach for Alana's arm, but she slapped it away.

"And now you have taken both from me!" she shouted. "All in pursuit of this shit of selfish lifestyle! My sister is dead. My mother is dead." She raised her drink and stretched her neck to the side. "Everything I did for you without questions. I put up with you and your sick circle of allies. I put up with your paranoia and distrustfulness."

Alexei cupped the wound in his chest.

"But uncaring gluttony is why you must die among the richness you coveted more than my family's lives."

The white of Alexei's eyes grew red as his heart pumped more blood through the gaping hole in his torso.

Alana stood, "Dlya sem'i."

She dumped her glass of wine over Alexei's body.

"Cyka…" Alexi huffed.

The 'bitch' stood above him, aimed, and pulled the trigger.

Once for her sister.

Once for her mother.

And once for the father that tried to protect them all.

Alexei's body jolted, tensed, then stilled.

Alana Kerkovich wiped her prints from the wine glass, left the premises, and did not look back.

CHAPTER

54

Brack had heard it called 'soul-searching' though he never really understood its meaning. The term always conjured visions of some giant white tent in the desert with incense, sitting cross-legged next to a guru in meditation. But that wasn't it at all.

Dax had gone through something similar, which he'd termed a 'crisis of conscience.' Brack felt that was also like what he was feeling. Though, not quite. No, soul-searching fit better.

He was in the best shape of his life, both mentally and physically. He'd all but stopped drinking and overly concerning himself with Gezzle and his men.

But perhaps it was simply that the mind and body were indeed connected? He could do 100 pushups without a break and often jogged on the beach to and from the hotel to Dax's office twice in the mornings.

Was it that a clear head could not occur without a clean body? Maybe he'd stumbled on a universal truth these past few weeks? Possibly this was the guru's technique in those smoky canopies out in the desert?

He removed the crumpled Whataburger bag from the bathroom's vent and tucked it into the gray briefcase. He wore most of the suit he'd put together for his outings, tossed a fifty on the bed for today's maid service, and headed downstairs.

Charlie saw him in the lobby. The hotel's owner wore painter's clothing dotted with oil stains and a matching hat. Despite the grubby

281

outfit, the hardworking man was as upbeat as always.

"And what's on the agenda for today, Mister David?"

Brack smiled, "Hey Charlie, is there a credit union around? Like a bank only it services the community?"

"Why, of course. It's just down the road. Walking distance, really. Of course, if you just need an ATM, there's one at the diner, but I'm sure you already knew."

"No, my friend. Today we're making a deposit."

"Going to be with us for a while more, then?"

"I'm thinking so. Yes."

"Excellent. Corina refreshes rooms today, and we'll be sure she takes care of yours extra special since you'll be with us a while longer," he made a note on his desk pad. "And please don't forget about the cocktail party tomorrow at 5pm sharp."

"Five, sharp. Wouldn't miss it," Brack said. "And I'm bringing a couple of guests."

Charlie grinned. "Perfect, Mister David. I'm also bringing one who I'm thrilled to have you meet."

"This reminds me, Charlie. I do have something I want to discuss with you tomorrow night if you have a moment?"

"Oh?"

"Five, sharp," Brack teased.

"Tomorrow evening, then, Mister David," Charlie bowed.

A short walk later, David Brack found the Shoreline Credit Union, opened an account, and deposited all $4,000 and change from the Whataburger takeout bag.

While waiting for things to process, he was treated to coffee and a magazine. Inside the publication, he found an advertisement for a watch, which he discretely tore from the magazine, folded, and put into his pocket.

It wasn't long before he was given a checking account, a savings account, and a bank card in his real name. Then, using the laptop, he began moving money from the silver cold wallet ledger to a crypto exchange, which he at once transferred to the credit union.

It was time to stop running for good.

If Gezzle's men did find him, he'd face that music when it came. The stress of moving from one place to another wasn't worth the long-term troubles. Not anymore. Besides, now he had some cash and could make a deal for any debt if they ever caught up with him.

On the way back to the hotel, he stopped at a clothing store and bought three pairs of more fitting casual trousers, four shirts, and other amenities to go with the outfits.

He took a long walk on the beach barefoot to Dax's office. Inside, his friend was hard at work on one account or another.

Brack set his things down at his desk.

Dax looked over at him, "Done some shopping, I see?"

"Just picking up clothes more akin to the area here. And something casual for the party tomorrow."

"Yeah, about that. Mind if I bring a guest?"

"I don't think that's a problem. Who are you bringing?"

Dax shook his head, but his cheeks blushed, "That's my business, Mr. Brannon."

"Oh, I see. Guess I'll wait until the party, then."

Dax let out a hearty laugh. "Yes, you will."

Brack removed the folded watch advertisement from his pocket, trimmed off the rough edges with scissors, and adhered it to the blotter on his desk.

Dax rose from his chair for a look, "What's that?"

Brack pressed the ad's surface and ran a finger over its taped edges.

"Ahh, the old Rolex submariner. A classic."

Brack fingered a crease, "Yeah."

"Take a few returns to earn enough for that one," Dax pointed.

Brack shook his head, "Oh, I don't want one."

"Then why?"

Brack motioned toward the flattened ad, "It's a reminder."

"Reminder?"

"Kind of like your paperweight."

"How do you mean?"

"Don't worry, my friend. We've got plenty of time to discuss all that one day."

"I see. Got some stories of your own, do you?"

"Ha-ha. You could say that."

Brack smiled, and Dax did too.

CHAPTER

55

The afternoon brought skies overcast.

Bennett picked up his Desert Eagle and examined the chamber. "Sometimes I can't figure you out, amigo."

Kendrick slipped on his overshirt. "And what were we supposed to do with that device, Detective Riley?"

"I don't know. But my plane needs new windows."

Kendrick gave a slight chuckle.

If Alana's presence had shown one thing, it was that this web of Symon Pellgrin, Gary Oliver, Rick Melton, Yuri Melnyk, and others had several casualties. It was more than moving goods from one place to another. These shipments held an impact on the lives of any place they touched. What was sad is that somewhere in all this madness, there didn't seem to be anyone who cared for the souls these illegal goods destroyed. The weapons, the drugs, and everything else. It was all about the money.

"We're dealing with some very selfish people who don't seem to worry who they step on to get what they want," Kendrick said. "At least we had a chance to make one of them whole."

"Ahh, I'm half kidding," Bennett shrugged. "I think you did a good thing there. That guy and his girlfriend seemed honest. And the more we dig into this, I wonder how many people those lawyers screwed over."

"Not just them," Kendrick raised his brows. "This entire thing is…"

285

"Yeah, I know," Bennett said, looking out a window.

The night before last, they'd sent the password sheet to Adler. Though, they'd not heard back from him since the exchange.

Kendrick again thumbed his mobile to check for messages. There were none.

"Alright." Bennett clapped his hands. "What's on the agenda for this evening?" He adjusted his hairline in the window's reflection. "You want to break in someplace else? I know you were disappointed when we found the backdoor already busted open at the lawyer's office."

Kendrick scoffed.

"Just asking if there's an itch to scratch, amigo. Don't want to keep you down."

"Stuff it, Marine."

Bennett snickered.

What they needed to understand was who Symon Pellgrin's customers were. Who'd wanted the human cargo? How wide was this web of customers? And where had they taken those girls?

However, they'd completely run out of suspects. Their only link to answers was the data Adler had in his possession. And, while Kendrick had complete trust in the young man, the more time passed without a call or text from him, the more worried Kendrick became.

While he and Bennett did get a partial lead from the mystery woman at Pellgrin's house, it didn't give him much to act on. A woman called Nia would visit the docks when shipments came in. Assuming the ports were those in the freeport, then the 'when' of the matter was anybody's guess. Kendrick also had no description beyond her name.

If they'd only had a few more minutes with the mystery woman.

So many damn questions that only left him guessing.

With Symon Pellgrin now dead, Kendrick also wondered whether any more of these 'shipments' would ever come again. Would they move operations to another port? Or shut things down altogether? Maybe there were one or two already in transit? They could try and scout the area, but that may take weeks or months and could very well turn up nothing.

"Can't do anything until we hear from your man." Bennett stood and stretched his neck. "And I think we need to prepare ourselves for the worst."

"The worst?"

"Nothing happens. Our friend Adler doesn't find anything of value, and we get stuck again." Bennett stared at him. "I know it's not the best outcome, amigo, but I'm just trying to keep you grounded."

He was right. That was a real possibility. It could mean these months he'd spent investigating were a complete waste of time. Adler was good, but could he crack the passwords and find anything on that laptop's drive? Moreover, would any of it point to something actionable? A person? A place? Without that, they were lost.

"Anyway," Bennett said, "I say we head back to that bar and throw back a few."

Kendrick snapped from thought. "Little early yet, don't you think?"

Bennett stretched his shoulders. "Bit of day drinking ain't ever hurt nobody. Kick back and listen to good music. Better than sitting inside."

Kendrick chuckled. "Alright. Let me –"

A rattle came from inside his pocket.

It was Second Lieutenant Adler.

Kendrick put the call on speaker.

"Sir, Second Lieutenant Adler. I've got some information."

Adler was speaking faster than usual. There was also ambient noise in the background and none of the typical keyboard clicking.

"Go ahead, Adler," Kendrick spoke over the phone's mic.

"Sir, something's happened here."

The last time Adler said that… the world shut down.

Kendrick held in a breath, "What is it?"

Car horns erupted in the background.

Adler was on the street.

"Sir, the passwords worked. I was able to open the files."

"Where are you now?"

"In a minute, sir."

It was exceedingly rare for Adler not to respond to his questions at once. It just wasn't who the young soldier was.

"This thing, it's deep, sir."

"Deep?" Kendrick turned wide-eyed to Bennett.

"When I cracked the files, I saw the records and tracked many shipments. Much of it is legal, regular raw materials. But there's an entire section on that laptop dealing with one-offs."

"One-offs?"

Adler's breathing increased, then a shout. "Dammit!"

Was he running?

"Apologies, sirs," he huffed. "Long-distance at street level is tough for me."

Kendrick wasn't sure what that meant but let the second lieutenant continue.

"I did some digging on the bigger systems. I investigated many of these connections and companies the laptop pointed me to get more information."

He often did this, and with his heightened network of service and military systems, the data he could supply was always unbelievably valuable.

"But then something happened, sir."

"What happened, Adler?"

The traffic grew louder, and so had Adler's breathing.

"My access was cut off, sir."

"What?"

"Sir, there are relationships, there are…"

The line faded out for a minute.

"Adler, I need to know your situation. What's going on? Adler? Adler?"

Bennett and Kendrick stared at one another for the better part of a solid minute. The hairs on Kendrick's arms tingled.

"Sorry, sirs. The buildings are… in and… get clear, one moment."

Adler was one of the most competent soldiers Kendrick had ever had the pleasure of working with. Why would he need to call them outside the office? Something wasn't right here, and Kendrick could tell by Bennett's confused expression that he felt the same.

What worried him most was if the young man were in some type of peril, he and Bennett were thousands of kilometers away, and it could be some time before they could help him.

A clicking sounded. Adler's line suddenly went dead.

Kendrick and Bennett stared at one another.

They'd put the man in this situation and were helpless to do anything.

Kendrick dialed once, then twice. He waited another minute and a half and tried again. This time the connection went straight to voice mail.

"Adler, it's your chum. Please call me back at this number at your earliest."

Kendrick hung up and attempted to text.

The message went unsent. So did the next.

Bennett's eyes were wide, "Oh shit, what's happened to the kid?"

"We've gotta find some way to –"

Kendrick's phone vibrated with an unknown incoming number.

He frantically hit the call icon, "Hello?"

"Sirs, my issued phone was cut off. I bought a burner from a shop, but the battery time is –"

Kendrick spoke quickly, "What do you need? What can we do?"

When Adler's following words came, they struck both Bennett and Kendrick with unsettling fear.

Adler huffed, "Sirs, I think I'm being followed."

Chapter

56

The courtyard pool at the Big B saw Charlie's new gazebo completed—which arched from one end of the patio, over the generous spa, to its other side. The ridged structure shaded poolside guests during the sunniest parts of the day, with plenty of room for lounge chairs beneath.

Charlie had also applied a deep golden-stain finish to the structure, which blended nicely with the shaped holly bushes and jasmine he'd meticulously clipped and cropped around its base.

This evening, the shaded space sat filled with tables of food and cold drinks for Charlie's guests under an array of tiny sparkling lights suspended from its rafters.

Brack drank sweet tea. He wore a casual coral shirt with tan slacks and a pair of dockside loafers.

Charlie was somewhere, and Brack asked his nephew if he could find him.

"Could you tell Charlie that Mister David has something to discuss with him?"

"Am I in trouble?" his nephew asked.

"No," Brack chuckled. "Nothing like that."

But for $25 an hour, you should carry luggage for the guests, you longhaired overpaid little shit.

Although, Brack held his tongue.

Under the new gazebo, he spotted Dax with a drink in hand, speaking to a curvaceous woman that Brack didn't recognize at first.

Dax had trimmed his hair for the occasion and was dressed in a handsome suit and polished shoes, laughing, and chatting. The woman in the tightish green butterfly cocktail dress occasionally touched his arm.

It was Deena from the restaurant diner across the street.

Brack smiled. Good for you, Dax. Good for you.

Nikki also showed. She wore a pair of fashionably ripped jeans and a cute summer sleeveless shirt. The exposed skin revealed arm tattoos. A band she liked, a rose on her shoulder, and the likeness of her son Curtis on her other arm. Overall, the ink was quite tasteful.

Brack approached.

"And how are we?"

"Doing excellent, Mr. Goodman. How are you?"

Brack smiled.

"Listen, Nikki. I've got something for you."

He fished the silver ledger from his pocket.

"Take this. I'll text you the PIN."

"What is it?"

"It's for you and for your son. I want you to buy the best laptop and finish your schooling."

"I don't understand," Nikki said, taking the small device.

"I think you will. I assume you know what crypto is?"

"Crypto? Yeah, but…"

"There's enough to help you with your education. Keep Curtis in a nice daycare facility and maybe a smidge more." Brack laughed.

The truth was, he'd taken only what he was owed with moderate interest. The remaining balance, which was on the ledger, depended on the crypto market's volatility. Right now, that balance was more than she'd make in twenty years as a driver.

"For me?"

"For you, Nikki. Do good things with it, okay."

Her eyes welled, and she nodded.

"Mister David," Charlie called.

Brack turned, and Charlie waved him over.

"There's someone I'd like you to meet, Mister David," Charlie said. "This is my partner, Eric."

Eric was a slender, well-groomed man about the same height as Brack, dressed in Bermuda shorts, a lavender t-shirt, and a matching sun visor.

Partner? He'd assumed Charlie owned the place outright and, with all the work he'd seen the man put in by himself, hadn't considered he might have another backer.

"Oh, okay," Brack said.

He cautiously shook Eric's hand.

Charlie tilted his head.

"You look displeased, Mister David."

Brack turned away for a second.

"If you don't mind my asking," he said. "What's your split?"

"Split? I don't understand," Eric blinked.

"Share. How do you divide the business?"

Charlie smiled uneasily at Brack.

"I'm sorry, Mister David, I thought you knew."

"Knew?"

Charlie wrapped an arm around Eric's shoulder.

"Eric and I are partners…" he cocked his head.

"Oh… oh. Partner-partner," Brack blushed. "My fault, crap."

"I'm sorry, Mister David. If you're disappointed or if this is uncomfortable…"

If time had taught Brack anything, it was that real love is a four-leaf clover found under a rainbow next to a unicorn. He'd never had it himself but appreciated anyone who did.

"Charlie, pal, I'm not disappointed. No, no. And Eric, it's damn good to meet you. Charlie's a good man, and I'm happy to know him."

Eric nodded with a grin.

"We really need a different word," Brack mumbled to himself. Then, aloud, "Let's restart this. Charlie, I have a proposal for you. If you'll indulge me for a moment—and Eric, I'd also like you to listen."

Both nodded.

"You have a fantastic location here. Beach access, solid bones, and your workmanship is excellent, Charlie."

"Thank you, Mister David."

"And if you can please stop calling me Mister David, that'd be good, too."

Charlie smirked.

"I have a sizable investment to make, and I'd like to make it with you."

"With me?"

"Yes, a business partnership."

"Ahh. Partner. Now I get it," Charlie chuckled.

"I see potential here, Charlie. Beach chairs for the guests. A full-service inside restaurant. Your nephew there delivering bell service for the bags of visitors. The place also has excellent facilities where its former food service section once was. But before that, we can work something out with the diner across the street to get your guests fed and refreshed until things open."

"Wow. You've really thought about this."

"It's what I do, Charlie. But we need to start with the name. I've been spitballing, and you both can tell me what you think."

"Spitballing?"

"Thinking you should rename the place. Give it a new vibe, more in line with the one you're working hard to deliver. Maybe call it 'Charlie's Seaside Inn?"

"Charlie's Seaside Inn. Oh wow, I like that. Charlie's Seaside Inn…"

"I like it, too," Eric said.

"And lounge chairs on the beach," Brack said.

"Lounge chairs?"

"With monogrammed towels, of course," Brack added.

"Oh, that's style… towels, I never thought of that."

"You'll run things," Brack said. "And I can work the finances for you. Though I want you to stay the face of this place. You've got a wonderful knack for hospitality."

"Why, thank you."

"We can work on the percentage of ownership, but I also want you to keep the majority no matter what we decide."

"Oh?"

"It's your sweat in the hotel, Charlie. I don't want to take that away from you. I just want to be part of it. Deal?"

"Mister David, sorry, David. I don't know what to say."

"Say you agree, and we can get started."

"Oh, I agree, of course."

Both Charlie and Eric grinned wide.

All three shook hands.

"We'll draw up some papers at Dax's office later, okay?"

Charlie nodded.

"But why? Why would you do this, David?"

Brack leered at his feet and then rose his head with a smile.

"Because I never had any good dreams, Charlie. Not like you have. A true friend once said, 'sometimes we're surrounded by better people than we deserve.' And to be honest, Charlie, you're a damn good man, and I want to be part of this dream."

Charlie's bearhug caught Brack by surprise and nearly crushed him.

Across the courtyard, a beautiful brunette enjoyed a cocktail in a short summer dress. She wasn't speaking with anyone, but it was the same person Brack had seen in the lobby chatting on her mobile phone days ago.

Did he know her?

She seemed so familiar.

Though, before Brack could get free from Charlie, the woman and her drink vanished.

CHAPTER

57

"I have the data in my possession," Adler said breathlessly.

Kendrick's heart raced and his palms moistened. He cared far less about Oliver's laptop data than he did for his UK friend.

"Adler, can you get someplace public?"

"Public, sir?"

"Not the tube, but a shopping center or a square, anywhere above ground?"

"Right now, I'm in a courtyard with shops and vendors."

"Good, stay visible. Make certain you have more than one exit should you need it."

"Copy, sir."

Bennett raced outside the room with his own mobile. Kendrick heard Bennett shouting on his call but couldn't make out any words.

Adler's situation was a nightmare. Some way, he'd put the second lieutenant in danger. What was he thinking?

Pellgrin had told them how deep this thing ran, that there were people who would kill to stop them. Or was it something else?

Adler was reporting to a Brigadier. Kendrick usually would've investigated the man. He did that with almost everyone else on any team he'd been on, ever. Why hadn't Kendrick done his diligence to protect Adler the way he'd done with others? Had he taken the young man for granted?

"Adler, do you have access to a vehicle?"

"Vehicle, sir. Yes. It's a –"

"I don't need the make and model, mate. I need you—when you can—to get to it safely. Use only cash. You have cash, don't you?"

"Some, sir. But…"

"Alright. No credit cards. Say it back to me."

"No credit cards, no sir."

"Adler, listen to me. I keep a place in Rumney. Can you get there?"

"Wales?"

"Yes, Wales. I have a cottage off Wentloog."

"It's a few hundred miles from my location, sir. But yes, I believe I can make it there."

"You need to do this in one shot. Fill up with petrol but do not show anybody your identification. And, above all, watch your speed."

Kendrick wiped the sweat from his forehead.

"Adler, we need you off the grid completely. Got me?"

"Yes, sir. Off the grid."

Kendrick was going to tell him to check for trackers on his vehicle in case someone had placed any. But he'd already given the young man too much to think about, and he wasn't finished.

"Make sure nobody follows you. We'll figure things out once you're safe, okay?"

"Understood, sir. I'll do exactly what you say."

"I'm going to text you an address. There's an old man that lives two houses away. You'll know his house, keeps all manner of plants around and… but that doesn't matter. He has the key. His name is Potter, which is scribed on his postbox. Miles Potter, got it?"

"Yes, sir. Miles Potter. Thank you, sir."

Adler was still breathing heavily.

"Don't thank me, Adler. Just get there as fast as you can. Park at Potter's house. He's an old friend of Bethany and me, and…"

Kendrick's heart skipped a beat. He'd said Bethany's name aloud for the first time in years. He centered himself for a moment before continuing.

"Park at Potter's place. Tell him I sent you and tell him your situation. He'll give you a weapon. Take it. Stay inside my residence but for food. Got me?"

A strange static interrupted the mobile's wireless connection but cleared.

"Yes, sir," Adler paused. "There's a man here. I think he might be clocking me."

"A man?"

"Sir, I should leave this spot. My leg's…"

But the call abruptly cut off.

Kendrick frantically dialed, but his phone would not connect.

"Jesus Christ!" He slammed a thumb on the mobile surface to redial. Then he noticed the bars on the screen indicator had fallen to nothing. "What's happening?"

Had someone remotely disabled his phone? Were they tracking him now? Had they eavesdropped on his call? Shit, the only person who had a chance at answering any of this was Adler.

Outside, Bennett paced next to the Chrysler.

Kendrick tried redialing Adler again.

"Your device is out of range. Goodbye," the soulless voice said.

"Fuck, fuck!"

What would they do? If Adler was caught or captured, what then? Had information from the recovered laptop sent things into this tailspin?

He'd promised to text Adler the address, but his phone screen no longer functioned properly. Had someone locked him out?

He'd given Adler the basic location. He only prayed the young soldier could quickly make his way to safety and follow those directions.

But this was a lot of hoping.

Could he use Bennett's phone?

He rethought this. If someone were tracing his, they surely had Adler's burner number now. Any inbound call was also bound to be caught in their web of surveillance.

Any communication medium might be compromised.

Would they track Bennett's phone next?

He knew Adler would have an answer to get around all of this. The young man was brilliant and indispensable.

Kendrick rubbed a palm to his forehead. He just wished he could help the poor lad right now.

Bennett burst through the door.

"We ain't taking the Riley," he said firmly. "Too short of range. But I called in a favor. They're filling up a C-20 now. Grab your shit."

Kendrick turned in disbelief.

"We're taking off from Barksdale." Bennett checked his watch. "Got a friend falsifying a scheduled lift-off now, and we don't have much time before someone with bars and stars finds out."

"I don't understand… are you sure we can do this? What if we're caught? It could mean…"

"Focus. We need to be in the air in 45 minutes." Bennett grabbed his duffle. "So, snap up and strap up, Major Kendrick. That's an order."

CHAPTER
58

Lorenzo was halfway through his second shift when two suspicious men entered Sigma-Sea's sort building at port 49L. It was very unusual for any of the white shirts to be on site this late in the evening, and Lorenzo took curious notice.

Working at the seaport, he was paid in cash. In a few short weeks, his English had also gotten conversational, and he had no trouble understanding their accents—provided they didn't speak too quickly.

But he also watched them. The ones in white collared shirts with the crooked black ties, mostly. The ones who carried electronic tablets and didn't lift, pack, or stack anything. They argued with the forklift drivers, scolded the handcart movers, and gave strict instructions to the truck drivers.

Beyond the yard's towering gantry cranes, massive cargo freighters traversed the Mississippi water channel. Plumes of diesel smoke swirled in the night air.

Lorenzo crept through the building's package processing machines, around the check weighers, air pillow systems, sealers, conveyors, strappers, and over wrappers, careful to keep himself out of sight.

The two white shirts greeted each other at the building's loading dock.

Lorenzo crouched behind a pallet and held low.

"Collins said he'd be here," the hard hat man said. "That shithead is always late."

The bald guy standing next to him agreed. He donned a necktie but no headcover.

Moments later, a large semitruck arrived at the loading dock.

"Ah, there's Collins now," hard hat pointed.

The driver Collins backed the truck and trailer into the loading bay in less than a minute. The chubby man exited the cab. He wore a red flannel with cutoff sleeves, a dirty ballcap, and jeans.

He hitched up his pants, came to the rear of the trailer, and opened the latch.

The insides were jammed with boxes stacked on pallets.

Two of Lorenzo's coworkers appeared and started the offload.

The bald guy, the man in the hard hat, and Collins walked inside an interior office.

Lorenzo snuck past more machines, toward the office, and remained low. He couldn't see them, but he heard everything they said.

"Rest of your load goes to Linkville," hard hat announced. "That's where the pickup is."

Collins grumbled, "Things on I-10 are getting dicey. Got that damn border patrol looking for illegals and there's fuzz all over the fucking place."

A fist slammed a table.

"No more fuckups! No more loss!" hard hat barked. "Johnson, you'll ride ahead in the van. Watch the map. At least two exits between you and Collins at all times. If you see any checkpoints, you get off and wait. Go during the night, the entire trip. There's less chance of being stopped."

"What about the weigh station?"

"That's what the van's for," Johnson said. "I can shuttle them past in groups, then we'll corral them back into the semi."

"In groups?"

"We need to make up for last time," hard hat said. "We have a total count of 59."

Collins refused, "No, no way. I agreed to 20."

"There're 59 heads coming in on the ship! That's your number!" hard hat shouted. "Or I can call Striker, and we can sort things out with him?"

"Fuck, okay." Collins relented. "Fifty-nine. But don't disturb the boss."

"That's what I thought," hard hat grumbled. "Ship's called the *Tiktell*. She's inbound now. Headed to a port, eight miles from your Linkville stop. Be there by midnight. They'll adjust your cargo to make a false barrier once the merchandise is loaded. They'll have your papers and such."

Collins, or maybe it was Johnson, grunted.

A brief time later, the two dock workers unloading the semi took in the last pallet to its station and left the area.

Lorenzo quietly made his way to the loading dock.

There was nobody around.

He crawled into the back of the truck's trailer and hid inside the hauler's remaining boxes.

Collins and Johnson conferred on the loading dock before the chubby man turned, tugged up his jeans, and headed to the semi.

Collins closed and latched the truck's trailer.

Lorenzo held quiet inside.

It was pitch dark when the semitruck's motor started.

The large vehicle rumbled forward.

Lorenzo's heart raced, and he shut his eyes.

Isabella, please be safe.

A Special Request

Your review really matters. Whether you bought this book in a magical mom and pop bookstore, online, or swiped it from a friend. Please tell me what you think!

I read each review, grateful, laughing, looking for character names.

Amazon.com

Goodreads.com

(Aiming your cellphone's camera at this QR code should take you directly to Amazon's review forum. Thank you and be well!)

Acknowledgements

Finances are complex, and the author takes full responsibility for all inaccuracies. For some reason I was taught Algebra and Geometry, not how to balance a checkbook.

Smarjie (number one fan!), and good friends Shelly and Bobby.

My big sister Cathy. The best CPA in any county.

Pickle and Paco, my little barking helpers.

Mike Peck for one of the best stories of survival I've ever heard.

Ken Yager for our financial chat at the Turtle.

Ashley (pleasure doing business with you!), Danni, Darlene, Deanna, Kaitlyn, Leshaye ('Trouble' has arrived), Suzie & Tammy, Doctors Costrini, Gibson, Luke, and Perkins—you are the best at what you do.

The harbor guys at The Palace.

Barry and Scofield at Knight's Pawn.

Captain Hicks, Nathan Coyle, and Robert Kozakoff at Fernandina Municipal Airport. Plus, the air jockeys on r/flying: JHG0 – thanks buddy! Itsjakeandelwood, KCPilot17, Wrenching4flighttime, UserName61585, and Findquasar. And let's hope there's no meowing on UNICOM.